The

Reich

Legacy

Also by Stanley Salmons

ALEXEI'S TREE AND OTHER STORIES

A BIT OF IRISH MIST

THE TOMB

THE CANTERPURRY TALES

FOOTPRINTS IN THE ASH

NH$_3$

THE MAN IN TWO BODIES

THE DOMINO MAN

COUNTERFEIT

THE
REICH
LEGACY

Stanley Salmons

ISBN: 1546642390

ISBN-13: 978-1546642398

This novel is a work of fiction. Any resemblance between the
characters and actual persons, living or dead, is entirely
coincidental.

For Paula, Graham, Daniel, and Debby

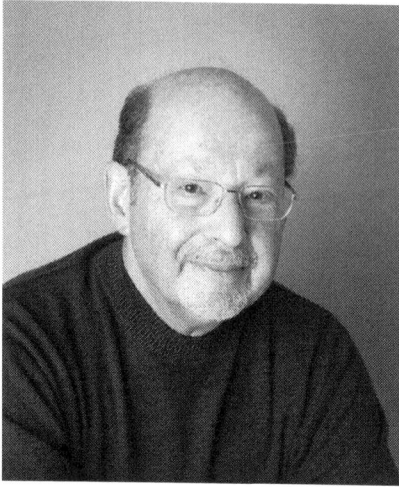

Stanley Salmons was born in Clapton, East London. He is internationally known for his work in the fields of biomedical engineering and muscle physiology, published in over two hundred scientific articles and twelve scientific books. Although still contributing to the real world of research, he maintains a parallel existence as a fiction writer, in which he can draw from his broad scientific experience. He has published over forty short stories in various magazines and anthologies. This is his seventh novel

GLOSSARY

ADC	Aide-de-Camp
BDU	Battle Dress Uniform (US Army)
BKA	*Bundeskriminalamt*, the German federal investigative police agency
blue on blue	casualties taken from friendly fire
camo	camouflage
CSA	Chief of Staff of the Army
flashbang	stun grenade
good-nite	short-acting gas grenade
klick, k	kilometre
incoming	incoming fire
infil/exfil	infiltration/exfiltration
MTP	Multi-Terrain Pattern (British Army uniform)
NCO	Non-Commissioned Officer
OR	Other Ranks
RPG	rocket-propelled grenade
SAF	Special Assignment Force (fictional Special Operations Force of the US Army)
SAS	Special Air Service (Special Forces unit of the British army)
stag	sentry duty
tab	march or jog with heavy equipment over difficult terrain
USACIDC	United States Army Criminal Investigation Command (also CID)
XO	Executive Officer (Second-in-Command)

1

"Jim, need you here. My office, 1000 hours. Confirm. Wendell."

The message had come up on my desk screen. No reason, no explanations, that's all there was – that and the date stamp: 04-04-2056, 7.03 a.m.

First things first.

I buzzed my ADC, Sergeant Bagley.

"Sir?"

"Bagley, you have the flight schedules. Can I get to the Pentagon for ten o'clock this morning?"

I waited.

"Yes, Colonel, you can if you leave now."

"I am leaving now. Book me on that flight. Then get me a driver from the pool. I should be back later today."

"Yes, sir."

I spoke my confirmation message to Wendell, then sat back and took a few moments to wonder what in hell this was about.

Operations for the Special Assignment Force come directly from Washington, through General Wendell Harken at the Department of Defense. That's a handy arrangement: Harken was CO of this outfit before I took over, so he knows whether a mission is appropriate and within our capabilities and resources. He's also well placed to defend our budget. The bean counters who sieve through the Department's accounts are apt to bellyache at regular intervals about how expensive the SAF is, and despite the successful operations we've carried out in the past – operations no other elite force could have tackled – memories are short, especially when they belong to bean counters. Harken is effective, and he's on his way up; I wouldn't be surprised if he makes it to the Chiefs of Staff. But that sort of wheeling and dealing isn't for me: I don't enjoy it, and I'm too blunt to be any good at it. It suits me to be the next link in the chain of command, looking after things at Fort Piper. So that's how it operates. If Harken wants us to take on an assignment, he phones or messages me. I go to the holoconference suite at the base, and we set up a secure link for a head-to-head. Then I'll plan the operation and make sure the men go into action adequately trained, equipped, and supported.

Except he didn't want a holoconference today. He wanted me in Washington. And he hadn't said why.

The heavy tramp of boots outside my window told me the guys were leaving for the 10 k tab with full pack. Normally I'd be with them. Dammit, I *should* be with them, not sitting on a bloody plane eating roasted peanuts. What kind of crisis was so important that I had to go to Washington?

Bagley's face appeared around the door, wearing his usual hurt spaniel expression.

"Driver's ready, sir."

"Okay, I'm coming."

I smiled. I liked poor old Bagley, although I was careful not to embarrass him by showing it. He wasn't SAF at all – he'd never have made it through the physical for one thing. Wendell brought him along when he became CO here and I'd inherited him. He lacked personality, ambition, or initiative, but he did his job and – no doubt with a monumental effort of self-control – he didn't actually moan about it, so we got along.

I picked my uniform jacket off the hook and headed for the car.

2

I've known sunny days in Washington, but this wasn't one of them. The air in the Capital was hung with a fine drizzle, in spite of which it was warm and humid. Most people would find that unpleasant but it was all the same to me; in North Carolina I usually trained with the men in conditions a lot stickier than this. The cab dropped me close to the Metro station and bus bays and I walked over to the Concourse entrance and into the cavernous reception area of the Pentagon. A security officer scanned my ID and asked why I was there and who I was planning to see. Of course I had no idea why I was there, so I just told him General Harken was expecting me. He picked up an internal phone, and after a brief conversation clicked it off again.

"Thank you, Colonel. Do you know your way?"

"Yeah, I know my way."

I caught the lift to the third floor and went through further security checks at each of the inner rings. Harken's windowless office was in D ring. As I took the corridor nearest his bay I was still wondering what had made him drag me up here. I reached the office, knocked on the door, and opened it.

Harken was sitting with his clasped hands resting on the big desk. It was a posture familiar to me from countless briefings, and just what I expected to see. What I hadn't expected to see was another man in the room. He was seated at the short end of the desk, which he'd covered with papers. Late thirties, clean-shaven, close-cropped hair, dark blue business suit. Despite the suit there was a look about him that said "army" to me. Both rose briskly to their feet as I came in.

Harken shook my hand. Despite the desk job he hadn't put on an ounce. He probably ran five or ten ks before going to work each day.

"Thanks for coming up here, Jim," he said. "We have a tricky situation on our hands. I thought you should hear about it at first hand. This is Mr Mark Godstall. He's a Special Agent with the CID."

For a brief moment my English background took over, and I wondered what the hell a plain-clothes detective from the old country was doing out here. Milliseconds later it clicked. CID was easier to say than either United States Army Criminal Investigation Command or its full abbreviation, USACIDC. I'd come up against some of these boys in the run-up to my court martial, when I was still Jim Forbes. Even without that history I'd have been familiar with this particular command. As a CO it was my job to know who did what, and who reported to whom. I'd know, for example, that Special Agents like this one could be civilian or military, but I was still backing the army for this guy.

"Colonel," Godstall said, extending his hand.

I took the hand warily. Some of his colleagues hadn't been too kind to me in the past.

At Harken's invitation I drew out the chair opposite him and the three of us sat down.

Harken turned to the agent. "Mr Godstall, would you like to lead off?"

The man nodded, then looked at me. "This is a sensitive matter, Colonel. Right now my job is simply to investigate and report back."

A sensitive issue involving the army. The army would certainly want to keep a sensitive matter within the family, so my guess was correct: he was army, an NCO in the Military Police Corps. And to talk to a General and a Full Colonel about a sensitive matter they'd send a Warrant Officer, or even a Chief Warrant Officer. That's why Wendell was calling him "Mister".

He continued, "I'll have to fill in a little background as we go along, so maybe you can help me out."

Helping these guys out usually meant falling for their tricks, so I waited.

"In 2052 you faced a General Court Martial, accused of murdering your fellow soldiers."

I must have looked as surprised as I felt. I'd learned to put all that behind me. Why was he bringing it up now? I quickly reassembled my thoughts.

"Wrongly accused," I corrected him. "I was exonerated."

"Yes – too late, unfortunately. You were found guilty and condemned to death. What's more, the sentence was carried out. Yet you're still here."

He paused to look at me, evidently waiting for an explanation.

I frowned. "You know the score, Mister. Executed murderers are used as organ donors, have been for years. Corneas, heart and lungs, liver, kidneys, bone marrow, blood – nothing wasted. In my case it was a whole body transplant: everything but the brain went to someone whose own body was failing."

"Sure, I understand that much. But normally the brain

that was taken out of your body – a brain that belonged to someone seen at the time as, ah, a non-contributor to society – would have been disposed of. Obviously that didn't happen; your brain was transplanted into another body. They call it a domino transplant – don't they? It's a difficult and expensive procedure, and I'm wondering if you could tell me why it was done in your case."

Harken interrupted. "The information is classified."

"I thought so," Godstall said, nodding at Harken. "That makes things harder, but I don't think we need to go into it now, or worry about who got the Colonel's original body."

Oh good, because as it happens I know who got it and I haven't the slightest intention of telling you.

This guy had got off on entirely the wrong foot with me. I was still chewing on "non-contributor to society". The phrase had been carefully chosen and better than some expressions he could have used, but I was still smarting. I'd contributed plenty to society, both before and after they operated on me.

"Mr Godstall," I said. "Is all this really relevant?"

"I'm afraid it is, Colonel. Bear with me a little longer." He looked down at the papers on his desk as if he needed to remind himself of something, which he almost certainly didn't. He looked up again. "These procedures we've been talking about. In the normal way they never become public knowledge. Surgery of this kind is only conducted by judicial order, and such orders prohibit the keeping of medical records. Secrecy would have been even more crucial in this case – I'm aware that the Special Assignment Force is mainly designated for black ops." He glanced quickly at Harken and back to me as if expecting a response. He didn't get one. Harken's face was set like stone, and I was still waiting to find out what he was leading up to.

"Your mission in Africa, though," Godstall resumed. "That attracted a lot of public interest."

Harken said, "The mission you're referring to was an outstanding achievement. Colonel Slater was promoted and awarded the Distinguished Service Cross."

Everyone had been pleased with the outcome. Harken was pleased because he was promoted from Full Colonel to one-star General. Bob Cressington, Director of National Intelligence at the time, was pleased because it cleared the way for his eventual appointment as Secretary of Defense. And the media was pleased because there'd been a dearth of major news stories during the anticlimax that follows a Presidential election, and when this dropped in their laps they couldn't believe their luck. So everyone was pleased – everyone except me. I was the target of so much media attention that from then on I was a write-off for operational duty. Perhaps it didn't make much difference. Harken's growing responsibilities in Washington meant he was spending more and more time away from Fort Piper, leaving me there as acting CO. Soon we both bowed to the inevitable and my role was made permanent.

Godstall nodded vigorously at Wendell. "Absolutely, sir. But unfortunately it gained Colonel Slater a certain notoriety. As a result he's been recognized." He turned to me. "In short, a party wants your body back. So as to give it a decent burial."

3

The room went deathly quiet.

So this was it. This was why I'd been summoned to Washington. This was what the preamble was about. Someone was claiming my body.

I got to my feet, turned, and walked as far from the desk as the confines of the room would allow. A bunch of worms was wriggling in my stomach. I knew they were watching me, and I put my hands in my pockets to hide the way they were shaking.

Head bowed, eyes closed, I relived the whole nightmare journey: the post-operative weeks and months, the long, ghastly process of waking up in a new body; the helpless anger and horror as I realized what they'd done to me; my revulsion at the hideous mismatch between the original body image stored in my brain and the body I was now stuck with. It was taller, and more heavily built. My hair had been brown and curly, now it was straw coloured with a slight wave. My lips had been thin, now they were full. The brown eyes were mine – they'd been transplanted with the brain as a single unit – but now they had someone else's eyelids and blond eyelashes. I hated this face and I hated the body it had come with.

Then rehabilitation. Relearning everything: to talk, to stand with quivering limbs between parallel bars, to take a few faltering steps. Then standing and walking unsupported, swimming, running, training with weights, on rowing machines and stationary bicycles, relearning my skills in unarmed combat. It was a full year before I was finally out on the street, a bitter man with scores to settle. And settle them I bloody well did[1].

I straightened up. This body had to see a lot of action before I could make it my own. If anyone wants to tell me it belongs to someone else now they can go to hell. Fuck them. It's mine. They can't have it.

I turned to face the desk.

"Why are we even talking about this?" I said. "When this guy was convicted he forfeited any rights to his own body. That's why the State could use it as a source of organs, isn't it?"

Godstall's tone was measured and patient. "The way the law was drafted, Colonel, the body can be returned to the family, minus corneas, heart, lungs, kidneys, and so on. In practice no one ever claims it; funerals and burial plots are very expensive. Even if there are friends or family they don't want to foot the bill, and most of them are happy to look the other way. This situation is slightly different. The law was passed before the whole body transplant came in, and it's never been redrafted. They're suing the US Army for the return of the body and technically, under existing law, they have a case."

I looked from Godstall to Harken and back to Godstall. "That's ridiculous!"

"Of course it is, but that's the way things stand."

"Come and sit down, Jim," Harken said.

---

[1] For the full story see *The Domino Man* by this author.

I walked forward and took the chair. "Who's bringing the suit?"

"His one-time partner," Godstall said. "She claims they were in a long-term relationship before his, ah, demise."

"Law suits are even more expensive than funerals. Someone must be bankrolling this. Who is it?"

He grimaced.

"Well?"

"I was trying to spare your feelings, Colonel."

"Why, because I'm inhabiting the body of a convicted murderer? Mister, if there's one thing I've learnt from this episode it's that the body doesn't have a mind of its own. Whatever this one was obliged to do before, it carries out my orders now. So just tell me."

"All right." He placed his wrists on the edge of the desk and put his fingertips together. "Because of the nature of the suit the claimant had to reveal the name of the donor. I don't suppose you want to know it?"

I was breathing hard now. "Damn right I don't."

"Sure, I understand. Well, as soon as we had that information we looked up the record of his trial. The man's victims ranged from small-time drug dealers to prominent gang leaders. The details didn't make pleasant reading. To judge by the methods and the nature of those targets the man was acting on orders. He wouldn't say where the orders came from."

"What, facing a rap like that?"

Godstall shrugged. "We assume he was a hitman for a powerful criminal syndicate, and he was trying to protect himself. These mobs have a long reach. If he'd plea bargained they could have had him killed before the trial or in prison afterwards. He had nothing to gain."

"Okay, go on."

"Large syndicates always have lawyers working for them. Someone must have come across your picture in the media and brought it to their attention."

"But that was well over two years ago!"

"They may not have made the connection at the time. But what it says to me is that this is no knee-jerk reaction. They've had the opportunity to prepare a case. No doubt that's where the money's coming from. As I said, formally the suit's being brought by his one-time partner." His lips tightened. "She may or may not have had a choice in the matter."

I shook my head. "What do they hope to achieve?"

"Their stated demand is for the body. The only way that could happen is if you agreed to another whole body transplant. I imagine there's little chance of that—"

"Not a snowball's chance in hell."

"Right. So in one sense the suit is frivolous."

"Glad to hear it."

"The claimants know that perfectly well, so there'll be a fallback position. We can only speculate as to what that might be, but it's not hard. They'd say that since the army is evading the bill for an extremely expensive operation—"

I pointed a finger at him. "And months of rehabilitation—"

"—and, as you say, months of rehabilitation, the least the court can do is award the costs of bringing the suit, together with damages for all the distress caused by failure to return the body – lack of closure for the grieving partner, bereavement counselling, and so on and so forth. Of course they're probably expecting it won't go that far. They'll hope the Army will settle out of court."

"And will it?"

"Absolutely not. We'd defend the case. But of course they don't know that."

There was a moment of silence. Then I said, "So I'm a test case. There's never been one like it before."

"That's right. There are very few of these whole body

transplants and the recipients tend to keep a low profile anyway. You were an exception."

"Terrific."

Harken entered the conversation. "Look, Jim, the service isn't going to contest that you were the recipient of this man's body, so at this stage there'd be no need for you to get involved. But there could be keen media interest, and they know where to find you. Mr Godstall and I discussed this before you arrived, and we think it'd be best for all concerned if you disappeared for a while."

I was trying to figure out what he meant by that when his cell phone buzzed. He picked it up from his desk, glanced at the screen, and said, "Excuse me, I'd better take this."

He got up, went to the far corner of the room, and stood with his back to us. Godstall and I waited in polite silence. Harken was speaking in a low voice, but I caught some of it, especially when he said, "I've got Jim Slater with me at the moment…" Then louder, "All right, be there in a few minutes."

Godstall was already gathering his papers together as Harken came back.

"That was Bob Cressington, Secretary of Defense. Something urgent's cropped up so we'll have to stop there. Thanks for coming, Godstall. When are the parties likely to meet on this?"

"Next week."

"You'll keep us informed."

"Of course."

We shook hands and Godstall left. I watched him go, then turned to Wendell. "I'll be off as well, then."

"No, Bob was pleased to know you were around. You're to come, too."

4

He led the way up to the fifth floor, E ring, where the most senior people hang out. As Wendell was a one-star General I thought security might wave him through. Not a bit of it. In fact they were still grilling us when Bob Cressington's PA hurried out to the checkpoint, had a brief word with security, and conducted us to Bob's office.

Bob rose from his desk and extended a hand. "Jim! Bit of luck you're here – two birds with one stone. Come and sit down."

Thanks to the lousy weather outside, the window admitted only a feeble light into the room, but the ceiling panels had boosted it to the regulation level. Bob's jacket was hanging over the back of his desk chair. His shirt still took a dead straight line as it disappeared behind his waistband; evidently he hadn't let himself go to seed since being appointed. Perhaps he and Harken ran those five or ten ks together. His hair was greying even more than Harken's but there was plenty of it, and his face was tanned and youthful. We took seats.

"Jim, Wendell, we have a situation in the Republic of Honduras."

I was familiar with most of the current trouble spots. Problems in the Honduras usually stemmed from drug cartels and people-trafficking. If someone wanted to involve the SAF it was probably people-trafficking.

"People-trafficking," Bob went on, confirming my guess. "Mainly women, of course."

Wendell said, "I thought that business had declined."

"Only if you believe the claims put out by their administration. In the past the girls would be offered well-paid jobs here in the States. When they arrived they'd be delivered to brothels. The government mounted a major educational program to raise awareness of what was going on. It worked well – too well, in a way, because it forced the gangs to switch tactics. These days they no longer persuade; they just snatch young women from the streets."

That did move it up a gear. The old scam could be managed by cheap pimps and go-betweens; now it would be in the hands of professionals. But this was an ongoing problem. I was waiting to know why we had to get involved.

"Yesterday evening a young woman was kidnapped in the capital, Tegucigalpa. Only this wasn't just any young woman; this one was the seventeen-year-old daughter of the United States Ambassador."

Oh, shit.

Wendell sucked his breath in through his teeth. "What in hell's name was she doing on the street?"

"I understand she's a rather independent, headstrong girl. She was bored with being confined to the safety of the Embassy compound, gave her parents a hard time over it. She'd studied Spanish so why couldn't she get out and absorb some of the local colour?"

Wendell said, "I imagine she's absorbed a lot more local colour than she bargained for. Where the hell were the DSS during all this?"

I knew what he was saying. It's the job of the US Diplomatic Security Service to protect the embassies and their personnel.

"The operatives are sourced locally, and cover is limited. The Ambassador had an official engagement – the funeral of a high government office-holder. The security detail went with him, leaving just one car and its driver. The young lady saw her chance. The driver was security trained and she must have persuaded him that was good enough."

"So what happened?" I asked.

"According to the driver they'd slowed to a crawl along a busy street. Then without warning she opened the door, shouted 'Wait here', and ran off."

"He should have gone after her," I said.

"Yes, he should have. He said there were cars all round him, horns blaring. He thought she'd be back in a couple of minutes, so he pulled over and waited. When she didn't show he phoned the Embassy and the Embassy contacted the police. No one's seen hide nor hair of her since."

Wendell said, "Any ransom note?"

"No. Which suggests the gang doesn't realize who it is they've lifted. At least not yet."

"I'd have thought this spirited young lady would have told them by now – in no uncertain terms."

"She may not have had the chance: they usually drug the girls to make them easier to handle. The Ambassador and his wife are frantic. They don't think the local police force or army can get her out safely; he wants our special forces to do it. He's used his influence with the Honduras government. They've agreed to a 'temporary foreign presence' so we can operate there."

Wendell looked at me.

I said, "What if they've spirited her out of the country already?"

"There's a good chance that hasn't happened yet. From what I understand the usual procedure is to collect a dozen or so of these girls together before sending them up the line – that way they can save on transport costs."

"Then we'll have to move fast."

"Correct."

"What's the girl's name?"

"Fiona. Fiona Rees-Williams. Can you handle it?"

"Well sure, but we have to find her first. Locating a kidnap victim in a city that size is like looking for one bullet in an entire armoury. Do we have any leads?"

Bob nodded. "The police went to the spot where she ran off and asked around. Had anyone seen anything? As usual nobody had. Then they offered a reward for information leading to… you know the kind of thing. After that everyone had seen the entire incident. Most of the statements were worthless, of course, but two accounts matched, and one man accurately described what the girl was wearing: an embroidered blouse and blue trousers. Seems she was bundled into a small car, a red Kabayashi."

"Registration?"

"He only saw the rear plate and it was covered in mud, probably deliberately. The police are out in force, and they've called in the reserves, too. They're cruising the city, looking for that car."

"How reliable was the sighting?"

"We think the guy was a good witness. She was certainly wearing the outfit he described. He was sure of the make of car because he's been thinking of buying a small hydrogen-electric himself. He said this one had a big dent in the rear offside wing."

I still wasn't convinced it was a job for the SAF. "Suppose the police find it. Why do they want us to extract her? The cops or army could throw a cordon round the house, then use a hostage negotiator."

Bob grimaced. "The police say they've tried that in the past. The gang will just come out holding a gun to her head. They'll use her as a human shield until they drive off and then we've lost her and we've lost the gang members as well. No, it has to be an extraction."

Now I was convinced. "Okay, I've got the picture. Where do we make our insertion?"

"Soto Cano Air Base. It's a Honduran military base, but the US Joint Task Force Bravo is headquartered there. They'll provide air support if you need it. You shouldn't need it."

"They'll have Rotofans, won't they? Don't you want to get them involved in the search?"

"No, I don't want to use them at this stage. If the gang sees one of those things overhead all sorts of things could happen. They may kill the girls and run. Or it'll click that they've pulled a high-value hostage, which could make things worse. In any case Rotofans aren't much help in an urban environment."

I was thinking it through. "We've already got what we need in the arsenal: body armour, night-vision gear, small arms, multirifles, flashbangs, good-nites…"

Bob blinked, and turned to Wendell. "What in hell are 'good-nites'?"

"Army slang for gas grenades," Wendell replied. "Disperse a highly volatile, short-acting anaesthetic gas. Developed for riot control but ideal for an operation like this."

"I'll need a special reconnaissance team," I said.

Harken nodded. "I'll organize that." He spoke quietly into his phone. The message would be on his desk screen when he got back to his office.

"We don't need any heavy vehicles," I continued, "just all-terrains. Better take ten, in case the recon team comes without any. Can I have a US Air Force Leviathon standing by at Raleigh-Durham?"

Harken said, "I'll arrange that, too." He spoke into his phone again.

"We may need to take over a few houses. Could be some damage. Will the residents be compensated?"

"Sure," Bob said. "The Embassy will cover anything like that."

I pushed my chair back. "Right, I'd better get things moving."

"Jim."

"Yes, Wendell?"

"In view of our recent conversation I think it would be a good idea if you took command of this operation yourself."

I stared at him in disbelief. "I'd normally coordinate something like this from my office, Wendell. Then I can provide logistical support in case of problems."

"This isn't a normal operation, and you're not in a normal situation. And having a recon team means there's another Battalian involved, so you'd have every reason to be in charge. Who would you normally assign?"

I answered without hesitation. "Tommy Geiger."

"All right, appoint Major Geiger as XO and let him do the coordinating while you go with the men."

Lead an operation instead of sitting behind a desk? I couldn't keep the grin off my face. "Yes, sir!"

Bob leaned forward, and he wasn't grinning. "Jim, we need a big success here. The whole incident's a nightmare – for the Honduran government and for us. Part of our mission there is to support democracy and human rights. Having the Ambassador's daughter abducted is a major embarrassment. The President herself wants me to keep her informed."

"I understand. I'll contact Tommy on my way back, and he can have the guys battle-ready by the time I arrive.

If the Leviathan's at the airport we can start loading in a couple of hours."

5

It was one o'clock in the morning when we landed at Soto Cano Air Base. The Base Commander was expecting us. We shook hands.

"Pat Banstead," he said. "I gather this is a hostage extraction."

He'd evidently been told that much, but not who the hostage was.

"That's right. Any word from the local cops?"

"Not yet." He waved a hand. "We're a bit tight for accommodation here but we've emptied a hangar. You're welcome to use that for the moment."

"Thanks."

We unloaded the all-terrains and lined them up, ready to drive out at a moment's notice. Then one of Banstead's men led us to the hangar. It was a huge space smelling faintly of oil and hot metal, and the concrete floor was patterned with dark stains. Still, it was dry in here, and retained some of the warmth of the day. My guys settled themselves in. They were used to periods of enforced inactivity during a mission, and they'd had to put up with a lot worse than this.

The delay weighed more heavily with me. We'd moved fast and gained an hour with the time shift, and now we had to wait around doing nothing. I checked my watch and started to pace back and forth.

An hour later Special Forces Reconnaissance Detachment Alpha landed in another Leviathan. I was standing on the apron as they disembarked eight men and two vehicles. Their Commanding Officer came forward and introduced himself: Major Ferenczi. He hadn't been fully briefed, so I filled him in. Then I led his people to the hangar where my guys were installed. They gave each other perfunctory waves and the recon team settled down in a separate group.

The waiting began again and dragged on, twenty minutes, thirty minutes, forty…

My two Captains, Cliff Marshall and Sam Govind, sauntered over.

"Okay, Jim?" Sam asked.

They'd obviously noticed my growing frustration. I grimaced. "Time's getting on," I said. "What are those cops up to? We need to get moving."

Cliff frowned. "You think they know where the safe houses are?"

"No. These gangs probably identify a suitable house, snatch the girls, and shift them out of the country as fast as they can. Two or three days and it's all over – creates too many problems if it takes any longer than that. And they won't risk using the same house again. People start to notice."

"So how are the cops going to find it?" Cliff asked.

"The red Kabayashi – that's the key. The girl was either unconscious or drugged when they took her inside, otherwise she'd have made a lot of noise and kidnappers don't like a lot of noise. They'd have had to carry or support her, which means the house they took her to must be close to that car."

"They could have moved it."

"Why bother? Right now they have no idea what they've stirred up."

Sam said, "Looks like we just have to wait."

"Yeah, but for how long? The Ambassador's daughter may be the first kidnap, in which case we have a bit of time. Or she may be the last, in which case we have no time at all."

He nodded. "See what you mean."

"And," I said, tapping my watch, "it's already getting on for three o'clock. Sunrise here is around six, and I want to go in while it's still dark."

Sam said, "Out of our hands, Jim. Just have to hope the local boys are up to the job."

Sam and Cliff rejoined the rest of the squad. Maybe I should have done the same but I couldn't relax. I hadn't been out on a mission for quite a while and I wanted this to go well – for us and for the Ambassador and his family. I looked at my watch yet again, bit my lip, and started to pace again.

Another hour went by. Then I heard the hiss of tyres on the approach road. I signalled to Sam, Cliff, and Major Ferenczi and we were waiting as the police cruiser rolled up. Two cops got out. One of them, presumably the more senior of the two, delivered the good news. They'd spotted the red Kabayashi.

Surprisingly, perhaps, it was parked in a fairly well-to-do residential area. Yes, there was a big dent in the rear offside wing and there was still mud on the number plate. No, they hadn't approached the car, they'd been told not to. They'd just called it in, and they had orders to come straight to the base and lead us there.

I turned to Ferenczi. "How's your Spanish?"

He shrugged. "I got the gist of it."

"Okay, we'll follow these guys. I'll come with you. Sam, Cliff, get your people and follow on. Drive with unequal spacing – I don't want this sounding like a convoy."

Minutes later the police cruiser was weaving through the night with a procession of all-terrains strung out at various intervals behind it. Eventually it slowed and braked to a halt. We pulled in behind it and the vehicles drew up one after another. I got out and went forward on foot with just the cops, my two captains, and Ferenczi.

The cops led the way. They walked past the front of the line of vehicles and turned right up a side street. We followed in silence. Finally they stopped and pointed out the car. It was well away from the nearest streetlamp but we could just make out the dent and the mud-covered number plate. We returned, walking out of step, although the composition soles of our boots made no real sound on the pavement. As we passed the streetlamp I got a better look at the houses. Unlike the chaotic jumble of low dwellings we'd passed on the way, these had two floors and all seemed to be built to the same pattern. The area had probably been developed quite recently. We reached the end of the street. I congratulated the cops on finding the car in such a remote place, and said it was very important. Then I told them they could leave it to us now, but they should come back with some of their colleagues and wait here quietly. There'd be some loud bangs when we went into action and we'd need them to keep the situation under control if it brought the neighbours out.

God knows how my Spanish accent sounded to them, but they nodded, got into their car and drove away.

I turned to Ferenczi. "Okay, you can send your team in. Maximum stealth."

He nodded and went off to brief his men.

Cliff, Sam, and I waited while the recon team worked their way along the street with infra-red detectors and directional microphones. Ten minutes later they came back to report to the Major.

"Okay, boss, we found the house. It's two up from where the car's parked. No lights in the houses each side, steady breathing from those, probably families asleep. Target house has lights on upstairs, puts out quite a bit of infra-red and we heard some moaning. That's it all right."

Ferenczi said, "Observation point?"

"There's a house th'other side of the street. From there we'll get a good line of sight for laser listeners on the closed windows and acoustic dishes on the open ones."

I intervened. "Okay, take that house over, but no noise. Show the people inside a lot of money and drive them somewhere fancy. They can all have a nice comfortable night in a hotel, courtesy of the Embassy. You have a Spanish-speaker with you?"

"Yeah."

"Good. Use him."

"It's a 'her'."

"Even better. What's at the rear of the target house?"

"It's built up against the hill, so out back there's only the upper floor windows."

"What about the roof?"

He nodded – he knew what I was driving at. "Pitch is shallow with a slight overhang. No chimney or anything to get a rope around but it's close to that hill, so you could bridge the gap. You got a ladder or a pole?"

"Yeah, we've got one."

"There y'go."

"Thanks."

Ferenczi issued some instructions and his team moved off, carrying their equipment. Two minutes later I couldn't see or hear anything of them.

They worked fast. Within half an hour the inhabitants of the house opposite had been moved and I was standing in their darkened front bedroom watching the guys in here at work. Both windows were open and they'd set up two tripods, a laser listening device mounted on one and an acoustic dish on the other. The operators sat on folding stools with headphones on.

Ferenczi came over. He spoke naturally in a low voice – the street outside was quiet, and whispers carry.

"We have more accurate infra-red readings off those rooms opposite. The reading on the right is way higher."

"Any idea how many in there?"

"Can't say exactly, but between six and twelve. Looks like that's where they're keeping your girls. No voices from that window, just a few moans."

"Okay, we'll have to play it safe and assume there's a man in with them. What about the other window?"

"We're getting more from the acoustic monitoring than the lasers. We picked up two distinct male voices, both from that side."

I crossed to one of the open windows and looked up at the roof overhang. It would be easy enough to swing in from there. I went back to Ferenczi.

"All right, we've got enough. Stand your men down and I'll brief mine. We're ready to roll."

6

Countless training exercises had familiarized my guys with this type of operation down to the last detail. Now they were enjoying the prospect of doing it for real.

I went back to the bedroom of the observation house opposite the target to watch the action from there. We didn't need the listening devices any more, so recon cleared the stuff away and I put two snipers in position at the open windows. It was a last resort, but if we had to use them those guys could hit a mosquito at this range.

The air was cool and even in a city this size it was very quiet at this hour. I was wearing night-vision goggles, switched from image intensification to infra-red, and I could see the bright green glows of my men as they emerged. The ones carrying grenade launchers moved silently into position on the hill behind and onto the street in front. Four more assembled on the roof, their machine pistols slung round their necks. The rest stationed themselves near the grenade launchers and on either side of the house. Everything was ready and the countdown began.

Ten... nine... eight...

Then I heard something I didn't want to hear: the unmistakeable sound of a loosened tile sliding across the roof. It seemed to be going on for ever and I prayed it would lodge somewhere. It didn't; it tipped over, dropped, and smashed. The noise was as loud as a gunshot. In my helmet set I heard the two captains calling an immediate suspension. I saw rapid movements from the men at the front and sides, and in a few seconds they'd melted out of sight. The guys on the roof were frozen in place. Minutes passed.

A new glow appeared at the front door; it had been opened a crack. I waited. The crack widened. A figure appeared, half-crouched, a pistol in his hand. The sniper on my left glanced my way, but I shook my head. The man at the door looked left and right and stepped further out. It would be hard for him to see anything; the moon had set more than an hour ago, and the distant streetlamp shed very little light up here. Then I heard a cat miaow. I was pretty sure it was one of my guys, but it was really convincing. The man straightened up and went back in. I realized I'd been holding my breath.

The men with the grenade launchers came cautiously back into the street and the others deployed as before. The ones on the roof got into position. The countdown restarted.

Three… two… one.

The first wave of grenade launchers fired and sent flashbangs in, front and back. The upper rooms flared brilliantly and there was an ear-splitting series of reports, followed by multiple echoes that almost buried the sound of glass showering onto the ground below. The launchers fired again and the lower windows blew out, followed by another volley of echoes. The second wave now fired good-nites, and they sailed through all the broken windows and detonated with dull thumps. The outlines on the roof disappeared together as the men swung into the rooms front and back. Moments later lights went on in the front rooms, and on the hill behind I could see the glow from the rooms at the rear. All rooms taken.

Then shots, the short snaps of a sidearm followed by two bursts of three from a machine pistol. Silence. A light came on behind the front door and it opened. Cliff Marshall was standing there. I went down the stairs two at a time.

I shouted, "Anyone hurt?"

Cliff was breathing heavily. His mask was hanging around his neck now – the anaesthetic gas would have dissipated very quickly. "One of the gang was in the kitchen," he said. "At the back. Came out shooting. Caught Morris."

"Is he—?"

I stopped short as Morris appeared, coming slowly down the stairs supported by Coutts. He gave me a wan smile.

"I'm okay, sir," he said, and pointed to a tear in the body armour. "Knocked the breath out of me, is all."

I breathed a sigh of relief. He'd have a lovely bruise tomorrow but the armour had done its job. "No other casualties?"

"Just the one who did it," Morris replied, pointing to the side of the stairs where a gang member was folded in a tangle of limbs. I didn't even bother to check him. The machine pistols were loaded with frangible ammunition to avoid any risk of shoot-through. A hit from a round like that is not recoverable, and this guy had taken several.

Coutts led Morris outside for some air and I went upstairs. On the landing I found a dazed gang member in the firm grip of two of my squad, their masks dangling, while a third frisked him thoroughly. They fastened his wrists behind his back and started to move him out. I was about to go into the bedroom, the one where we suspected the girls were being held, when two more of my men came out escorting another gang member, his hands already tied behind him.

"Any more in there?" I asked.

"Just the girls, Colonel."

I went in and did a quick count: ten of them. Six were lying on the floor or trying to raise themselves. Four had made it to a sitting position. Two of the four were just blinking their eyes, another was holding her head, and yet another was trying to clear her ears with her little fingers. That one was lighter-skinned, and she was wearing an embroidered blouse, unbuttoned, and blue trousers. I went over and squatted next to her.

"Fiona?"

She looked up, squinted, and retracted her head as if to get a clearer view of where the voice was coming from. It was a movement I'd seen on old drunks, but never on a sober seventeen-year-old. Her eyes came into focus and she scooped back thick chestnut hair.

"Fiona, I'm Colonel Jim Slater, Special Assignment Force. You're safe now."

She looked at me for a moment, then she started to cry. She didn't bury her face in her hands, she just sat there noiselessly, still staring at me, mouth slack, the tears running down her cheeks.

"Take it easy, now." I helped her to her feet, kept an arm round her shoulder. "Did they hurt you at all?"

She just sobbed and, as if I'd reminded her, she drew her blouse together over her bra and fumbled with the buttons, trying to fasten them.

I looked around. Most of the other girls were sitting or trying to stand now, pulling down the hems of their skirts or buttoning up their dresses. If nothing else they could get these guys for kidnap, false imprisonment, and sexual assault, maybe even rape.

Cliff was standing in the doorway. "Ambulances are on the way, Jim. And police have already moved up, ready to take those goons off our hands."

"Good work. Get a few men to help these girls downstairs. I'm going to call the Ambassador and General Harken."

I made the first call. The Ambassador picked up immediately – he must have been waiting by the phone all night – and I gave him the good news. I heard what must have been his wife in the background, saying "Is she all right?" and his reply "Yes" and there was a great sob of relief. He returned to me.

"Where is Fiona now?"

"She'll be taken to hospital with nine other girls. Don't be alarmed, sir, it's standard procedure."

"Colonel, I don't have the words to thank you—"

"Sir, you'll have to excuse me, but there's still a lot to do here."

"Oh. Yes. Of course. Well, thank you, and thank your men for me."

"I will."

I clicked off and stood there, thinking for a moment. Did I say enough? Physically I didn't think his daughter was seriously harmed, but she was badly shaken and she'd probably need psychiatric support. All that would come out later; right now the Ambassador and his wife would just be glad to have her back in one piece. I placed the second call. Harken sounded pleased.

"Nice going, Jim. I'll pass that on. Now get your people out of there. We don't want to outstay our welcome, do we?"

I went downstairs. The flashbangs and gunfire had woken the entire neighbourhood and lights were on in every house. They illuminated the scene outside, which had the curious effect of enlarging the space, so that the street now felt wider and the houses more compact. A knot of residents had gathered, coats donned hastily over their nightwear, to see what was going on. They were being held back by a police cordon.

Two groggy gang members were manhandled into the back of police cars. I had a fair idea what was in store for them, but the cops wouldn't learn much of any value. These people were just links in a chain and they wouldn't know anything beyond the location where they were required to deliver their human freight for the next pickup. Even if they gave that away it wouldn't help. With the amount of publicity this was going to generate in a few hours' time the pickup point would be abandoned long before anyone could get near it, and even that was assuming it was inside the border.

Two police cars drove away with their sirens wailing, which at this time of the morning seemed more like a declaration of triumph than an actual necessity.

The ambulances arrived and the girls, most of them still unsteady, were loaded into them. They took off. The sound of the vehicles died away, leaving everyone with a feeling of anti-climax.

I found Ferenczi. "First class operation, Major. My compliments to you and your men. I'll see that a commendation comes through at a high level."

"No problem, glad it worked out well." He looked around him. "Now it's all over I guess we can exfil."

"Sure, you go ahead. I'm going to get my squad to do the same."

They'd already mustered in the street as I went over.

"Okay, guys, great job. The Ambassador sends his thanks and congratulations. Let's pull out."

Sam Govind came over to me. "Could we hang on a bit longer, Jim?"

"Problem, Sam?"

"Yeah, one of the guys is missing."

"Okay," I said, loud enough for everyone to hear. "We'll give it another few minutes."

I wasn't too bothered. The man could be taking a leak or something.

Five minutes later I looked at my watch again and clicked my tongue. It was shortly after six o'clock and the sky was already glowing pink.

I said to Sam, "This man is a goddamned nuisance. I want to get going. I've a good mind to leave him to make his own way back. Who is it, anyway?"

"Sergeant Bill Archer."

I pictured him right away: stocky guy, very strong, flat nose, deep-set eyes, shaved head. He'd been with the SAF for several years. Attaching names to faces was something I was good at – I acquired the skills way back. You needed to know things like that when you were taking command of a new troop: it meant you could assign tasks to specific people and it made them feel like individuals instead of numbers. But when I saw this particular face again I was going to give him a right royal—

A tall soldier was jogging up the street towards us. He was camo'd but I knew who he was by the rangy way he moved.

"Colonel," he acknowledged, with a slight dip of the head, then immediately spoke to Sam. "Captain, one of the all-terrains has been taken."

Sam's mouth dropped open. "What do you mean, 'taken'? I left you and Sergeant Michaels in charge of them."

"Sir, he was SAF. He strolled along the line of vehicles, then quickly got into one. Sergeant Michaels said," he paused, glanced at me and licked his lips, "excuse me, sir, he said 'Where the fuck do you think you're going?' but

33

the man didn't reply. He just closed the door and drove off fast."

Sam closed his eyes. "Don't tell me: it was Sergeant Archer."

"Yes, sir, it was."

Sam murmured, "What the hell's he playing at?"

I caught the soldier by the arm. "Viktor, you said 'He strolled along the line of vehicles'. What was in the vehicle he took?"

"Armaments, mainly, sir. Multirifles, boxes of ammunition, grenades—"

"What kind of grenades?"

"All kinds: standard, flashbangs, good-nites, incendaries."

I turned to Sam. "He selected that vehicle on purpose. We need to find him fast."

"I know, Jim, but where's he gone?"

I looked down the street, biting my lip. The men were standing casually in groups, chatting, waiting for the order to pull out. I raised my voice.

"Who saw Sergeant Archer after the operation?"

Three hands went up.

"Over here." They came forward. I couldn't make out who they were through all the black camo. "All right, what was he doing?"

They shrugged. One said, "We were helping the girls out of the house."

"And…?"

Another said, "He's right in front of me going downstairs, supporting this girl with an arm round her waist, talking quietly to her. She's more with it than the others, and she's telling him what went on up there. From what I can hear, the bastards interfered with them, all of them."

"How did Archer seem?"

"Angry, real angry. We all were. They were only kids, some of them." He paused, then added, "He was swearing a lot."

"Was that unusual?"

He looked at his companions, and one said, "I'd say so, yeah. The guy's pretty laid back as a rule."

Then all heads jerked round. Soldiers know the sound of ordnance and what we'd heard was a grenade, no question about it. There was a second explosion, and it wasn't that far away.

I was already running. "Everyone to the vehicles!"

7

Our convoy threaded its way through a tangle of streets. We drove as fast as we dared, but some of the local inhabitants were already on the move and the last thing we wanted now was an accident involving a pedestrian. My driver hardly needed to be told where to go: the sky in that direction was a bright orange and it wasn't from the sunrise. Ten minutes later we saw smoke pouring from the end of a street and drew to a halt. I hopped down and walked forward, and through gaps in the smoke I could see a line of houses, all burning fiercely. I went back to speak to the two captains.

"It looks like—"

We turned our heads at the sound of approaching sirens. A fire engine rolled up. For a few moments nothing happened and I guessed they were radioing for more appliances. Then the police arrived. Their car came in at high speed, braked sharply as it encountered our small convoy of US army vehicles, and pulled up in front. A rear door opened and a short, wide police officer got out, straightened his uniform, and walked back to us with the deliberate gait of someone prepared to enforce the law. It was never a good idea to wait in these circumstances so I lifted my helmet visor and went forward to meet him. I couldn't tell what rank he was, but there was a lot of gold braid and stars on his jacket. He gesticulated at the fire and asked me in colourful Spanish what the hell we were doing there.

I had to shout over the roar of the fire. "We just extracted your hostages and detained two people-traffickers," I explained patiently. "We think one of our men may have done this. He has perhaps gone a little crazy?" I made a circular motion of my forefinger at one temple. "We came to get him back."

"No." He stared down the street, as if our man was going to be standing there, and said, "You must leave this to us."

"He is a citizen of the United States—"

"And he is destroying property and killing citizens of the Republic of the Honduras!"

"Sir, your government gave us permission to operate here."

"For a hostage extraction. This is not a hostage extraction. Go home. Now."

He said this with a flip of the hand, turned his back on me and returned to his car. No doubt he was going to call in police reinforcements, probably the army too.

Another couple of fire engines pulled up. There were people everywhere now and the air was full of the heat and smoke and noise of the fire, heavy motors throbbing and the shouts of firemen as they unravelled hoses. A slow, grinding crash told me the roof or floors of one of the burning houses had collapsed, and seconds later a cloud of sparks rose within the smoke above the buildings. Then another crash and another cloud of sparks and smoke billowed across the road, stinging my eyes and nose. It was hard to see what the firemen could do about this at the moment beyond stopping the fire from spreading to neighbouring houses and the next street.

I rejoined Cliff Marshall and Sam Govind at the car. "They're not going to let us take over."

"Idiots!" Cliff said. "They have no idea what they're up against."

"I know. Question is, what can we do? This is their territory. They may manage to catch up with Bill Archer and they may manage to kill him, but he's going to take out a good few of them first. I only wanted to bring him in – the guy needs help. My God." I wiped some blown ash off my face and my hand came away black with camo paint. "How does something like this happen? One moment we've got a diplomatic triumph on our hands, minutes later it's turned into the makings of a full-on international incident."

Cliff said, "Where do you think Bill is now?"

"Not here, Cliff. This is just a distraction – he's gone off to create havoc somewhere else. They'll realize that sooner or later and deploy army units all over the city, looking and listening out for him." I sighed. "Guys, I don't know what the legal situation actually is but my gut feeling is that, diplomatically speaking, we could make things worse rather than better by trying to intervene. And if their soldiers spot our soldiers all hell could break loose. We'd better pull out. Sam, take one of the all-terrains and come with me. We'll stick around just in case we can help. Cliff, take the rest of the guys and the gear back to the air base. Make yourselves comfortable if you can; I don't know how long this is going to take."

*

The men left for the air base and Sam and I drove a short distance away in the all-terrain and stopped again to decide on a strategy. The NavAid was showing a street map of

Tegucigalpa. I changed the scale so that we could view the city in its geographical context.

"The question is, Sam, does Bill Archer have an exit strategy? If we can guess what it is it'll give us a clue to where he'll strike next." I pointed at the screen. "There are mountains up here to the north-east and some open country to the south-west. Either one would be a good bet, but right now he only has to go a couple of ks to the east and he'll be that much nearer the mountains."

"He's not acting rationally, Jim. He may not be thinking that far ahead."

I heaved a sigh. "Well, we've got to position ourselves somewhere. Our only chance is if we can get to him before the local cops and army do. You got any better ideas?"

"Not really. It's a toss-up. He may not even move that far; he could be in the next street – he could be anywhere. The first we'll know is when we hear grenades or gunfire."

"Decision time, Sam. Let's take a gamble and drive a couple of ks east."

*

Some gambles pay off, some don't. This one didn't.

We parked on high ground and got out of the all-terrain. Sam took his helmet off; I did the same and rubbed a hand through the sweat on my scalp. We stood there, scanning around and listening to the sounds of a city waking up: the increasing hum of traffic and honking of horns against the growing background noise of shutters and doors opening, dogs barking, and people bustling along pavements. The conflagration we'd just left seemed to have died down, marked only by a column of smoke, brown against the rising sun. Fifteen minutes went by. Half an hour. Then the sky lit up way over to the south-west. I counted off nearly twelve seconds before we heard the explosion. It was all of four ks away.

Sam pointed. "It's down there."

"Shit, got it badly wrong. Let's go." We replaced our helmets and I climbed into the driver's seat, Sam slammed the passenger door behind him and I accelerated away.

I couldn't keep up any sort of speed. It was already seven o'clock, the roads meandered, and on the major routes the traffic was really starting to build. Sam had restored the street map on the NavAid and he shouted detours; still we seemed to be no nearer. We kept the windows open but there was little chance of hearing much over the traffic noise. Even if we did, sound would bounce off roads and houses, so we wouldn't know which direction it was coming from.

We went up another hill and I stopped the car to get out and listen. We could hear automatic gunfire, still some way off. Then a clattering which grew louder.

"What the hell's that?" Govind shouted.

"Sounds to me like they're using an old helicopter. That could speed things up for them. May also guide us in."

We went back to the all-terrain and drove on. From time to time the sky peeped between the rows of houses and we got glimpses of the helicopter cruising back and forth, training a searchlight. Then it began to hover. We figured we must be getting near. Now nothing could conceal the sounds: more grenades, automatic fire from a lot of weapons. We reached an army roadblock with barriers across the street and two armed soldiers. I stopped the all-terrain and they levelled their automatic rifles at us. We got out slowly, hands held high, and I shouted to them in Spanish.

"I am Colonel Jim Slater of the United States Special Forces and this is Captain Sam Govind. It is one of our men in there. Maybe I can speak to him, get him to turn himself in."

Two pairs of eyes drilled into me. They said nothing. The rifles were still levelled. Had they understood? Surely my Spanish wasn't that bad? They probably understood English, so I tried that.

"Come on, guys, we're unarmed. We may be able to help. It sure won't do any harm. One of you can come with us."

They moved together, exchanging words out of the sides of their mouths without taking their eyes – or weapons – off us. I couldn't hear what they were saying over the rattle of the gunfire and the clatter of the helicopter. The muzzles of the rifles dropped a little. One shouted back at us, "A police negotiator tried already. All he got was bullets."

"Yeah, but I know this guy. He may listen to me."

They looked at each other, then the one who spoke said something to his partner and jerked his head to us. We followed him down the street. It didn't look to me like much talking was going on. To our right, rifle muzzles were poking out of every window and whether these guys had a target or not they were blazing away, raking a tall house opposite. The Honduran soldier pushed us close to the right-hand wall and we walked doubled over to lower our profiles. The helicopter passed overhead, its searchlight sweeping the house and its surroundings and revealing yet more soldiers. They were everywhere we looked, crouched, rifles at the ready. Further along the street several cars were on fire, sending flames and black smoke soaring. If one of those vehicles was the car with the loud hailer we were wasting our time.

We stopped and I studied the house, watching for muzzle flashes. One. Two. Three. He was single tapping, moving from room to room, choosing his target each time. The soldiers continued to fire. Seconds ticked by but now there was nothing coming back. What was he up to?

The soldiers on the ground were slow to realize it, but gradually the firing eased off, then stopped altogether.

There was an ominous silence. Had he quit the building? I assumed there'd be soldiers on the other side of the house ready to pick him off if he made an appearance there, and the helicopter would spot him if he got onto the roof and tried to jump houses.

Then I flinched as every room in the house lit up brilliantly again and again in a series of loud explosions. Glass fragments rained down, tinkling as they hit the road. Sam and I looked at each other. Even before the after-image from the explosions had faded completely from my retinas I could see the flickering light of flames. Soon they were licking from the upper windows.

"Grenades," Sam said.

"Yeah, and at least one of them was incendiary."

I straightened up and looked around to see where that salvo had come from, but all I could see were automatic rifles, no grenade launchers. Now the only sounds were the crackling of the fire and the helicopter clop-clopping back and forth overhead. Someone shouted a command and the soldiers began to move, converging on the house from all directions, running fast through any exposed areas. From the helicopter they would look like ants heading back to their nest. A soldier shot out the front door lock and kicked it open and they stepped inside. There was a rumble of collapsing timbers and a shower of dust and sparks billowed from the broken lower windows. The soldiers hurried out and seconds later the blaze engulfed the entire house. As they backed away an army officer strode across the road to them. Before our Honduran escort could stop me I'd run over to speak to him.

I identified myself quickly. "I came here to get him to surrender," I said.

His lip curled. "You are too late. He just blew himself up."

"That…?" I swallowed. "I thought it was your men."

"No, not us, we were waiting for him to run out of ammunition. He did it himself."

The house was now an inferno, sheets of flame pouring from every window, soaring into the sky and illuminating the entire scene. The heat was intense and we both moved away. In the reddish light I could make out bodies lying in the street, and another hanging out of a ground floor window in the building opposite. The officer followed my gaze, nodding grimly.

My body went slack. All I could say was, "I am sorry. I am very, very sorry."

The helicopter banked overhead and flew off. Then, in the distance, the siren of a fire engine rose and grew louder.

By the time it got here there wouldn't be much left of the house or of Bill Archer. He must have pulled the pin on every grenade he had, then just waited.

It seemed he had an exit strategy after all.

8

This time I wasn't surprised to be called to Washington. Three days ago I went there to be told someone wanted my body back. This time someone wanted my head on a plate. So one way and another it seemed like things hadn't changed all that much. Even the weather was replicating the last trip, a warm, penetrating drizzle that didn't merit a waterproof but made clothes and everything else damp to the touch.

Harken had called me before I left. He'd said nothing about the operation, just gave me the room number for the meeting and reminded me to wear my medal ribbons.

At the Pentagon reception desk they seemed to be expecting me. After scanning my ID the young man said, "One moment, please, Colonel." He made a call and there was a brief exchange. He clicked off.

"Please come with me, sir."

"I can find the way, soldier."

"I've been asked to escort you, sir."

Escort? This was getting worse by the minute. I

followed him into the elevator, which he took to the fifth floor, and along a corridor, traversing one ring after another, speaking to security at each checkpoint, with a more thorough check at the E-ring. We turned right and I was shown into a conference room. Unlike the rooms on the inner ring this one had windows. If I hadn't lost my sense of direction – and I didn't think I had – these would provide a nice view out to the Lagoon and over the Potomac in fine weather, but his wasn't fine weather and the windows looked grey and opaque. Not that it mattered to the four at the table, as they had their backs to the windows. On the left was a four-star general, who I'd never seen before. He had a florid complexion, his buzz cut and moustache were silver-grey, and he filled a tunic that was almost totally obscured by gold braid and medal ribbons. Who the hell was he? Maybe I should have known but the truth was, I tended not to interest myself in guys as high in the stratosphere as that. Next to him, working my way to the right, was Helena Brooke-Masters, Deputy Secretary of State, who seemed to be chairing the meeting. Although we'd met before she offered no greeting, just indicated the chair opposite her with a peremptory wave of the hand. I'd never found her a friendly prospect; her small dark eyes were too close together, she had a beaky nose and thin lips, emphasized by a startling shade of red lipstick, and her hair was curly and cropped short. Today she looked even more grim than usual. That was easy enough to understand: the State Department would have their hands full right now trying to mend fences after this debacle. Sitting next to her was Bob Cressington, who gave me a rueful smile, and on the end was Wendell Harken, whose expression changed not one iota. There was a glass, a jug of iced water, and a smart notepad for each one. Not, I noted, for me.

Helena Brooke-Masters introduced everyone by name

and title, including herself, as if I couldn't possibly know any of them. I was simply wondering who the four-star general was. She left him to last.

"And this is General George Wagner," she said, "Chief of Staff of the Army."

My God, the CSA.

This guy was a seriously big hitter. In the army, it didn't go any higher.

By now everything had slipped into the background except for the four faces in front of me, the slippery leather upholstery of the chair I was sitting on, and the gleaming wood finish of that table.

Helena Brooke-Masters said, "I expect you can guess what this meeting is about, Colonel. We're endeavouring to sort out the unholy mess you left behind in the Republic of the Honduras."

I waited.

"Well, what have you got to say about it?"

"What do you want me to say, ma'am? It was an unmitigated disaster."

She blinked and recoiled slightly. Was she hoping for a stream of lame excuses? If so my candour must have been a disappointment to her.

Bob Cressington coughed lightly. "In fairness, ma'am, the Colonel's outfit pulled off a considerable coup before that. They rescued ten kidnapped girls, including the US Ambassador's daughter. They also killed a member of the gang and detained two others. The Ambassador has spoken to us in glowing terms about the conduct of the operation. There were thirty-two soldiers involved in that hostage extraction. This tragedy was the work of just one man."

It was generous of Bob to intervene. I noted the formality, though. He probably had cocktails with this woman, but here he addressed her as "ma'am". Then I returned my gaze to Brooke-Masters. On second thoughts he probably didn't have cocktails with her.

She sighed. "I think, Colonel, you'd better tell us in your own words exactly what happened."

I was prepared for this. I gave a full account, up to the point where the windows lit up with grenades and the house went up in flames.

"Sergeant Archer committed suicide?" she asked.

"Yes." My reply was hardly more than a grunt. I felt again the sadness of that wasted life.

"You're sure of that?"

"Ma'am, the Honduran forces had the house under close surveillance from the ground and the air, and he wasn't seen coming out. On the contrary, up to a few moments earlier he was returning fire, so there's no doubt he was in there. At least one of the grenades was incendiary, probably more than one. The house quickly became an inferno – it burnt to the ground with Sergeant Archer inside it. Not a thing remained."

"Not a thing," Brooke-Masters repeated acidly, "except for fifteen people dead: nine soldiers of the Honduran army, two members of the Honduran police force, and four innocent Honduran civilians who failed to escape from their burning houses. Plus a dozen or so injured or wounded, currently being treated in hospitals. Add the damage to property and we're facing millions of dollars in compensation."

I didn't care for the way she brushed aside the death of a man who up to then had served his country well, but it wasn't a point I could make in these circumstances. "Ma'am, this man's combat skills and experience were way beyond anything their police and armed forces had ever encountered. We might have been able to prevent at least some of those casualties if they'd allowed us to tackle him, but they refused point blank."

"You didn't challenge them on that?"

"The granting of a 'temporary foreign presence' was for us to carry out the hostage extraction, not this. I thought we'd be skating on thin ice if we intervened where we were so clearly unwanted. So I sent the men back to the air base, just kept Captain Govind with me to observe events."

General Wagner pushed his smartpad out of the way and rested his arms on the table, a gesture sufficient to attract Brooke-Masters' attention. "General?" she said.

His voice was gruff. "This man Archer. Did you know him?"

"Of course, sir. I was his CO. I know every man in my command."

"And you suspected nothing, nothing that suggested he was capable of doing something like this?"

"I saw no prior indication, General. Neither did his closest friends. During the hostage extraction he played his part efficiently and obeyed orders to the letter. The men with him said he became very angry when he learned how those gangsters had interfered with the girls. But there was nothing remarkable about that; we were all angry. The girls were young, and these men were sexual predators. It was then that he went off the rails."

He pursed his lips and nodded slowly. Then he said, "Isn't it the case, Colonel, that your outfit is made up of some pretty wild bastards?"

The question wasn't delivered aggressively, it was more like a casual swipe.

"No sir, it is not. We only have room for highly trained, highly disciplined bastards."

The language had brought a sour expression to Brooke-Masters' countenance, but the CSA was smothering a smile.

"It sounds to me like this man suffered a delayed response to the stress of the operation. What kind of psychological screening do you carry out before you take these people on? You know, just to make sure you get the right kind of bastard."

It was my turn to smother a smile, not least because Brooke-Masters' expression would have curdled milk by now. I was becoming aware of the CSA's extraordinary charisma and I was really warming to him.

"All applicants undergo a thorough psychological profiling, sir, and Archer was considered perfectly sound. As for conduct under stress, I believe the selection process for the SAF is more rigorous than for any other force in the world. Take, for example, the training in case of capture. General Harken devised that part, so perhaps he should outline it to you."

Brooke-Masters turned to Harken. "General Harken?"

Harken nodded and went straight in. "The type of mission given to the SAF can present the risk of kidnap or capture. In that event there are two vital things to know: who your captors are, and where you're being taken. Let's start with the first. All our soldiers are fluent in at least one language other than English, often two or three. In addition we want them to recognize other languages, particularly ones found in trouble spots, and in the case of languages like Spanish and Arabic they need to be aware of local variations in accent and idiom. We instruct them, then test them with short recorded snatches of conversation. The second thing is where they're being taken. We drive candidates around a winding route, and at the end they trace it on a map. We repeat the exercise, but this time they're hooded. Then we take them on an unknown route, also hooded, to see if they can identify where they are at the end of it. Finally we go abroad with them somewhere and put the two exercises together."

The CSA said, "Sounds pretty tough."

"It is. And remember, this comes after candidates have

passed all the usual tests: endurance, survival in the jungle, combat training, and resistance to interrogation. Most of the drop-outs occur during this last phase of selection. Those who remain can certainly cope with stress."

"And Sergeant Archer passed all these tests."

"Yes, sir. If he hadn't he wouldn't have been with the force."

"Thank you." The CSA turned back to me. "Colonel, in your account you said a police negotiator tried to communicate with the soldier – presumably in Spanish. Would Sergeant Archer have understood him?"

"Yes, sir. Sergeant Archer had spent a lot of time in South America. He was a fluent Spanish speaker, and he was familiar with local variations, too."

"So you can't explain why this man should suddenly go on the rampage."

"No, sir. If we'd succeeded in getting him out, as I'd hoped to do, we'd be a lot closer to finding out what made him snap. As it is I have no explanation. I wish I did."

Brooke-Masters' mouth was making impatient little movements. She sniffed in a quick breath.

"May I ask what you propose to do to avoid repetitions of this disastrous turn of events?"

The room went silent. Everyone present was acutely aware that she'd asked a really stupid question, no doubt including Brooke-Masters herself. How do you answer a stupid question without pointing out that it's a stupid question? I just said:

"Ma'am, I'm open to suggestions."

The CSA pushed himself away from the table. "I think we've gone as far as we can with this, don't you agree, Helena?"

She sniffed again. "Very well. Colonel Slater and General Harken, you are excused."

9

As Harken and I left the conference room he said, "Coffee, Jim?"

"Coffee would be good."

We rode the elevator to a Starbucks in the second floor Mall. Harken said nothing until we sat down with our coffees.

"Well, Jim, after this I shouldn't think the Hondurans will be in any hurry for us to carry out another mission on their patch."

"If the Ambassador sends his family home, or at least keeps tabs on his daughter, it shouldn't be necessary. What about our air base there? That's also classed as a 'temporary foreign presence'."

"I gather they're making threatening noises, but no one expects them to go as far as that. A good chunk of their national income comes from that base. If we pulled out it would hit them harder than us."

We sipped our coffees. Then he put his cup down and looked at me, his mouth twisting in a wry smile.

"You were bold in there, Jim."

"Quite honestly it didn't seem like I had much to lose. If Helena Brooke-Masters wants me thrown out it'll happen anyway."

"It wasn't a disciplinary hearing. She wanted one but the CSA insisted on assessing the situation first. What has that woman got against you?"

"To my knowledge we've only crossed swords once. You remember the Cuprex International business? A clear case of the Russians looking to get a commercial advantage by assassinating a rival. I wanted the State Department to take it up diplomatically, but they were deep in trade negotiations. The last thing they wanted was someone like me upsetting the apple cart. I seem to recall I made some pointed remarks about human rights in the Russian Union."

"That was a while ago."

"Evidently she has a long memory… Is that Bob?"

Bob Cressington came away from the counter and strolled over. He set down his coffee and pulled up a chair. "Thought I'd find you here."

Harken said, "It's over, then."

Bob shook his head. "Yeah. Sorry you had to go through all that. The Honduran government filed an official complaint and the Secretary of State's foaming at the mouth. His whole Department's bearing the brunt of it. Helena wanted a scapegoat, and Jim here looked like a prime candidate. But the CSA wrote it off as a freak occurrence. It couldn't have been foreseen and it was beyond the control of any commanding officer." Bob took a sip of coffee and smiled at me over the edge of the cup. "Seems he took a bit of a shine to you, Jim. Anyway he insisted there were no grounds whatever for disciplinary action, so Helena closed the meeting. She was none too pleased."

"Good of you to tell us, Bob," I said. "And thanks for

your support in there. I appreciated it."

"No, you did the job we asked you to do. The rest was, well, just unfortunate." He looked at me. "It's a strange business, all the same. Just between us, Jim, you didn't hold anything back, did you?"

"Not a thing. Sergeant Archer was a damned fine soldier. I've no idea what made him go off his chump like that." I grimaced. "Now we'll never know."

We chatted a bit longer, then Harken looked at his watch. "You'll have to excuse us, Bob. I arranged for Jim to meet someone in my office."

I looked quickly at him, but he didn't meet my gaze.

Bob said, "Sure, I'd better get on, too."

Harken and I shook hands with him, then went up to Harken's office. I followed, wondering who else I had to see.

Harken waited until we were inside before telling me.

"Mark Godstall is consulting with the Defense Legal Services Agency at this moment. He said he'd meet us here around midday."

Oh, that. I nodded. "I take it things have moved on."

"Yes, but I need to know if there are any fresh developments."

There was a knock at the door. My watch said three minutes to twelve. Right on cue.

Harken indicated a chair, which Godstall took. He had a document case with him but he placed it at his feet.

Harken said, "You'd better brief us on the current situation."

Godstall turned to me. "This party that's suing for the return of your body. In a nutshell, we got it wrong. They aren't seeking a quick settlement at all. They actually *want* it to go to court."

My heart sank. "Why? What's in it for them?"

"They can smell a rat. A whole body transplant is a

hugely expensive operation, usually reserved for the very rich or very influential. Yet the individual who received this man's body was an ordinary soldier, namely you. They sense there's a lot more to it. That gives them two opportunities. First it's a chance to cause major embarrassment for their old adversary, the Army. Second, it'll pay dividends. This business is classified, and that's all they need to dangle in front of the media. You know the kind of thing: if it's been suppressed – never mind the reasons – it must be something of public interest. The media can create a long-running story, for which the syndicate will no doubt be very well rewarded. They've probably got the contract lined up already. This action will pay for itself."

"You say 'the syndicate', but the action's being brought by the man's girlfriend, isn't it?"

"She won't see any of it. The only benefit for her is that she won't be gang-raped in some warehouse or have her face slashed to ribbons." He sucked in a short breath. "These people aren't known for their subtlety."

Harken bit his lip. "We can't allow this to go much further. There are issues of national security involved."

"I guessed there were. We could get the case dismissed on those grounds alone, but that would attract even more notice. It would be better to get it thrown out at an early stage. I've just been discussing who we should use as a Defense Attorney."

"Whatever happens the media will have a field day."

"The army intends to keep the whole thing under wraps for as long as possible. Unfortunately the other side is unlikely to see it the same way."

Harken nodded briskly. "All right, Godstall, the Colonel and I need to talk about this now. No need for us to detain you."

"Very good, sir."

We rose, shook hands, and Godstall left the room. We sat down again.

Harken said, "Godstall told me what was going on a few days ago. I didn't bother you with it then because I thought the other side might have a change of heart. Clearly they haven't, so my contingency plan needs to come into operation. I've arranged for you to be transferred temporarily to your old Regiment, the 22 SAS."

For a moment I felt a sense of shock. I was loyal to The Regiment when I served with them, but I'd been with the SAF for nearly ten years and I'd identified completely with them. And it wasn't just that.

I squinted at him. "Straight after this mess in the Honduras? People will assume I'm being relieved of duty!"

"I can make it clear to anyone who matters. I'll say it was part of a long-standing commitment."

"It'll still look like I'm running away from the problem."

"It can't be helped, Jim. The alternative is having a media circus descending on Fort Piper and hanging around your neck all day, every day. It'll be impossible for you to function effectively as CO under those conditions. We need to get you completely off the scene."

I heaved a sigh. "I suppose that makes sense."

"It does. And it would be a good idea to make your move sooner rather than later."

"Point taken. Which squadron am I assigned to?"

"'A' squadron, Hereford."

"And who do you want as XO back at base while I'm away? Tommy?"

"Yes, Tommy Geiger will be fine. I'll leave you to brief him."

I said nothing for a few moments. Then, "Suppose things had gone differently upstairs? I could have been out on my ear long before this other thing came to trial."

He shook his head. "There was never any real possibility of that. Helena was way off base. The CSA wouldn't want the entire Army to take responsibility for the actions of one crazed individual. That's certainly the way it looked, and the meeting upstairs simply confirmed it."

I nodded. My thoughts were running ahead now, turning to the SAS. Things would have moved on since I was transferred from there.

"Do you know who the CO is at Hereford?"

"Colonel Owen Gracey."

"Never heard of him." I hesitated. Something occurred to me. I thought I knew the answer, but I needed to be sure. "I take it he doesn't know I've served with them in the past."

"Good God, no! All they know is, a court case is coming up that could bring down a lot of media attention on you, so you'll be waiting it out with them. Neither he nor anyone else at Hereford has a clue about your previous identity."

Okay, now I was sure. "Would I know anyone else there?"

Harken nodded. "I thought you'd ask me that. I looked up the longer-established people, ones you might have served with." He called up a page on his desk screen and read out the names. "Lieutenant-Colonel Bruce Harrington and Major Scot Hayward. Remember either of them?"

I smiled. "Yeah, I remember them."

*

I boarded the flight for Raleigh-Durham and took the window seat. I always liked to sit by the window, even when I was a kid.

What was I saying? I meant when Jim Forbes was a kid. It could be confusing, carrying around memories from a time when your brain was in a different body.

I barely heard the announcements. The morning's events had unwound almost too fast for me to keep track and I was replaying them in my head.

Thinking it over now, Harken was right. The timing wasn't ideal, but getting me out of the picture made sense. Although I didn't like relinquishing my command, Tommy Geiger was a good XO, so it would be in safe hands. As for the law suit, I was glad to leave that behind me. It wasn't just the media attention I was anxious to escape from; I had – with good reason – a healthy dislike of anything to do with courts and the legal process. Normally I fought my own battles, but this was one I was glad to let the Army fight for me. And since it was out of my hands I refused to let it prey on my mind.

The engines roared briefly, then settled, and we rolled away from the apron and out towards the runway. As the aircraft turned I could see the queue for take-off ahead. This was going to take a while.

It would be interesting to rejoin my old outfit, the 22 SAS. Harken said Lieutenant-Colonel Bruce Harrington and Major Scot Hayward were at Hereford. I had an immediate mental picture of both of them, at least a picture based on the way they looked ten years ago. Bruce Harrington was a Captain back then. Clean-cut guy, slim, smart, good leader of men.

Further up the queue a plane took off. I couldn't see it from this side, but I could hear it all right. It thundered along the runway and the airframe in contact with my shoulder trembled with the sound. After a pause the engines of our own craft roared, then died, as we moved up one place. A minute later the whole sequence repeated.

Scot Hayward was a Lieutenant when I was with the Regiment, same rank as me. We always called him Scottie, but there was nothing Scottish about him – he was more South London than Glasgow. Big guy, big voice. Wide, flat features, and a five-o'clock shadow that made its appearance at ten o'clock in the morning.

Of the two, I'd known Scottie the longest. We met on an assignment in Libya. That was back in 2043...

10

Libya 2043

There's been yet another outbreak of civil war and the UN's sent a delegation to broker peace. How the hell they're going to do that I have no idea; by now the combatants have splintered into so many rival groups that even they don't know who they're fighting – or why. It doesn't seem to matter to them. So long as they have plenty of arms and ammunition they want to use them, and so long as they're firing bullets there may as well be someone or something on the receiving end. Armed, unarmed, man, woman or child, dog or cat, it makes no difference: if it moves it's a target.

The UN delegation's holed up in a disused Embassy building and the SAS is there to protect them. We're just part of it, though: the security detail has to be international as well as everything else. It creates some problems because of differences in language and training, so we make the best of it by ensuring that four of our guys stay together at all times. I'm one of them. Scottie is another. Our main job is to guard the building because there are people around here who don't want peace at any price and not all of them are at the negotiating table.

One night Scottie and I are on stag at the front. The improvised sentry box does nothing to keep out the cold night air, but that's okay because the low emission clothing we're wearing tends to hold in the heat. The clothing is a precaution against snipers with infra-red sights, and there's nothing paranoid about that: the street is full of shelled out buildings, concrete rectangular monsters with vacant eyes where the windows once were, prime firing positions for anyone in the mood for a little target practice. At this moment there are two bad boys in a building a block up on the left. We've been keeping an eye on it, seen the muzzle flashes on the sixth floor, counted the windows along, stored the information.

We're the second team of the night to be on duty. There's plenty of depth to the backup but we're the most exposed to anything that comes along, which is why they call it early warning and we call it shit duty. The sky's just beginning to lighten and my night vision glasses have compensated by dimming somewhat. I detect movement, nudge Scottie, and point. I've spotted two figures on the other side of the street. They're moving slowly, staying close to the walls and backing into doorways wherever they can. Automatically we reach for our sidearms. As they get nearer I can see it's an old guy and a woman. The old guy has a long beard and he's wearing a djellabah. She's all wrapped up in some sort of shawl with another one over her head, and she's carrying what looks like a wicker basket. We don't holster the sidearms: there's enough room in the basket for a serious amount of explosive. There haven't been that many suicide bombings yet, and normally they wouldn't waste two people on one attack, but we're on our guard all the same; there's the basket, and the old guy could be wearing belts. Some of these groups aren't averse to giving such people a choice: "Do this. If you refuse we kill you and your whole family. If you accept, we spare your family."

I speak into my helmet microphone. "Open Channel Blue."

"Channel Blue is open." A pleasant female voice. It doesn't belong to anyone here, more's the pity.

"Blue, this is Red."

"Yes, Red, we are receiving you." The Germans are on. It sounds like Dieter.

"Two civilians approaching."

"Hostiles?"

"I don't think so, but stand by."

We watch them carefully but they don't look at us, just work their way further down the road. Maybe they're simply two people who need to be somewhere else and figure it's safer to travel in the dark. Which is a mistake.

When they're just about level with us they look around them and start to cross the street. A shot rings out and the woman drops. The old man steps towards her and there's another shot and he seems to leap sideways, landing in a heap of angles. Neither one moves. The basket rolls slowly across the road with a curious up and down motion, teeters, then tips up just yards from us. The contents spread out on the road: olives, vegetables, fruit, tajeen-bread, now spattered with blood and brains. We have our answer. Just an old couple taking a meal home. We've seen bodies like that in the streets before but it's different when it happens right in front of your eyes. The black puddle of blood around each head thickens.

We're both breathing hard.

"Fuck," Scottie says. "That can't be right."

"Bastards," I murmur.

He switches off his helmet comms and pulls up the mask of his low-emission outfit. "Back soon."

I nod. All our communications are recorded. That one won't be.

Ten minutes pass. The sky lightens some more and the sides of the buildings to my left start to glow a pleasant peachy colour.

There's a flash followed by a bang coming from the sixth floor of that building. Stun grenade. Something dark appears at the empty window and drops to the street with a long, wailing howl. Then another one appears and goes the same way.

Five minutes later Scottie strolls up and joins me.

I say nothing.

*

I was looking out of the window at a cotton-wool cloud landscape. Above it the sky was a clear blue. It reminded me of a lovely Spring day back in England. Well, I'd be experiencing that at first hand soon enough.

The engine note dropped. I checked my watch. It wasn't a long flight and we were already starting on the descent. It was odd but I couldn't even remember taking off. I'd been thinking about Scottie. Libya was the first of many tours I did with him. Whatever the deployment was, Scottie and I would always team up – it went without saying. And although we were still Lieutenants, Scottie was already showing the leadership qualities of a Captain. Like that time in North Waziristan.

North Waziristan 2044

We've had reports of insurgents holed up in a village and we have to do a house-to-house. We're working in two-man teams but staying close enough to provide support if there's trouble. It's tense, dangerous work, but doing it with Scottie makes me feel more confident, and I think he feels the same way. Jim Forbes and Scottie Hayward – we're invincible, aren't we? I can see the others strung out along the street behind us. Each of us is carrying a multi-rifle, the under-barrel loaded with a grenade.

We clear two houses, both strangely empty, and go to the next one. We move slowly and quietly, listening at doors, trying to snatch a peek through windows. Scottie nods and points. He'll take this one from the front, me from the back. I get in position, my heart thudding inside my chest. This is the moment you could meet nothing or a hail of bullets. I crouch low on the hinge side of the door, level the rifle, and burst in. Scottie and I have worked together so long we have a knack for gauging each other's moves, and sure enough he comes in from the front at the same instant. No bullets, just an old man, two old women, three young women, and eight young children – boys and girls. The women have their arms tight around the children and they're all huddled in a corner, fourteen pairs of dark eyes, all fixed on us, all wide with terror. We make placatory signals with our hands but it doesn't seem to help. We go back outside.

Scottie speaks out of the corner of his mouth, although his eyes never stop roving.

"I don't like this, Jim. Word must have got out."

"You think so?"

"That looked like more than one family, got together for protection. How did they know to do that?"

"True."

He's still looking around, and now he narrows his eyes. "And where are the young men?"

"Run to the mountains, probably. Afraid they'll be killed – or recruited."

"Or with the insurgents waiting to jump us."

"Maybe we should get our Pashto speaker in here. Ask them what they know."

He scowls. "They'll be too terrified to say anything. He should be following us up, all the same. Those people need reassuring. You see their faces? Poor sods think we're going to kill them or rape the women or carry them off or something. Where's our glorious leader? I'll tell him."

He uses the helmet comms to speak to the Captain. The rest of the troop is mustering because we've finished this street. Up there among the mountains the air is fresh and cold, but all of us are sweating bricks. That's what it does to you. It's coming to the end of the afternoon and the Captain looks like he's ready to call it a day, but there's one more street to clear. If you can call it a street: it's just a dusty open area at the end of the village, with a few houses on one side.

Scottie and I are patrolling in our usual fashion, one walking forwards in front, the other walking backwards behind, both fanning our rifles. This time it's Scottie in front and he stops so suddenly I bang into him. I open my mouth but he puts his fingers to his lips and stabs a forefinger at the house at the end.

"I'll go round the back," he murmurs. "Wait for the flashbang, then use your grenade launcher. Target that window."

Following his example I keep my voice low, but I've got to say it. "Scottie, there could be civilians in there!"

He just shakes his head and moves off between the houses, doubled over. I take up my position.

A minute later the windows all light up and there's a loud bang. I fire and the grenade smashes through the window and explodes. I rush in at the front and Scottie meets me coming in at the back. Smoke hangs in the air in layers, barely disturbed by the thin rain of plaster that's still falling from the ceiling. The walls are pockmarked by the shrapnel, and the tang of Celonite explosive stings my nostrils. There are five bloody and mangled bodies lying under the windows. A grenade at close quarters does a lot of damage to the human body, especially in a confined space. This is even worse, because the fragments of glass from the window were still airborne when it detonated and they've been driven by the blast. Shards of it are sticking out of the wall and up from the floorboards and you can bet that plenty sliced through those bodies. An automatic rifle lies close to each of them. Treading carefully to avoid the glass, we turn the bodies over with the muzzles of our rifles. Heavy ammunition belts sag to one side. On the floor nearby there are two wooden boxes of hand grenades, open, ready to throw. We check the other rooms. Empty.

When we go outside the rest of the troop are running up. The Captain goes into the house and comes out again. He nods to us. "Well, done, lads." Then to the others, "All right, go in and collect up the munitions; we don't want them falling into the wrong hands, do we? Then we can pull out."

"Watch out for the glass," Scottie calls after them.

Our armoured vehicle is a couple of klicks to the east and we strike off in that direction. Scottie looks very calm. I feel anything but calm. I'm gripping my multi-rifle hard, trying to stop the shaking. I'm thinking how easy it would have been for me to walk right into that trap. I'd be stone dead now if it weren't for Scottie.

I lean towards him and say quietly, "How did you know they were in there?"

He gives me his lop-sided smile. "Heard them breathing."

*

The engines roared out in reverse thrust and the aircraft slowed to taxi to the apron.

Harken was probably right: if I was going to make the move, the sooner I did it the better. If I hung around, the media could pile in before I left and if they were really persistent they might even follow me. So I'd start my preparations as soon as I got back to base. In two days' time I should be on the supersonic, leaving behind Fort Piper and the US of A, heading for England.

11

I'd packed the bare minimum: toiletries, a change of clothes, and my running kit. I took no paperwork, and the contacts I needed were on my phone. If I lacked something I figured the base would provide it or I'd buy it. So when I disembarked at London's Heathrow Airport my only baggage was a soft carry-on.

They said they'd send a driver to meet me, and I looked for him as I emerged into the Arrivals Hall. There was a crowd waiting eagerly at the barrier. Behind them, at a respectful distance, was a tall guy in MTPs. He was standing feet apart, hands behind his back. He wasn't holding any identification – he didn't need to, the sand-coloured beret with the downward-pointing flaming sword said it all. I wasn't in his chain of command but he saluted me anyway.

"Take your bag, sir?"

"I've got it."

He led me to the car and held open the rear door. I'd have preferred to sit up front with him during the ride to Hereford but it seemed he preferred it this way. Normally protocol was less strict inside The Regiment. But I wasn't inside The Regiment. I was sitting here in the uniform of a Colonel in the US Army. Once on the base he conducted me straight to the CO's office, saluted me again, and left me with the aide-de-camp. The ADC took me straight in, then withdrew, and I heard the door close behind him.

Colonel Owen Gracey rose from behind his desk. He looked a bit older, but a good deal heavier, than Harken. If the funding situation was as bad as when I left the outfit he was probably doing the equivalent of my job and Harken's combined. Which wouldn't leave much time for running five or ten ks before going to work.

It wasn't a large office. There were the usual bookshelves and filing cabinets, a map of the Brecon Beacons on one wall, and a venetian blind on the single window. The carpet was an orange-brown cord – cheap and hard-wearing.

Gracey was even taller than me. He leaned forward to shake my hand. "Welcome to the 22 SAS, Jim."

Very informal, no salutes, first name terms right away. I followed suit. "Thanks, Owen. Sorry about this. I'm sure you're busy enough here without having to babysit an officer from another force."

He gestured to a chair in front of the desk and resumed his own. "Not a bit of it. We're familiar with your outfit – even do combined ops from time to time. We get the news here, too, so I know about your exploits. Congratulations."

I stiffened. Congratulations on what, exactly?

He'd caught my blank look. "The Africa mission. Major coup. Well done. We should be honoured – you're quite a hero."

That was a relief. The African operation was general knowledge; for a moment I thought he was referring to the counterfeit business. I was hoping that particular one would remain my own little secret.

I shrugged. "Like you, we do what we have to do. Usually no one notices; this time the media got wind of it. The publicity blew me for future operations. Bad luck, that's all."

He nodded. "I'll level with you, Colonel. I understand that mission also brought you a fresh round of interest from the media. I haven't been told any more than that, and I have sense enough not to ask. Anyway, I agreed to look after you until things have died down."

"Thank you, Owen. I appreciate it."

There was a glint of something else in his eyes. "Is that the trace of an English accent I hear?"

Harken says I do have a weird transatlantic accent so there's no point in denying it.

"Yeah, I was from England originally. Emigrated way back."

"You have any family or friends over here, people you want to visit?"

"No…"

"So there'd be no reason for you to leave the base."

Ah, that's where he's going. "Are you saying I'm confined to barracks?"

He laughed. "No, not exactly. It's just that, as CO, I need to know where my people are, and as of now you're one of my people." I opened my mouth to say something, but he added, "That may seem irregular, even unpalatable, for someone of your rank, but it's expected of me. Needless to say you'll have the run of the base. Just that if you go anywhere else I'd like you keep me informed."

"Sounds reasonable. I'd probably say the same thing in your position."

He smiled. "I don't suppose you've had a chance to look round yet."

"No, I thought I'd better report to you first." It's protocol, he knows that.

"I'll get Captain Parry to take you to your billet, show you the facilities, and so on. I have some urgent stuff to cope with right now otherwise I'd do it myself. If you should need to holoconference securely with your people back home, the suite is in this building. Any other problems, just let me know." He pressed a button on his desk, then spoke to his ADC. "Get hold of Captain Parry, would you? Ask him to come here to meet our new, er, guest, take him to his quarters, and show him round."

I stood up. "Thanks again, Owen."

We shook hands, more firmly this time, and our eyes met.

This could work out better than I'd expected.

*

When Captain Parry showed up he took me to my billet first, so I could dump my stuff. The room was adequately furnished: a bed, a chair and table, a wardrobe, and an armchair. The walls and paintwork were white, and looked reasonably fresh. The carpet was navy blue, but otherwise looked like the same government-issue as the one in Gracey's office. The window looked out across a strip of thin, yellowing grass, a paved pathway, and another strip of undernourished grass, the view ending in the wall of an identical building opposite. There was an en suite bathroom with a toilet, sink, and shower. I opened the wardrobe door and was pleased to see a uniform hanging there. I wasn't planning to swan around the base in US Army BDUs, and we'd arranged for the UK equivalent to be ready for my arrival.

Parry was waiting outside. I didn't pause to unpack but went out to accompany him on the grand tour. First, however, he pointed to the office next door to my room.

"Colonel Gracey said you can have the use of this office while you're here, sir."

I had a quick look inside. It was about the same size as my room and sparsely furnished, just a desk and a couple of chairs. But there was a computer terminal and it looked like it was networked, which could be useful. At some point the office had been painted with white plastimulsion, but one wall was covered with grubby marks where things had been posted up and later torn down. I went back outside.

"Who had this office before, Captain?"

"It was Lieutenant-Colonel Heptinstall's office, sir. He's moved on to D squadron."

"Right. Carry on."

We walked briskly. I could hardly believe the weather. There wasn't a cloud in the sky, and although there was some heat in the sun the breeze had a bite to it. After so many years in North Carolina I'd forgotten what a fine Spring day in England could be like.

It was nearly ten years since I'd last seen the base and it had expanded in that time. The firing range, parade ground, obstacle course, and the chapel with the SAS dedicated window were unchanged, but the gym and the mess were in totally new buildings. Finally we took a walk through the main building, although at my request he just pointed out the various offices and facilities. We didn't open doors because I wasn't ready to meet anyone yet. We ended up outside my room again.

"Thanks, Captain. I'd like to have a shower and change before dinner."

"Of course, sir." He consulted his watch, standard issue. "Shall I pick you up in an hour, then? I can come with you to the mess, introduce you to whoever's around."

"That would be good. See you then."

I had a shower and changed into the uniform they'd left for me. I had mixed feelings about coming back. In any other circumstances it would have been great to see Bruce and Scottie again, but the guy they knew was Jim Forbes and his brain inhabited a different body now. Jim Slater didn't look the same and he didn't sound the same and they wouldn't have a clue who he was. I just had to pretend I never knew them. It was surprising how much that hurt.

*

At dinner the Captain and I sat with Lieutenant-Colonel Bruce Harrington and a Major Nigel Greenaway. Bruce's hair was silvering at the temples now, but he looked fit and he was as suave as ever. He didn't know me, of course, and we had the same sort of strained conversation that any visiting serviceman might expect. Greenaway looked young to be a Major, but there was something steely in his manner that told me he'd seen a bit of action. There were others at the table, and some regarded me curiously but averted their gaze when I looked up. I realized this wasn't going to be a comfortable posting unless I did something to break the ice. After we'd eaten I got the training schedule from Captain Parry, read it, and went to bed early.

There was a six o'clock reveille and I was down there with them for the off. A 10-k tab with full pack, followed by the assault course. They were surprised to see a Colonel doing it with them, more surprised still that I could finish it. I'd have been disappointed if I couldn't. I still trained regularly with the men back at Fort Piper, and it was easier here than in the heat and humidity of North Carolina. I did it the next day, too, and the day after that; everything the men did, I did with them: tabs, assault course, circuit training, firing range, navigation in featureless terrain, the lot. I missed the adrenaline of planning and resourcing actual missions, but the activity helped to take my mind of it.

Then I had an idea. I found out who was in charge of unarmed combat. It was a Warrant Officer, name of Ed Halloran, and I sought him out.

He looked me up and down. "And what did you have in mind?"

"Seems like you're on your own here. I thought I might give you a hand with the training."

His expression was half amused, half incredulous. "You have your kit with you?"

"No, I travelled light."

"Okay, I'll find you some and we'll see what you can do."

We changed, then went on the mat. We circled a couple of times, then he tried an attack. I knew he was making allowances but that's not what I wanted so I dumped him on his back. A flash of annoyance crossed his face and he got up.

"All right, then," he said, and this time he came in firing on all cylinders.

That was more like it. There was a flurry of blows, parries, a quick throw, and I stopped the kick an inch short of his Adam's Apple. When he got up he was grinning all over his face.

"You're fast. Where the fuck did you learn to fight like that?"

I grinned back. "Got it from people like you."

More than once: in the British army, again when I joined the SAS, and yet again for the SAF – different instructors, different moves each time. Then after the transplant I did it all over again, and that time I really went for it. When I was reinstated in the SAF I became the instructor and ran courses for the new recruits. I hadn't yet met the man who could whip me on the mat.

"All right," Halloran said. "You could be handy, at that. We can split the class, do demonstrations. Start tomorrow? Attackers with knives – real knives."

"One-on-one or more than one-on-one?"

"Jeezus." He shook his head. "Just plain ol' one-on-one to start with."

"Okay." I shook hands, alert in case he tried anything,

but he didn't.

So I added training in unarmed combat to the portfolio, and folk were getting to know who I was.

When I needed a break I'd borrow a car from the pool and drive to Hereford or Leominster or Hay-on-Wye, just to stroll round the towns, browse the shops, have a coffee and watch the civilian world go by. We tend to be quite sequestered at Fort Piper so this was something of a novelty to me. A lot of the youngsters were wearing Virtual Reality goggles. Nobody took much notice, but watching them gave me the strange sensation of being in a world that was half under water. They didn't bump into streetlamps so I assumed that whatever it was they were viewing was superimposed on real life. Other times I'd just go for a spin to enjoy the countryside. Driving on the left was never a problem for me; I'd learned to drive back in England, and since then I'd driven in many countries where it was the norm.

I knew I was just filling time but I had to be patient. Sooner or later the court case in the States would be resolved, the media would lose interest, and I'd be able to return to my unit.

Only that's not the way it turned out.

12

Up to now I'd spent a little time with Bruce but I'd seen neither hide nor hair of Scottie. I'd been careful not to show undue interest, because I wasn't supposed to know him, but on the way back from a navigation exercise in the Brecon Beacons one day I mentioned it casually to the three guys I was with.

"Pete, I was told there's a Major Scot Hayward on the base. I haven't seen him at all. Is he around?"

Pete's face darkened and he exchanged glances with the others.

I looked from one to the other. "Something wrong?"

He glanced at my cap badge. "Look, I don't want to be unfriendly, Colonel, but this is an SAS matter."

I didn't like the sound of this. Normally he called me "Jim" – I'd asked him to. "Come on, Pete, right now I'm SAS, like you. If there's a problem that affects The Regiment, it's my problem, too."

"It's only a rumour."

"Yeah, all right, it's a rumour. Go on."

We began to struggle up a steep grassy slope. The weight of gear we were carrying meant we had to place our feet carefully to avoid sliding, so we focused on that and he said nothing until we reached the top. We paused to get our breath back and take in the view, several miles of open moorland descending to a town, a small cluster of Monopoly houses which was the pickup point we were heading for.

Pete said, "Scot Hayward was on a posting in Africa. The others have been replaced but he stayed on. He wasn't supposed to stay on. He's gone off the radar."

I felt a flash of alarm. If someone had been killed or captured, his mates wouldn't just come home without him. "What do you mean 'gone off the radar'?"

"Look, I think it's best if you ask someone else. Colonel Harrington can fill you in better than we can."

"Okay."

I didn't press it further, but at dinner that evening I made a point of sitting down opposite Bruce Harrington. I brought up the subject during a lull in the conversation.

Bruce cleared his throat, gave me a penetrating look, and said, "What's your interest in Scot?"

I thought quickly. "I heard somewhere he'd served in Libya. I was there on operations, too. Thought it would be interesting to compare notes."

Bruce's face tightened. "Scot's somewhere in northern Nigeria. He's gone mental."

A chill ran through me. "How do you mean?"

"He was there on a mission. One of his patrols was ambushed – killed, all of them, in various very unpleasant ways. Seems that sent him over the edge. He stole an all-terrain and a shedload of weapons and ammunition." He paused, running his lower lip through his teeth, then spoke quickly, as if to get it over with. "He's going from village to village killing everyone he comes across – not just hostiles: men, women, children, every damned living thing."

It felt like all the nerves in my body were firing at once.

It couldn't be – not again.

I remembered those trigger-happy rival militias in Libya, and I knew very well what both of us thought of them. Scottie behaving that way? I was so incredulous I blurted out "Bullshit!"

I managed to stop myself from going on. I was about to say that I knew Scottie and he'd never do anything like that. Not against non-combatants.

Bruce was frowning at me, so I did my best to cover up.

"Sorry, er, what I mean is, that's totally out of character for an SAS man. Are you sure of these reports?"

His face recomposed and he sighed, a long, weary sigh. "Afraid so."

"Well, we need to get him back. Find out what's gone wrong."

"You think we haven't tried? I wanted to go out there myself but Gracey couldn't spare me." He leaned over to the group on his right. "Nigel, could you join us for a moment?"

Major Nigel Greenaway broke off his conversation, said "Sure", got up and sat down with an amiable smile next to Bruce.

Without taking his eyes off me, Bruce said, "Jim here is asking about Scot Hayward."

The amiable smile vanished. He looked quickly at Bruce and back to me.

"Bad business," he said.

Bruce prompted, "You located him, didn't you?"

Nigel gave Bruce another uneasy look and said to me, "He was damned hard to find."

"Of course he was," I said. "He's trained like the rest of us. He'll know every trick."

"Yeah, well a reconnaissance drone picked up the all-terrain after another of his bloodbaths and we went in.

Made contact, tried to reason with him. You know what the answer was?"

"A lot of high-velocity?"

"Correct. Accurate, too. We were glad to get out of there alive."

There was an uncomfortable silence. I didn't know how long Nigel had known Scottie but I knew damned well how long Bruce had known him.

"What's your take on this, Bruce?"

He sucked in a deep breath. "No idea. Scottie could be a bit off-the-wall at times, but I never knew him do anything like this."

I nearly said, "Me neither."

But Bruce rumbled on. Normally stiff and correct, he seemed to have disappeared into a world of his own. "Bloody waste. Finest officer I ever served with – him and a guy named Jim Forbes."

The mention of my former name made my heart beat faster and my eyes darted to him, but he seemed to be far away. I detached myself as soon as I decently could and went back to my room.

It had been a strenuous day and I was tired, but sleep was impossible. I lay on the bed. A shaft of moonlight entered through a gap in the curtains and as time slipped past it moved slowly across the ceiling. I was replaying everything I'd been told about Scottie Hayward, over and over again. Did I believe what was being reported? I had to believe it. Was this behaviour consistent with what I knew of Scottie?

No way.

Could I be sure? It was ten years since I last saw him. People can change in that time.

Crap. People don't change as much as that.

Don't they? Sergeant Bill Archer changed in about ten seconds, not ten years.

The thought was disturbing. Was it possible I'd stumbled across another case like his? What kind of coincidence was that?

I tried to relax my mind, but all it did was open the gates for other memories to flood in. Memories of the last job Scottie and I were on, shortly before I was seconded to the SAF.

The Yemen. Yeah, the Yemen. What a fuck-up that was.

The Yemen 2046

The RotoFan flies us in from Saudi. The jihadis in Yemen have good eyes and ears, so we're following normal practice, ground-hugging and following a wadi to minimize visibility and engine noise. This lot have been a running sore since way before I was born. Now a bunch of them have kidnapped the Saudi Foreign Minister. He's a member of the royal family and they want him back. We know where they're holding him at the moment, and we have to act fast before they can move him on.

There are eight of us on board – which is standard for operations out here – ten if you include the pilot and copilot. Being a Captain, Bruce is in command, but we all know what to do. It's a routine infil. We'll rope down at five klicks and tab the rest, coming in west of the target with the sun behind us. It'll be hot, and we're toting a lot of gear, but we've trained for it, so that won't be a problem. There will be one problem, though. We never get there.

As luck would have it, they have a patrol out right under our flight path. One moment the only sound is the drone of our twin engines, the next the air is full of clatters and thuds as incoming hits the metal and fibre-reinforced plastic hull of the RotoFan. The pilot jinks the craft left and right and shoots flares, which is completely pointless because these guys are just using small arms. Then one of the bastards gets lucky. There's a loud bang and the RotoFan cants over to the right and stays that way. Starboard engine out, no lift that side.

The pilot's voice comes through on our comms helmets. He sounds very calm. "Brace for impact. We're going to ditch."

I'm on the port side, so all I can see right now is sky. RotoFans aren't pretty to fly on one engine. Standing rules for this situation are to fly on as far as you can go, so you have a chance to regroup before the hostiles catch up with you. The pilot is doing his best but he's lost control; we're going in steeply – I can see that from the angle of the fuselage. I cover my head, try to make myself small, then there's an almighty, rending racket which goes on and on, and the whole craft is jerking like mad, this way and that, throwing me hard into my harness. Finally there's one very large bang and things go quiet.

I'm looking at the sky again but this time there's no window in the way. Moving slowly and carefully I look myself over. Two legs, two arms, all present and correct. I get to my feet carefully. The ship has split like a pea pod, and we're the peas, scattered all over the desert.

Bruce is sitting up. He's lost his helmet and he's blinking hard and holding his head with one hand. Scottie is on his knees, taking it all in. There are bundles of clothes everywhere. Then I realize the bundles of clothes are our guys, strangely inert. Scottie gets to his feet and we go to them, one after another. It looks like all the casualties are on the starboard side, plus Ted and Andy, who'd been up front on the port side. The cockpit is so badly damaged there's barely any point in looking inside, but we do; sure enough the pilot and co-pilot are dead, too. We find Ryan lying near the wreckage, dazed but alive. He joins us while Bruce is retrieving his helmet.

"Christ, Jim," Ryan says to me. "We're the only ones left. Why the hell did they dump the crate here? We'd have made it if there hadn't been a rock in the way."

I scan around. There are fucking rocks everywhere.

"Who had the sat link?" I ask him.

"Ted."

We check it out. There are a few dents in it but it looks like it's in working order.

Ryan says, "Shall we call in the evac?"

I look at Bruce. He's supposed to be taking decisions like this but he's still holding his helmet in one hand and rubbing his head with the other. I say, "No, that bloody patrol could down that one, too. We need to take them out first."

Scottie is on his way back. He's staring around him like he can't believe all this has happened. And now he loses it.

"The bastards!" he says. "The fucking bastards! Look what they've done. There's four of my best mates lying there." He hefts his multi-rifle. "I'm going after them. They've got it coming to them. I'm going to slaughter every last one. I'll hack their fucking heads off and feed them to the vultures. I'll—"

I cut in. "For Christ's sake, Scottie, will you stop playing silly bastards, shut the fuck up, and listen? We don't need to go looking for them; they'll come looking for us. They knew we were going down."

Bruce blinks and murmurs, "That's right."

I say, "How far did we fly after we were hit?"

Ryan says, "Four or five ks. Not more." He looks at me. "They're probably in one of those open recce vehicles. They could be here in a few minutes!"

"No," I say. "They can't drive fast in this terrain, and they'll want to stop at least 2 ks away so we don't hear the engine. That means we've got maybe thirty minutes to prepare for them." I look around, then point. "They'll come in on that ridge. It's the highest point and it'll give them a good view of the wreckage. If they have half a brain between them they'll know there were ten on board and they'll be counting. So let's make it look convincing. We need four more heaps of camo. Find something."

Scottie's face is as red as a beetroot and he looks like he's going to put up a fight. Instead he goes slack. "Sorry, Jim. Got to me, that's all."

"'Course it did, you old bugger." I punch him lightly on the arm. "Come on."

The four of us start to search in the debris. In the cabin we find some camo tents, intended for temporary shelter, and we heap them up to look like four more casualties. We separate the two pilots a little from the ruins of the cockpit to make them more visible.

"Right," Bruce says, "that'll do." He's still a bit dazed but he's functioning again.

"All very well," Scottie says, "but where's the cover for us?"

Ryan looks about him. "Behind the big rock? The one we hit?"

I shake my head. "No, we'll be exposed on the other side. They'll circle round the whole site before they come in."

We continue to look, but the answer is staring us in the face and we come up with it together.

"The wreckage."

13

The Yemen (contd)

The two largest pieces of wreckage are the cowling from the starboard engine pod and the port half of the cabin, which is lying partly on its side with one or two windows miraculously intact. The curved overhang of the cabin will provide cover from a high viewpoint and some welcome shade from that burning sun. The cowling isn't quite as good, but it'll have to do.

We spend fifteen minutes adjusting the two pieces of wreckage so as to give us a good arc of fire when the insurgents come in to examine the bodies. The cabin's a bit unstable so we pack small rocks under it to hold it steady. Then we stand back.

Scottie says, "They'll see us when they come in."

"Not immediately," Bruce says. "The crash lies north and south. The sun's bright and we'll be in shadow."

Ryan says, "They'll see the muzzle flashes when we open up, though."

I say, "Our job, Ryan, is to make sure that by then it's too bloody late."

He says, "Suppose they toss in grenades?"

"Unlikely," Bruce says. "I know how these people operate. They want to have some fun with anyone who's survived, and do nasty things to the ones who haven't. Grenades mess things up for them. They won't use them unless they have to."

"So," Scottie says, "Three under the cabin and one in the pod?"

I shake my head. "Too risky. If they take out the cabin we're three down. And it's better if the fire's coming from different directions. It'll cause panic, give us extra seconds. Ryan's the smallest. He can get inside that pile of debris by the co-pilot. We wait till they're all down here, and then let them have it."

Scottie says, "It's not ideal. We could kill each other in the crossfire."

Bruce says, "It's not an ideal situation, Scottie. No raking. Aimed shots, single taps. You take the engine cowling. Jim and I will take the cabin. But first pick up some of our guys' water bottles. It's hotter than hell out here, and they won't be needing them now. Let's move."

We take up our positions. After that it's a matter of waiting and watching.

The desert isn't still, it moves constantly in the hot air. The cabin hull provides some shelter from the sun but it only multiplies the heat underneath. Another ten minutes go by. Not long now. Flies come out of nowhere and start to buzz in clouds around the bodies of my comrades. I stiffen. Four of those piles have no cloud of flies. I've seen it and if I have so will the ragheads.

I crack a tin of emergency rations, nip out quickly, and smear the meat paste on the camo bundles. Then I get back under cover as fast as I can. It solves the problem. Now there are flies bloody well everywhere, including on us.

I'm just in time. The ridge line is waving in the heat but

something dark disturbs it. I see the flash of binoculars. I wait. Ten minutes later the ridge line breaks up some more and they start to come down the dunes like a line of beetles. I count six.

There should be seven. Where the hell is number seven?

It's a trade mark of this band that they go around in sevens. Maybe they think it's their lucky number. I know that and my mates know that, so they'll be looking out for the missing man, too.

I watch them, breathing quietly through my mouth. One of the six makes hand signals and they fan out, keeping a good distance, three circling one way, three the other. Now I've lost sight of them. A deadly calm settles on me. The only sound is the buzzing of those bloody flies.

Then the faint crunch of boots on the sand. They're coming in cautiously. I can see five. I glance at Bruce, but he's waiting calmly. I hope Scottie and Ryan don't open up too soon; if there are any left outside our circle all they need to do is toss in a grenade. And where the hell is number seven? Minutes go by. All six are here now, poking at the heaps with the muzzles of their rifles. They haven't found the dummy heaps yet, but when they do…

Single taps from one of our weapons. Now it's bedlam. They're shouting, running around, dark faces, black beards, firing bursts at unseen targets. Bullets zip through the air, flinging up fountains of sand, smacking through the hull over my head, and all the time I'm sighting and firing, sighting and firing, and I can hear the steady tap, tap of the other guys' weapons. Then everything goes quiet.

Are they all down? I think so. Then I hear a cry of *"Allahu akbhar!"* and there's a mighty explosion and something hits my face, and then there's a second explosion. What in fuck's name was that? I can usually tell different bits of ordnance apart by the sound but not when they're that close.

In the aftermath of the explosions my hearing feels dull. I wipe a hand over my face and it comes away bloody. It doesn't hurt.

I rise a little higher, take a cautious look, start to count bodies, see only six. But now Scottie is standing, a six-foot-four massive target. If he can do that the coast has to be clear.

We regroup.

Bruce says, "Where's Ryan?"

We go over to the cockpit wreckage, Scottie ahead of us. He throws aside his helmet and multi-rifle and steps forward. Then he drops to his knees and buries his head in his elbows, and he's saying, "Shit, shit, shit" over and over again.

I look into the cockpit. Ryan is lying in there with half his head missing.

I lean over Scottie, squeeze his shoulder. "What happened?"

He uncurls slowly and looks up. "Number Seven," he says. "Came out from behind the big rock. He's got a grenade and he's about to toss it in the middle. My high-velocity jams so I use the grenade launcher."

"You killed him with a fucking grenade launcher?"

"Well if I hadn't he'd have taken out the whole damned lot of us."

"Why didn't Ryan drop him?"

"Ryan was in the cockpit – this guy was behind him, so I saw him first. Anyway, it worked. It blew the bastard to bits." He draws a breath. "Only one of those bits was his hand and the grenade was still in it with the pin out. It landed in the cockpit."

I'm not listening any more. I find the sat link, fire it up, give the evac team our coordinates, and tell them to bring seven body bags. They're for our guys; we'll leave the insurgents for the vultures to pick over.

*

Even after the evac team land in their RotoFan, even after we help them get the bodies of our dead comrades on board, even after we take off, leaving that godforsaken place behind us, I'm still torturing myself over what's happened. Scottie's made it clear he wants to be on his own, so I give him some space, just leave him brooding in a seat further forward while I sit with Bruce.

I keep my voice down. "Bruce, are you going to report Ryan as a blue on blue?"

He shakes his head. "No. Blue on blues are much harder for the families to take. It was enemy action all right, just bad luck the way it panned out."

"Right."

I'm still thinking about it as we fly back over the desert, and I was thinking about it all over again now, lying on my bed at the SAS base at Hereford, my body aching for sleep that wouldn't come.

Did Scottie's rifle really jam, or was that just his excuse for taking out an Arab with a grenade launcher? Is that what he wanted: to see the guy blown to pieces?

What if he did? A grenade in the centre of the wreckage would have ripped us all to shreds. Scottie was right to take him out. He saved our lives. Who cares how he did it?

And I remembered my reaction when I got back to the base camp in Yemen and looked at my face in the mirror. The blood wasn't mine. Nor were the pink bits of flesh clinging to my uniform.

Scottie got his revenge all right.

14

By the following morning I'd made up my mind. I found Owen Gracey in his office.

He smiled, waving me to a chair. "Problem, Jim?"

I sat down, back straight. "This business involving Major Scot Hayward…"

His face fell. "You've heard about that."

"Yes. I gather he's gone berserk."

He nodded. "Afraid that's putting it mildly."

Again I had to fight the urge to say that something smelt wrong about the whole thing, that I knew Scottie, that he wouldn't…

"Owen, I don't understand why it's been left like this. If there's one thing you learn in the SAF and the SAS – and the regulars, for that matter – it's that you look after your buddies. If one goes down you bring him back. You don't abandon him."

"He hasn't 'gone down', he's turned into a human demolition machine. He kills anyone he sees, makes no difference whether they're hostiles or non-combatants, friends or enemies. I can assure you I'm no more happy about the situation than you are. He's been a good soldier, solid, dependable, and I have a huge regard for him. But we tried out there, believe me, we really tried. His own mates couldn't get anywhere near him."

"I know. That's why I'd like to go out there myself. Find him. Bring him back."

His laugh was closer to a cough. "You're not serious!"

"I'm deadly serious."

Half-smile, eyebrows raised. "And what makes you think you can succeed where the others failed?"

"I know the psychology; we were trained for this kind of thing." Lies, but all in a good cause.

He blew out his breath. "All right, so you were trained for it. Have you ever used it?"

"Sure. Last time I talked down a guy who held up a drug store. Took a child as hostage when the police showed up." More lies, still in a good cause.

He shook his head slowly. "Jim, I've been asked to keep you safe, not put you in the firing line."

"Look, Owen, I've been stuck behind a desk for I don't know how many months, planning missions for other people to carry out. I come here and I'm not even doing that much. The inactivity is killing me. Much more of it and I'll go bananas myself."

"You've been training with the ORs, haven't you? And Ed Halloran tells me you've been a tremendous help with the combat classes."

"It's not the same as being on an assignment. I'm experienced, I'm fit, and I have skills I'm not using. You have an officer in deep trouble. If there's a shadow of a chance of saving him, I'd like to take it."

A few moments of silence passed. I was looking at him, and he was looking at me, drumming his fingers on the desk. I knew what he was thinking. We were the same rank. He might be the CO of this outfit but he couldn't stop me. Only I didn't want to play that card. He'd been helpful and accommodating. I didn't want to abuse his good will.

He said, "It's probably too late by now."

My heart missed a beat. "What do you mean?"

He sucked in a breath. "What Scot has been up to is a major embarrassment, to us in The Regiment, to the UK, to the West. The current President of Nigeria is not particularly sympathetic to our presence there. This could be the last straw. If he starts demanding that all foreign troops leave his country – and right now that seems increasingly likely – it would be disastrous."

"Why? Oil? I thought the developed world had moved to a hydrogen economy."

"That's largely true, but there's still plenty of value in oil as a raw material for the chemical industry. And Nigeria has useful mineral deposits, including niobium, tantalum, and uranium. Western companies have been quick to move in, and the previous administration welcomed them. But the jihadis in the north are still active, and companies won't stay there, or invest further, unless there's adequate protection. That means a military presence: UN boots on the ground, mainly US and UK boots. If we have to withdraw now there isn't a company that wouldn't pull out. After which, of course, China would set up shop."

"The companies could put in private contractors."

"Mercenaries? Too expensive, especially when the profit margins are slim, and in many cases they are."

"What's the SAS doing out there anyway?"

"Officially we're wearing blue helmets, escorting company employees and patrolling the perimeters. Unofficially we're carrying out covert operations, taking the fight to the jihadis. It's all part of a necessary security operation."

"I see. So if someone like Scot runs amok—"

"The whole house of cards collapses. That's why he's got to be stopped." He met my eyes. "Jim, I hate to lose a man, especially a man as highly skilled as Scot. I've tried to protect him, but we're talking about international diplomacy here. These decisions are made at a higher level." His lips tightened. "The Americans are planning to send in a drone to take him out."

I blinked in disbelief. "My God."

He lifted open hands. "I know. And there isn't a bloody thing I can do about it."

My mind was racing. Scottie and I were a team. Twice he saved my life, once in Waziristan and again in that Yemen fuck-up. Do I have to sit behind a desk while the Americans get ready to blow him to bits?

"Owen, that only strengthens my case. I have to get him out while there's still time."

"You're determined to do this, aren't you?"

"Yes, I am."

He sighed. "All right. I'll set it up. The troop out there is under the Command of Captain Stephen Pascale. The rest will be up to you."

"Thanks, Owen." I got to my feet. He engaged me with his eyes.

"Jim?"

"Yes?"

"For Christ's sake, try not to get yourself killed."

15

I flew civilian from London Heathrow to Lagos and on to Kano. I snatched several hours' sleep on the first leg, but the second flight was cramped and crowded, and when I disembarked the following morning I felt hot and sticky, and in need of a shower and a change of clothes.

Captain Pascale had told Gracey that he'd send a driver to pick me up and I was relieved to see him waiting for me. I found myself automatically looking for his name tab, then remembered that most British Army uniforms didn't carry them. He introduced himself as Corporal Masters.

"This way, Colonel."

"Thanks."

A wall of heat met me as I emerged from the airport building but the air wasn't humid, just hot enough to make my skin prickle. On the way to the car park I asked Masters if he knew Major Scot Hayward. He looked at me.

"The man who…?"

"Yes."

He shook his head. "No, we never met. He was with the other troop."

I didn't push it.

The car park came into view, shimmering in the heat, and now I could see the vehicle he was heading for. It was an Army Endeavour, complete with four-wheel-drive, massive tyres, and an exhaust pipe that exited above the cabin. I wondered why we needed it in a town like Kano.

I stopped wondering as soon as we went off-road. This was much older equipment than we'd use in the SAF, but it certainly did the job. Twice we plunged across shallow rivers and up slippery banks, spattering the side and rear windows with mud, and the vehicle just took it and asked for more. But after that there wasn't any more rough ground, just mile after mile of featureless grassland. Corporal Masters referred to the NavAid at frequent intervals, and I let him concentrate on the route while I watched the scenery go by. I guessed this was the type of terrain Scottie was operating in, and I was thinking about how he'd go in and out of cover.

Eventually we pulled into the temporary base, which consisted of a couple of large tents and a cluster of smaller ones. Masters drove the Endeavour under a canopy, where it joined some other vehicles. He switched off the engine and turned to me.

"Captain Pascale is expecting you, sir. Would you like to see him now?"

"I think it's a good idea." I was fatigued after the flight and the rough journey but it was protocol to introduce myself, and I wanted to know what kind of help I could expect. As we walked back I noticed another canopy, and under it a familiar sight: a Rotofan, this one camo'd for jungle operations.

We found Captain Stephen Pascale in one of the large tents. He came forward right away to shake hands, then nodded to Corporal Masters.

"All right, Masters, that'll be all."

"Sir."

As he left the tent I turned and said, "Thanks for the ride, Corporal."

Pascale looked fresh as a daisy, which was quite an achievement in this heat, and probably a good distance from the way I looked right now. He was straight-backed and blue eyed, with blond hair that was just about short enough to comply with regulations. The sun had lent his pale skin a pink tinge rather than a tan. He gestured to a couple of chairs, and as we sat down he said, "Not a very comfortable ride here from Kano, I'm afraid."

"Good for the kidneys, they say. Thanks for making room for me on the base. Did Colonel Gracey brief you at all?"

"Yes indeed. Look, Colonel—"

"It's Jim."

He smiled briefly. "Jim, let me say straight away, I'm more than happy to help. I imagine I'm as anxious as you are to get Scot Hayward back."

"Because…?"

"Well, for his sake, obviously, but there's more to it than that. Thing is, we're conducting operations in the same area, and the last thing I want is for one of my patrols to stumble into him by accident."

"Right. So you do have some idea where he is."

"Yes, let me show you." He got up, then glanced sideways at me, no doubt taking in the red-rimmed eyes and creased uniform. "We could do this tomorrow if you prefer."

"No, I'd like to do it now."

He had a lap top open on his desk and I joined him behind it.

"I've been downloading images taken by a military satellite," he explained, as I watched the screen over his shoulder. "High-resolution optical and infra-red. The sweeps aren't frequent enough to catch him on the move, of course, but you can often see the villages he's been through. There'll be smoke, or collapsed huts, even bodies in the open."

I swallowed. "That bad?"

"Yes, that bad. The previous troop sent a reconnaissance drone up there to locate him. Scot Hayward shot it down. They still didn't give up. One of the officers took a patrol to the spot to try to get him back."

"That would have been Major Nigel Greenaway."

'That's right. He'd served with Scot Hayward for quite some time but it was hopeless even for him. In fact his patrol got such a hostile reception he advised me to stay clear."

"Any idea of the route Hayward's taking?"

"He seems to hit a couple of sites in succession, then goes off in an entirely different direction."

"He's trying not to establish a pattern."

"Yes, but there's a lot of open grassland and scrub and he has to hide the all-terrain whenever he stops. So my feeling is, he dodges in and out of the jungle up here." He ran a finger over the screen without touching it.

"Good analysis, Stephen. Only one problem."

"What's that?"

"The Americans must have been thinking along exactly the same lines."

He nodded, and drew a breath between closed teeth. "That's the other problem. I don't want some gung-ho Yank targeting my people by mistake." He stopped short and shot me a curious look. "Sorry, I, er, assumed you'd disapprove."

Gracey had obviously said something about my being on loan from the SAF.

"Damn right, I do. This guy needs help, not their kind of solution. Where was your last sighting?"

He pointed. "Here, two days ago. What do you need?"

"A dozen of your people – men or women – if you can spare them. We can rope down near that village. See how far we can track the all-terrain from there."

"You don't want them to engage, do you?"

"Hell, no. I'll do that part myself. Do you have a professional tracker?"

"Yes, I can let you take Nwosu. He's a local guy attached to the troop. He's good."

*

At daybreak they pushed out the Rotofan. Rotofans are perfect for operational conditions like these; they can take off vertically from a space not much bigger than you'd need to park that Army Endeavour. The twelve of us boarded and it flew for about thirty minutes in a north-easterly direction to a spot five ks from the village Stephen Pascale had identified. There it slowed to a hover and we roped down and continued on foot, the double whine of the Rotofan's engines fading as it returned to base. The air was cool as we started off, and although the temperature soon began to rise it was a dry heat and quite tolerable. The route took us through savanna and it was hard to move quickly with the long grass dragging at our legs and boots. An hour later we sighted the village and proceeded with more caution. It looked like Stephen Pascale's satellite images were on the mark. There wasn't any smoke now, but even from here I could see that one of the huts had been reduced to a heap of ashes and another lay in ruins.

Lieutenant Akbar was at my elbow. "You want to search it, Colonel?"

"Not yet. Let Nwosu finish his recce."

We waited. A light breeze refreshed us, then changed direction, bringing with it the rancid, all-too-familiar smell of death. Decomposition starts quickly in hot climates.

"Colonel, sir?"

Nwosu had crept soundlessly up to us.

"Yes, Nwosu?"

"He stop the all-terrain just outside. Come in on foot. Some he shoot in the hut. One hut he burns, shoot them as they come out. They lying out there. The big hut, he hit that one with a grenade. Then he go back to the all-terrain and head out that way." He pointed.

"Good work, Nwosu."

So Scottie was headed out. Or did he just make it look like he was headed out? I was pretty sure he'd moved on, but I wasn't taking any chances.

"Okay, Lieutenant." I pointed to the village. "No need to put your men at risk. I'll go in there alone."

He opened his mouth to protest but I didn't wait for it, just turned and headed off.

I went in quietly and worked from hut to hut. The only sound was the buzzing of flies, lots of flies. I buried my nose in the crook of my elbow to shut out the stench. In the entire village nothing had been left alive. Men, women, old, young, livestock, all dead. I came across a mother and baby, ripped to shreds by bullets.

I felt the tears welling up.

Why? Why did you do this, Scottie, why? What in hell's name got into you?

I wiped my eyes and composed myself before rejoining the men.

"All right, Nwosu, we'll rely on your tracking skills again. But remember: Major Scot Hayward is good, too. Sooner or later we're going to lose him. When that happens we break into three patrols: Red, Green, Blue. Kelly, you lead Green; Akbar, you lead Blue; I'll take Red. Stay in touch, okay? We're on a select frequency, so he won't hear our transmissions. If any group picks up the trail again, they tell the others right away. No engagement, understand? Right, Nwosu, you lead, we'll follow."

The all-terrain had been travelling over hard-baked earth and grassland and there was seldom anything as obvious as a tyre track, yet Nwosu stayed on the trail for eight ks before he finally lost it. By that time the temperature was up in the high thirties and with a full load on we were cooking in the exposed landscape. I let the men settle down in a deep patch of grass for a rest and a drink while Akbar, Kelly and I looked at satellite views of the area. We agreed on three promising routes, all of which took in patches of jungle. Then we split up as planned. I mustered Red patrol and we moved off.

It was late afternoon when I got the call. Nwosu was with Blue. They hadn't just picked up the trail. They'd spotted Scottie's vehicle.

16

We rendezvoused with Blue and Green.

The all-terrain had been left in thick forest bordering a grassy plain. When I first joined them I couldn't see anything. Then Nwosu pointed, and I saw something glinting in amongst the foliage; the low sun had penetrated far enough into the trees to reflect off a headlight. The vehicle certainly wouldn't have been visible from the air or by infra-red satellites, even if the motor was hot. There was no sign of Scottie.

I smeared more black camo on my face and hands for good measure. Then I told everyone except Nwosu to stay put, and the tracker and I made for the forest. To the right of the all-terrain the trees emerged from a dense understorey of tangled shrubs, and no one would have chosen to go that way. Nwosu clearly had the same thought because, keeping a good distance from the vehicle, he traced just a half-circle around it, looking for signs – perhaps disturbances in the leaf litter, crushed grass, broken twigs – reading the ground like a map. I stood still, watching him, and soon he straightened slightly and began to walk into the trees to the left of the vehicle. I followed him and quite soon daylight streamed through the foliage ahead of us. That explained it: this was just a finger of forest projecting outward, with grassland on either side. Nwosu raised a hand and pointed with a crooked forefinger. That was the direction Scottie had taken.

I walked cautiously towards the edge of the trees. It was quiet and rather beautiful out there. The sun was shining through the tall grass, illuminating a constantly moving cloud of insects. There were intermittent screeches from birds somewhere in the forest behind me. I had the feeling Scottie wasn't far away. He could be relieving himself, or making something to eat, or scouting ahead, or preparing a bivvy, he could even be waiting and watching, I just felt he was out there.

I beckoned to Nwosu and we went back to the others. Keeping my voice low, I said, "Okay, help me deploy the equipment in there, then you can start walking. I want you a good 8 ks from here before I try to locate him."

There was a soft murmur. Lieutenant Akbar said quietly, "You'd be safer if we stayed with you, Colonel."

"Thank you, Akbar, I appreciate the offer but we need to do this my way."

"He could come back, drive off. Why don't we take out the all-terrain?"

"No, that'll antagonize him and scotch any chances of getting him back."

Lieutenant Kelly said, "We could place a tracking device on it, though. Make it easier to find."

"Kelly, have you heard of pencil mines? You can arm them, even explode them, with a radiofrequency link. That all-terrain could be well protected, and I'm not risking any of you people trying to interfere with it."

Ten minutes later they moved out. I spent quite a bit of time finding myself a good hide. Finally I picked out a tree that divided into a fork low down. If I hunkered down behind it and looked between the trunks it afforded a good view of the open ground. I'd be in deep shade, and very hard to see, whereas everything outside was bathed in brilliant sunlight. It wasn't very comfortable, but right now that was the last thing on my mind.

I settled down to wait.

*

I was on maximum alert. It would be stupid to assume Scottie didn't know what was going on. My guys were well camo'd and stealthy, and they'd stayed among the trees while they were here, but ten people create a certain presence, which he'd almost certainly picked up. I remembered that house in Waziristan.

Heard them breathing.

The afternoon wore on. I shifted uncomfortably, but tried to minimize my movements. From time to time I thought I saw small disturbances in the grass, but it could have been caused by a reptile or a small animal. Even so, I was convinced he was still out there, watching and listening. Before he could use his all-terrain again he'd need to know what was going on over here.

Two hours went by. Then the earpiece in my helmet buzzed. Lieutenant Akbar's soft voice.

"We're in position, Colonel."

"Okay, Lieutenant. Stand by."

I wouldn't shout to Scottie from where I was – that would be suicide. I was using the equipment, a small public address system, the microphone in my hand and the speaker hidden in the undergrowth a safe distance away.

I brought the microphone up to my lips.

"Major Scot Hayward. Talk to me, Scottie."

Silence.

"Scottie, I know you're out there. Talk to me."

This time the answer came: a burst of incoming. I half expected it, but I ducked instinctively. From the way the tree branches whipped away and came back it was at about head height. Behind me I could hear the bullets snapping their way through the leaves into the distance. There was a clattering of wings as birds rose in alarm from the forest. The noise stopped. My heart beat faster.

I tried again. It would be safe to use my old name, the name by which Scottie knew me, because the troop was out of earshot. Which was precisely why I'd set things up this way. I steadied my voice.

"Scottie, this is Jim. Remember me? Jim Forbes. We served in Libya and the Yemen together. We were both Lieutenants back then."

There was a short silence, then a voice exploded from quite close at hand. "Like fuck!"

Another hail of bullets.

I ran my tongue over my lips, breathing hard now. Of course, I sounded different to Jim Forbes. I looked different, too, but I'd deal with that when the time came. Right now I had to keep at it. I tried to sound casual.

"Sorry about the voice, Scottie. I had a throat operation. But it's me all right. It was me when you chucked those two guys out of a sixth floor window in Libya – the ones who used an old man and woman for target practice. Remember that? And it was my life you saved when you took out a raghead in the Yemen, my life and Bruce's. Only you did it with a grenade launcher and it got Ryan killed. I'm sure you haven't forgotten that either."

His voice came from a totally different direction. He was moving fast, not giving away his position. "All on record. Fuckyoufuckyoufuckyou! Fuck all of you!"

He fired again, a long traverse. To my left a branch sheared off and dropped heavily into the undergrowth. A couple of rounds plunked into the trunk above me, and for a few moments the forest behind was alive with the sounds of bullets whipping through the foliage.

There was a hysterical sob in his voice. I remembered how he lost it when our Rotofan came down in the desert, but this was worse, much worse, and I wasn't sure I could reach him.

I took a deep breath. He was trying to kill me, but he was my friend. Only I could help him now. I lifted the microphone to my lips.

"Come on, Scottie, you know very well none of those things were reported."

Another silence.

"I'm on my own, Scottie. I'm not here to harm you. I came here at my own request. I want to talk to you."

Silence. I went on.

"You need help. We can get help for you. What you're doing – this isn't you, Scottie. Some demon got inside you, sent you off on a killing spree. Was it that patrol, Scottie? Is that what did it?"

A long silence. He was on the move again. My eyes darted around, watching for the slightest sound or movement, a crackle in the undergrowth, the rustle of a leaf, motion in the long grass. Nothing.

He's good, he's really good.

His voice, from another direction. "Fucking murderers, I'll kill them all, every last fucking one of them. You too."

"This isn't the way, Scottie. This way will just get you killed. I don't want that, none of us wants that. Come and shake hands and we'll go back together. You're my friend, I owe you."

This time the answer was another stream of bullets. Again I ducked, but they were directed at the loudspeaker.

He thinks it's a loudhailer, and that's just what I want him to think. But none of this is working. He doesn't trust me, doesn't believe I'm Jim Forbes.

The voice from another direction. "You're dead, fucker, I'm gonna kill you, you hear? You want a grenade up your arse, you can have a grenade up your arse."

I took a deep breath. This was getting serious. He almost certainly had a grenade launcher on that multi-rifle. If he used a smart grenade, fused to explode somewhere overhead, I'd be toast.

Another burst of gunfire raked the forest, lower this time, near enough to lash through the bushes not ten feet away. That did it. I'd had enough.

"For Christ's sake, Scottie, will you stop playing silly bastards, shut the fuck up, and listen?"

Silence. No bullets, no grenade. Had I said something that struck a chord?

The voice, still high-pitched. "Jim?"

I breathed out.

"Yes, Scottie, it's Jim. I told you it was Jim. Now be a good boy and come over here. We'll give each other a hug and you can come back with me."

"Can't do that, Jim."

"You can, Scottie, you can. All you have to do is—"

I hunched into my collar as something passed low overhead. What the hell was it? I peered out between the branches, caught a glimpse, recognized the profile. It was banking, coming round, swift and silent. US Airforce markings.

He was a sitting duck out there. His infra-red signature would be lighting up the terrain map in that drone like a bloody signal flare.

"Scottie, for Christ's sake run for cover!"

He shouted, "You bastard! You led it here!"

"No—"

I saw a dark figure rise from the grass and race away, heading for the trees. Not far now, another thirty seconds and he might make it—

The rocket came in right on target. A ball of fire expanded from the spot where I last saw Scottie and an almighty explosion shook the ground and sent a shockwave out that bent the grass like an ocean wave and swept through the trees, releasing a shower of leaves. A wall of hot air passed over me, and above my head small branches snapped and dropped, clattering through the trees and littering the ground. Again I hunched into my collar as something light bounced off my helmet. The pattering stopped. The only sound now was the crackle of burning grass.

I emerged cautiously into the open, just in time to catch a glimpse of the drone as it gained height, heading back. A feeling of blind panic gripped me and I started to run towards the spot. The smoke was rolling over the ground and the air was full of the bonfire smell of it, stinging my nose, cutting my lungs. I was coughing and running and shouting "No-o-o!" and "Scottie!" and I don't know what the fuck I was shouting any more. Then the breeze veered and pulled the smoke away in another direction and I stopped dead. There was nothing there, nothing whatever, just a blackened circle more than thirty feet across, a crater at its centre, the grass still burning all around the perimeter. My body went limp. I couldn't move because my limbs were too heavy. I could feel the tears streaking my face, and I told myself it was just the smoke, even though I knew it wasn't. There was a great emptiness inside me. Scottie was my mate. Twice he saved my life. Why, oh why, couldn't I save his?

My earpiece buzzed. "Colonel? Colonel, are you all right?"

I swallowed. It was a struggle but I managed to keep my voice calm. "Yes, Lieutenant, I'm okay."

"What the hell was that?"

"Drone came in. Scot Hayward's dead. Give me your coordinates and stay there. I'll come to you."

I worked it out on the way. Gracey must have warned

the Americans I was going in, asked them to hold off. They treated it as an open invitation, hacked our communications link, or maybe tracked my team on infra-red, pinpointed my position to the metre.

I brushed my sleeve across my eyes. I was hoarse from coughing and crying. All I could do was say it over and over again.

"I'm sorry, Scottie. I'm so, so sorry."

17

"I'm so sorry." This time it was Gracey saying it. "Really sorry, Jim. This shouldn't have happened."

"Damned right, it shouldn't."

His eyes narrowed. "You look like shit, Jim, if I may use the expression."

"Haven't been sleeping too well. This whole damned business is one big nightmare."

He took a deep breath. "I can't believe they sent in a bloody drone when they knew we had men operating out there. It could have been you it took out – they wouldn't have known the difference. Have you thought about that?"

"It's crossed my mind. What's going to happen about this?"

"I've lodged a complaint, but I'll be honest with you: I don't know how high it will go. As far as the suits in Westminster and the Capitol are concerned, it's a relief; the problem's gone away. That's all they care about."

"We're supposed to be sharing security information, Owen. How can we do it if one side takes unilateral action? That's something the suits *should* care about." I looked at my hands, then straightened up. "You know what hurts, what really hurts? He died thinking I'd betrayed him. And I did. I led the bastards right to him."

"You couldn't have known, Jim, none of us could. Don't blame yourself, it wasn't your fault. You did everything you could." He contemplated me, head tilted. "If it's any comfort the word's gone around. Your stock has gone up with every soldier on this base, myself included."

But it wasn't any comfort. I walked slowly back towards the barracks, still thinking about that last interaction with Scottie. What made him behave that way? How did his mind slip out of gear so disastrously? I was half-way there when I thought of the resident medic, Major Wicklow. He'd given me a medical before I left for Nigeria. I took the path that led to his office.

*

Major Alan Wicklow got to his feet and shook my hand.

"Heard all about it. Fine effort, Jim. Great shame it didn't come off." He hesitated, then said, "I'm afraid some of us are pretty pissed off with your compatriots."

"*You* are? *I'm* pissed off with them, Alan. I went in to get Scottie, er Scot, Hayward out, not see him blown to bits."

"Dreadful business." He pointed me to a chair and sat down himself. His office was the same size as Gracey's but the furniture had been laid out differently because there was a second door, presumably to an adjacent room. For a moment or two neither of us said anything. I knew he was looking me over with a professional eye, taking in my drawn, sleep-deprived appearance. Then he said, "Look, do you need—?"

"No, this isn't about me, it's about Scot. I'm trying to put it together. I'm trying to understand why a guy like that suddenly goes stark raving bonkers. You knew him. Would you say he was unstable?"

"Of course not. He had flashes of temper – who

108

doesn't? He regained control – often apologized afterwards."

That was my experience, too.

"But you know," he went on, "odd things can happen in a war zone. Close comrades get killed and there's anger and a strong temptation to seek retribution—"

I interrupted. "It's been driven home to them over and over again. God, I've laid it on my own guys often enough. Article 13 of the code of conduct: 'The civilian population is to be excluded from hostilities. Even if you suspect they are harbouring combatants, giving them food and shelter, they may be doing it under duress. Involving them in the conflict aggravates the situation, and doing so deliberately is a breach of international law.' Scot was as aware of all that as anyone."

"Yes, I know," he sighed. "But it's all very well getting a briefing in a nice, comfortable, safe environment like this. You still can't be sure how you're going to react on the spot."

We sat in silence again. Then I said, "In your experience, how often does this sort of thing happen?"

"Within the army, specifically?"

"Yes."

"The armed forces carry out pretty thorough psychological screenings these days, so it's certainly rare. I've never encountered it," – he grimaced – "at least, not before this."

"Well I have."

"You have? When?"

"Just before I came out here. Pretty much at first hand. And it wasn't unlike this one. If I've seen two cases it can't be that uncommon."

He shrugged. "The SAS is a highly selected force so my experience may not be representative."

"Okay, Alan. Thanks, anyway." I got up. "I might do a

little digging. There's a computer in my office. Do you think that would have deep access to British Armed Forces records?"

"Is that Heptinstall's old office?"

"That's what they told me."

"Then it'll have full access." He smiled. "Owen Gracey evidently trusts you."

"Yes, I believe he does."

*

I sat down at the terminal. The screen came up. It wanted a fingerprint or a backup password. Great.

There was a knock at the door. Alan Wicklow was standing there. He handed me a scrap of paper. Lower case and upper case with some figures in between. The backup password.

"I forgot," he said. "You'll need this."

"Thanks, Alan."

"No problem. Let me know how you get on."

I watched the door close behind him. It occurred to me that Alan Wicklow was as interested in getting to the bottom of this as I was.

The first thing to do was search the Courts Martial. It took me a while to find the database, but when I got there I started to read through the last five years. Any time I encountered a mortality I made brief notes on the case in a text app, including the date and location of the offence.

I wasn't aware of time passing. When I glanced at my watch I saw that lunch had long gone, but I wasn't hungry. I reviewed what I'd got. There'd been several murder cases in the last five years. Most of them involved a single perpetrator and a single victim. An infantryman stationed in Germany murdered the girl he was having an affair with. It was complicated because both were married to other partners. Another one stemmed from an argument in a pub in South London which ended up with knives. And a street brawl – that one was in Germany, too. A soldier and two civilians died, but from all accounts the soldiers were set upon. I didn't get as far as the verdicts; my interest was in how these soldiers behaved, and none of them had gone out of his skull the way Scottie had.

I sat back and thought for a while. Someone who went on a rampage wouldn't necessarily show up at a court martial, would they? They could be killed. Bill Archer took his own life. Scottie Hayward was killed by his own side. Others could be killed by hostiles.

But there'd surely be an inquiry.

I jumped back to the keyboard and accessed Courts of Inquiry, looking specifically for cases involving deaths.

A young soldier went berserk in a barracks, opened up with an automatic weapon and killed six of his comrades. Then he put the muzzle in his own mouth and pulled the trigger. I noted it down, adding the base in Scotland, five years ago.

A soldier died of hyperthermia during a training exercise. I noted that down, too, then deleted it because it was irrelevant.

I was getting nowhere. I stood up and paced the room. Maybe Alan was right. Maybe incidents like the two I'd witnessed really were rare, and it was merely coincidence that I happened to be around for both of them. I wasn't convinced.

The US Armed Forces were much larger than the British ones. Perhaps there'd be more cases to look at there. As CO at Fort Piper I had a high security clearance, and I could access the records with my own ID and password.

Fifteen minutes later I had the figures for courts martial in which the defendant was charged with murder. There were quite a few like the ones I found before: single perpetrator, single victim. One fit the pattern, though. Five years ago an infantryman serving in Sudan went out on his own with a grenade launcher, killing civilians as well as combatants. It was added to the notes.

In courts of inquiry I found more cases. I finished, logged out, and pushed the chair back. My head was spinning. I needed a break.

I left the office and returned to my room, changed into the running vest and shorts I'd brought with me from the States, pulled on my trainers, and went for a run. The sun was getting low now and there was a chill in the air. I emptied my mind, just concentrated on breathing steadily and listening to the rhythmic thump of my feet on the paths and across the fields. The sky was dark with clouds the colour of wet slate, and the remaining light had the luminous quality that presages a rainstorm. It came soon enough, accompanied by a wind that cut to the bone. I ploughed on.

An hour later I padded back along the paved path to my room, went straight to the bathroom, shucked off the soaking wet kit, and had a hot shower. I felt a lot better; cleansed and glowing. I put fresh clothes on, fastened my bootlaces, and then straightened up and paused. I'd seen a way of getting a little more order into those notes. I hurried next door.

The idea was simply to place all the incidents in date order. If I'd thought of this before I'd have put them in a spreadsheet, but after shuffling them around for a bit in the text app I had the results. I stared at them, blinking.

Five years ago there were just the two court martial cases, one in Scotland and one in the Sudan. Of the inquiries at that time none involved murder, so nothing appeared in my notes. Four years ago, there was one case, ill-treatment of detainees resulting in the death of one of them. Several people were involved, so again it didn't fit the pattern. Three years ago, nothing involving deaths.

Two years ago, seven cases of individual armed personnel going out on a killing spree, attacking civilians as well as suspected insurgents. Seven! In the last year alone there were two recorded cases. To which I could now add two more, Bill Archer and Scottie Hayward.

I sat back, chewing my lip. Eleven cases in the last two years, and hardly anything before that. What did it mean and why hadn't anyone picked it up? I suppose the inquiries would have been held in different locations and involved different personnel. Perhaps the soldiers involved were on particularly stressful tours. It wouldn't take much of a change in the political landscape to create a rash of missions in one geographical region. Where did the incidents occur?

I went back to my notes and checked the locations. Colombia, Guyana, Nigeria, Angola, Pakistan. Did that make sense? Not really. We had boots on the ground in Morocco, Libya, and Syria. Those tours would be just as tough, but of the eleven cases not a single one came from there.

I was out of ideas. I logged out and sat back. I was feeling hungry and I realized I hadn't eaten all day. It was a little late, but they'd still be serving. As for what I'd found, I'd sleep on it and have a word with Alan Wicklow about it in the morning.

Outside my office I stood still for a moment. The weather had cleared and the air had the clean, cold taste it gets after it's been washed generously with rain. I took a good lungful. Above my head the sky was a dark blue, but as I followed it over to the west it lightened to the palest green and below that a dying sun bled orange light into the horizon. A lone blackbird was singing.

Why did I ever leave England?

18

Alan Wicklow looked across his desk at me.

"Eleven cases in the last two years?"

"Yes."

"And where, again?"

"Colombia, Guyana, Nigeria, Angola, and Pakistan."

He thought for a moment. "Could be stress-related. Those are all danger spots."

"Alan, that just doesn't compute. The armed forces are only ever sent to danger spots, and those are no worse than some of the others."

"We've got a bigger presence in those places. That could increase the incidence."

"Yeah, but that's been true for – what? – five years? That's how far back I started searching the records. There were just two cases in the first three years: one in Scotland, one in the Sudan."

"Well, I don't know then. Any other thoughts?"

"Not really. But something must have changed two years ago."

He rubbed his lower lip. I said nothing, letting him think. Then his eyes widened. "Mmm…"

"What?"

"No, it must be a coincidence…"

"Come on, Alan, spit it out."

"South America, sub-Saharan Africa, and Pakistan are tropical regions. Personnel sent there would be routinely dosed for diseases endemic to those places, including mosquito-borne diseases like malaria. yellow fever, and dengue fever."

"Okay, but so what? Like you said, it's routine, has been for years. Why should things change two years ago?"

"Well, the drug combinations can change. I had to respond to a new notice only a few months ago. Hang on, I just want to check something."

I got up and strolled over to the window while he went to his computer terminal, which was on a table against one wall. Outside there was an asynchronous tramp of boots and I watched a squad trot by, fully loaded, no doubt making for the assault course.

I turned back. Alan wasn't looking at the screen any more. He was staring into space.

"Alan? What is it?"

He took a deep breath. "Two years ago the American Armed Forces approved a new cocktail of drugs for tropical diseases. The main change they made was to replace an existing drug with one that's more effective against dengue fever and lasts longer."

"Right, but—"

"Wait, I haven't finished. Four months ago the British Armed Forces finally gave their approval to the same measure. So what have we got? Up to two years ago, cases of US soldiers going on killing sprees were rare. Since then, eleven cases to date. Until recently cases of UK soldiers going on killing sprees were rare. Now, one case: Major Scot Hayward."

"And Scot—"

"Yes, Scot had the new cocktail. I administered it

myself. And before that he'd had it for another mission."

My mind was racing. "This drug, Alan, the one that's more effective against dengue. What's it called?"

"Prescaline."

"Is it possible for a drug to do that – send someone right off the deep end?"

"It's unusual but it's been known. About forty or fifty years ago the US military – and ours – were using an anti-malarial called Lariam. There were increasing reports of rare, but occasionally severe, adverse effects, and the US Special Forces Command banned it. Eventually we followed suit."

"What sort of adverse effects?"

"Neuropsychiatric effects: anxiety, hallucinations, depression, paranoia, suicidal tendencies, that sort of thing. There was at least one incident of the sort we're talking about, and people blamed that on Lariam."

I turned it over in my mind. "We're deployed in other regions that have those diseases. Why haven't we seen any cases from there?"

"Like I said before, Jim, it's a question of numbers. People react differently to drugs: some don't get any ill-effects at all, others suffer from one side-effect or another. If you're looking for a particular side-effect – a less frequent one – you're more likely to see it where there are a lot of boots on the ground."

He got up from the terminal, but he didn't take the chair at his desk. Instead he just stood there, hands in pockets, staring at the floor. Then he looked up, shaking his head. "I can't understand it, Jim. An effect as serious as that should have shown up during clinical trials. If it had, it would never have got past the FDA, let alone the US Army."

"Who makes this drug, this Prescaline?"

"It's a German outfit, I think. Hang on, I've got some

of it back here." He opened the door that I'd noticed previously and disappeared into the adjoining room. Moments later he reappeared with a small box. He read off the manufacturer. "Lipzan Pharmaceutica." He opened the box and removed a vial. "Here, take the box and the leaflet if you like."

"Thanks." I pocketed it and got up, ready to go.

"Jim…?"

"What is it?"

"I don't like this, I don't like it at all. I gave that cocktail to Scot Hayward. What happened – well, I feel I'm to blame."

I reached out and squeezed his shoulder. "Come on, Alan, you weren't at fault in any way. You were observing best practice."

"But it's still best practice! We have people going out to tropical regions all the time." He scratched the back of his neck. "I don't know, maybe I should revert to the old combination."

"I don't think you have grounds for doing that right now. And if one of those soldiers came down with dengue fever, there'd be a lot of questions asked and you might end up taking the blame. Let me look into it first."

"Yes. All right. I suppose so. Keep me posted, won't you?"

"Sure."

As I got to the door I said, "By the way, I saw you before I went to Nigeria. You checked me over and gave me an injection. Did that—?"

"Standard prophylaxis, Jim. And yes, it did include Prescaline."

∗

I headed back to my quarters, but not to my room; instead I went into the small office that had been assigned to me. I pulled up a plastic chair and sat with my elbows on the desk and my head in my hands. I'd only gone in there to turn things over in my mind, but soon the black thoughts came flooding in like an unstoppable tide. I was seeing it all over again: the dark figure rising to its feet, starting to run, the explosion, the smoke, the grass burning around a blackened patch of ground where my buddy Scottie Hayward had been just a few seconds before.

Am I heading for the same fate? It's only a distant possibility, but I'm not taking any chances. No practising on the firing range, in fact no contact with weapons of any sort until several weeks go by and I can feel I'm in the clear.

I raised my eyes and looked at the blank wall with the grubby marks where posters or notices or maps had hung. I used the spacing between the marks to try to figure out what they might have been. And it occurred to me that this was what I had to do: fill in the pictures on a wall that was currently blank – blank except for one possible clue: a drug called Prescaline.

I took the box from my pocket, shook out the leaflet inside, what these companies sometimes call the ticket or the label. I read through the indications and possible side effects. Going berserk and killing innocent people wasn't among them. I learned that Lipzan Pharmaceutica GmbH was located in Taufkirchen, Federal Republic of Germany.

I woke up the terminal and started searching. Taufkirchen was about ten kilometres south of Munich. I found some entries about the company. It was research-based, produced pharmaceuticals, also active ingredients for the cosmetic industry. I read about some of the drugs and additives they marketed. Nothing struck me as exceptional until I noticed the date the company was established. 1947.

More than a hundred years ago? I was expecting a start-up, maybe a spin-off from a university, formed this century, not half-way through the previous one. And 1947? In the aftermath of the Second World War? Not the most propitious time, you would have thought, to launch a brand new company.

I still wasn't much wiser. But if these side-effects were genuine it would be interesting to know how this drug ever got approved by the FDA. The only person I knew there was Norman Harries. Harries had made a very helpful contribution in the counterfeit medicine affair.[2] He was a formidable individual, the sort of guy for whom light conversation was a ridiculous indulgence. I don't usually stand in awe of people, but I was hesitant about contacting this one directly. Last time, of course, we were introduced by Stefan Dabrowski of the US Public Health Service Commissioned Corps in Washington. This time it was different and I couldn't justify going via Stefan again. I checked the time. 12.30, that was 7.30 in Washington.

I'll bet he gets in early.

The contact details were still on my phone. The call was picked up on the second ring.

"Harries."

"Er, Dr Harries, sorry to disturb you first thing. This is Jim Slater."

There was a pause. "Colonel Jim Slater?"

"That's right. Do you have a moment?"

"Yes, Colonel, for you I do have a moment."

It was the closest to warmth I'd ever heard from him. Perhaps Stefan had told him about the outcome of the counterfeit medicine business. He'd have been pleased about that, if he was ever pleased about anything.

"I'm in the UK at the moment, seconded to the 22 SAS. One of their people went off his head in Africa, killed a lot of civilians. I'm looking into a possible

---

[2] See *Counterfeit* by this author.

connection with a drug he was given. I wonder if I could get your opinion on it."

"What drug are you talking about?"

"It's a prophylactic for dengue fever: Prescaline."

There was a long silence. Then he said slowly, "If we're going to discuss Prescaline I think it would be better to have this conversation on a secure link. Do you have a holoconference suite there?"

"Yes."

"Contact me from there in half an hour."

19

I hadn't used the holoconference suite here before, but it was designed along pretty much the same lines as everywhere else: a small, windowless room with the projector on a low table in the centre, and a chair with a console in front of it. I picked up a few folding chairs and stacked them against the wall. The last conference had obviously involved several people. Mine was a one-to-one and I could just as easily have used a video link on a computer. The great advantage of the holotransmission was that it was totally secure. Perhaps it would be more correct to say I knew of nobody who'd succeeded in hacking into one, but that was good enough for me.

I made the connection and Harries' holo-image appeared, head and shoulders only, straight black hair neatly parted, face as gaunt as ever, lips set tightly. Some people had a charisma that drew people; others, like Harries, made them feel permanently on edge. But I'd seen him wipe the floor with a cagey CEO, and when it came to drug safety I had huge respect for his expertise.

I didn't spend time on pleasantries; I knew he wouldn't

appreciate it. I just gave him my suspicions, based on the data that emerged from my trawl of the records, and waited.

"Prescaline," he said, with some deliberation. "This one did come across my desk, because of the prospect of Government procurement. I had a look at my notes after you phoned. The committee wanted to approve it; I expressed doubts."

"Why was that?"

"The data from the clinical trials. You know, Colonel, I see a lot of this material, so I'm used to the incidence of side effects – nausea, rash, drowsiness, arrhythmias, all that sort of thing. There was absolutely nothing unexpected in the figures submitted by the company. That satisfied the committee, but it raised my suspicions. I don't say they hadn't recorded such side-effects, they had. But I applied the average figures for incidence of side effects to the size of cohort they'd recruited for the trials, and the figures aligned precisely with what the company had submitted. Too precisely. I said I thought the data had been manipulated, but I was accused of being supercritical and over-ruled. From what you say, my suspicions may have been justified. Of course, what you've uncovered is terribly circumstantial. Statistically speaking, you'd need a far stronger case before you could mount a challenge."

"You mean a lot more soldiers going on the rampage and killing people?"

He inclined his head. "You could put it that way."

"What if you could obtain the original data from the clinical trials – before they were doctored?"

He gave a short, humourless laugh. "If they're falsifying data are they going to invite you to examine the original records? I don't think so."

"Take your point. Do you know anything about them?"

"Lipzan Pharmaceutica? Not a lot. Based in Germany,

isn't it? An independent, not big pharma. Lucrative contracts from the US Department of Defense would make a big difference to a small company like that, so there'd be a strong temptation to cut corners."

"Well, thank you very much, Dr Harries. I don't want to take up any more of your time."

"Before you go, this may be of interest. Another of Lipzan's drugs has completed Phase III trials, and it's with the FDA at the moment. It's done very well up to now, so it could go through."

"That is interesting. What's it called?"

"Xylazib. It seems to be very effective in extending immunity to Yellow Fever, so if it's approved it's sure to be of interest to the military."

"X-Y-L-A-Z-I-B?"

"That's correct."

I wrote it down. "Thanks very much."

His thin lips tweaked in a slight smile. "Not at all, Colonel. As I understand it, your past actions have probably saved a lot of lives. I hope you have some success with this one."

*

I closed the door of the holoconference suite and walked back to my quarters, thinking about the conversation I'd just had. The picture was filling out a bit, but in other ways I wasn't much further on. One thing Harries said stuck with me, though.

If they're falsifying data are they going to invite you to examine the original records? I don't think so.

What if they were obliged to let you do just that? Suppose there was some sort of misdemeanour, financial or otherwise, that justified a full investigation, preferably a surprise visit so they couldn't wipe the computer records? It was worth poking around a little. Max Keller was ex-FBI. I phoned him at Cuprex International as soon as I got to my room.

"Jim! How the hell are you, old buddy?"

"I'm good, Max. How are things with you?"

"Oh, same old, same old. Say, is this a social call or do you need a favour? I'm here for you, either way."

I chuckled. "It's good to talk to you, Max, but yes, I do need a favour. Is there an outfit in Germany that's roughly equivalent to the FBI?"

"Sure, that'd be the BKA, the *Bundeskriminalamt*."

"When you were with the Bureau did you ever have dealings with them?"

"I did, but Jim, that was way back. Why?"

"I'm looking into the dealings of a company called Lipzan Pharmaceutica, based near Munich. I'd like to know if the Federal Police out there has a file on them."

"Shouldn't be too hard to find out. I'll ask around. Can I phone you back?"

"Sure, I'll text my number to you. Whenever you like, Max, day or night. I say that because I'm in the UK right now."

"What the hell are you doing in... never mind, some other time. Talk to you soon."

*

It was six hours later when the call finally came through. I'd just sat down to dinner with Bruce and some of the other guys, but I excused myself and went outside.

"Yes, Max. Any luck?"

"I don't know what you're up to, Jim, but could be you're opening a real can of worms with this one. There's a guy at the BKA, name of Schröder, Viktor Schröder. He's put together some kind of dossier on this Lipzan outfit. He'd prefer to discuss it with you in person. He's based in Berlin. Any chance of you hopping over there?"

I thought for a moment, but only for a moment. "Sure. Any particular time?"

"He'll make time. I'll send you his contact details."

"Thanks a bunch, Max. By the way, do you know what branch of the BKA this guy is in?"

"Yeah. Counterterrorism."

20

I wore my US Army dress blues, complete with ribbons. As an afterthought I added the water-repellent nanovelour cape, which was a good call because when we landed at Berlin's Tegel Airport it was bloody cold and pouring with rain. I'd given Viktor Schröder my arrival details and he'd sent a Merc to pick me up. It arrived, big, black, and beaded with water, and stopped in a roofed-over pick-up zone. The driver pointedly opened the rear door, so I took the hint and got in the back – if he didn't want to talk it was fine with me. He drove the car smoothly away and the moment we left the shelter of the pick-up zone the rain set up an incessant thrumming on the roof. From where I sat I could see little more than a watery urban landscape and a blur of red tail lights. All I knew was that he'd be heading for the GTAZ, the Joint Counterterrorism Centre in Treptower Park. We joined an autobahn and the windscreen wipers slap-slapped at double speed for the whole journey.

When we reached the GTAZ the pass on his windscreen opened the main gate. He rolled slowly through and pulled up outside the building. It was still tipping down and we both ran for the entrance. The driver shepherded me through security and with a stiff bow left me waiting at the reception desk. Minutes later I was shaking hands with Viktor Schröder.

Schröder was tall and spare, with straight brown hair and startlingly blue eyes. He said, "Thank you for coming here, Colonel."

He'd assumed we'd be speaking in English, which was a relief as my German was very limited.

"Thanks for the ride from the airport. I had no idea it was this far." I was leaning on the American half of my accent. For this interview I wanted to come over as SAF, not SAS.

"Yes, it is not so easy to get here otherwise. I may offer you coffee?"

"I'm good right now, thanks."

"Then please come."

I followed him to his office on the first floor. The room was light and airy and the windows looked out onto a pleasant landscaped area. The trees displayed the fresh green they reserved for springtime, and their leaves glittered in the pelting rain. In weather like this it was easier to admire them from indoors. He didn't go to the desk but gestured politely to a couple of easy chairs next to a low table; I took one and he took the other. He placed his elbows on the armrests and interlaced his fingers.

"Now, Colonel. You have come here because you are concerned about a company called Lipzan Pharmaceutica."

I didn't need to give him the full story. I told him the US Army had standardized on one drug from this company and we were considering adopting another. A contract like this was valuable and normally we'd deal only with large companies with an established reputation. I felt that the security checks conducted on the previous occasion hadn't been sufficiently thorough. It was a small company and we needed to be sure it wasn't under investigation for any reason.

He nodded his understanding.

"Tell me, Colonel, does anything about this company appear to you to be unusual?"

"Not really. Well, yeah, there was one thing. Lipzan was established in 1947. That was just after the Second World War. Most of Europe was on its knees, so it seems like a weird time to be setting up a brand-new company. How did it stay afloat – and how did it avoid being taken over by one of the major pharmas?"

He smiled, half closed his eyes. "Yes, all this is relevant. Do you know something about the Second World War?"

"Yeah, as it happens, I do. I was interested in it at one time."

During my officer training we studied some of the classic campaigns and land battles. That was enough for the others; it wasn't enough for me. I wanted to understand where those actions fitted in the context of the overall conflict. I read up a history of the war, and then another one. I was hooked for a while. I'd never paid much attention to history at school, but this was really interesting. It was about to get more interesting.

"Allow me to give you something to read to, so to say, set the stage."

He took a book from the table. There were a couple of paper markers stuck in the pages and he opened it at the first one and passed it over. Two paragraphs were indicated with a long pencil mark in the margin. I began to read.

It is the 29th of April, 1945. After four-and-a half long years the end of the war in Europe is nigh. Germany is shrinking before the advance of the Allies in the West and the Russians in the East. The Red Army has reached the outskirts of

Berlin. The streets of the city are grey and
deserted except for a few women hurrying away
from the invading army, scarves wrapped
around their faces, babies or bundles of precious
possessions clasped to their chests. They flinch
at every sound: the rattle of small arms fire, the
regular percussion of heavy artillery. They keep
to the road, skirting or climbing over piles of
rubble, all that remains of buildings which have
collapsed and toppled over the pavements. Dust
rises from broken concrete, bricks and plaster. It
hangs in the air, jerking with the louder
explosions. It obscures the sky.

It was a scene I'd imagined myself, and my own
experience of urban warfare made it the more real to me.
It went on:

At Vosstrasse 6, the Reich Chancellory lies in
ruins. A little further north, eight and a half
metres under the ground, Hitler and his
entourage are in the Führerbunker. Hitler is
apoplectic with rage. He rails against the
generals whose divisions have failed to arrive.
He accuses Reichsmarschall Göring and
Reichsführer-SS Himmler of betraying him by
attempting to negotiate with the Allies and
bringing shame on the whole nation. Eventually,
in a quieter mood, he consults Goebbels and
arranges matters to follow his death, which is
now inevitable.

He then returns to his rooms and records
these decisions in a Last Political Testament,
which he dictates to his secretary, Traudl Junge.
Among other things he blames 'International

Jewry' for starting the war, and hopes for a renaissance of the National-Socialist movement with the realization of a 'true community of nations'. He cancels the decree naming Göring as his successor and sacks him from his state offices and from the party. He does the same with Himmler, then appoints a new cabinet. He also dictates his Last Will. The documents are signed and witnessed by Hans Krebs, Wilhelm Burgdorf, Joseph Goebbels, and Martin Bormann. Bormann is appointed sole executor. Within days all these people will be dead.

I handed the book back to Schröder. "I don't get it. It says in there all the witnesses to Hitler's final documents were dead within days, so how come we know all this?"

"Some details came from interrogation of Hitler's personal valet. The rest – well, we have the Wills."

"What – you mean here, at the BKA?"

Schröder laughed politely. "No, not us, I mean the British and Americans. You see, there were three original copies. These were given to messengers to smuggle out of the city. The first messenger was Heinz Lorenz, Hitler's deputy press attaché. He was travelling under an alias as a journalist from Luxembourg, but he was intercepted and the Wills were discovered; they were sewn into his shoulder pads. He revealed the existence of two more copies and their messengers were arrested by the Americans."

It was interesting stuff but at the same time I was beginning to think I was in the wrong room, talking to the wrong person. What had any of this got to do with Lipzan?

I said, "You've done a lot of research on this..."

He held up a hand. "Perhaps you are thinking that

these things, which happened over a hundred years ago, could not possibly influence events now?"

"Well, yeah, I guess I am."

"You must be patient a little longer, Colonel." Schröder got up, crossed to his desk and came back with a few sheets of paper stapled together. "This is an English translation of the Private Will. Much of it needs not to concern us. Please look at this paragraph." He held out the document and pointed. I took it from him, and read Hitler's words:

What I possess belongs – in so far as it has any value – to the Party. Should this no longer exist, to the State, should the State also be destroyed, no further decision of mine is necessary.

I placed the sheets on the low table and looked up, eyebrows raised.

"Do you notice," Schröder said, "*in so far as it has any value*? You see, Colonel, Hitler liked to give the impression that he was a man of modest means and that he had never benefited personally from being the country's leader. His one concern, he said, had been his people. If this was true, then the Will would be to us of historical interest only." He met my eyes, and his own acquired a new intensity. "But it is not true. Hitler was worth a fortune."

"He was?" This was new to me.

Schröder picked up the book again, and opened it at the second bookmark. He placed a finger on the page, then said, "I just give you some examples. His book *Mein Kampf*. From 1933 every couple in Germany who were married were presented with a copy. The State paid for the books, and he received the royalties, worth millions of dollars. He said he got no fees from the book, but he did." He glanced down at the page. "People paid for admission to his meetings. He said the fees went to the Party, but they went to him. He had his image copyrighted, so he received a commission from every picture that was hanging in every office around the country, and from every postage stamp with his face on it. And so on." He closed the book. "He paid tax on none of this. When he was sent a tax form he put lines through it. He said the Chancellor does not pay tax and," he gave a short laugh, "for some reason no one wished to disagree." He tossed the book on the table. "When Hitler took his own life on the 30th of April, 1945, he was worth, in today's money, billions of dollars."

I whistled softly. "Where did it all go?"

Schröder pointed at me. "That, Colonel, is the question. The property, of course, could not be concealed: the apartment in the centre of Munich, the mansion, the villa at Berchtesgarden. He purchased that villa as a small house, then built houses for his henchmen, an SS barracks, anti-aircraft emplacements – this project alone cost millions of dollars. Then there was his art collection. Over eight thousand paintings were recovered from a disused salt mine at Ataussee in Austria. They had been hidden in forty miles of tunnels fitted with shelving. But these things accounted for a fraction only of his wealth."

"And that's assuming he paid for them himself."

"Quite." He inclined his head. "It is clear that there was much more to be found, and this interested the Americans very much – naturally, yes? – the war had cost them a great deal of money and they wished to get some of it back. The funds had been placed in what you call 'safe havens', a complex arrangement of bank accounts in Switzerland and Holland. America's Office for Strategic Studies – these days you would call it the CIA – found one of them: a Swiss bank account which alone would be worth well over a billion dollars in today's money. There were known to be other accounts but Max Amann, the financial wizard who made the arrangements for him, died in 1947. The secret died with him."

He sat back and crossed his legs. I picked up the translation of the Will and the Testament and read it through quickly. Then I looked at him. His expression was neutral, if anything slightly amused. Clearly he was waiting for a prompt.

"So that's it? That's the end of the road?"

He leant forward and tapped the table with a forefinger. "We believe not. We believe some – perhaps all – of the money was used to establish a pharmaceutical company. A pharmaceutical company called Lipzan."

21

Schröder sat back, watching me again with that Mona Lisa smile, awaiting my reaction.

I looked at him through narrowed eyes. "Let me get this straight. You're saying this legacy of Hitler's – worth billions of dollars – was used to start up a drug company?"

"Yes."

"In 1947."

"Yes, that is when it was registered."

I frowned. "I thought US policy after the war was to dismantle German industry."

"At first this was true, Colonel, but only at first. In 1947 President Truman reversed the policy. The Cold War was beginning, and America needed a strong Europe as an ally."

"So this guy – this master banker or accountant or whatever he is – registers Lipzan and then dies. Kind of convenient, isn't it?"

He shrugged.

"How do you know that was where the money went?"

He held up a finger. "Ah, we do not *know*, Colonel; we *suspect*. You see, the documents show that the company was set up with a Charter to transfer fifteen per cent of all profits to an organization called 'The Guardians of the Reich'."

That much German I *did* have. "Guardians of the Empire?"

"'Reich' also can mean 'Realm'. No doubt they would prefer this interpretation. It is a registered charity for assisting the families of German soldiers killed in combat."

A Charter.

I thought for a moment. If the Charter was drawn up in such a way that it couldn't be bypassed it would explain why the big pharmas had no interest in taking over the company. With fifteen per cent of the profits being siphoned off, it would be an unwise investment. Still…

"With a drag like that on them I can't see how they'd stay afloat."

"There could be two reasons." He counted them off on his fingers. "One, remember that this organization had a large injection of capital at the very start. Two, they have an excellent record of getting their drugs onto the market. You know, most new drugs fail at some stage: they cause unacceptable side effects or they are not compatible with other drugs, and so on. Lipzan has had very few such failures."

I thought about Harries' suspicions. A record like that could be no accident. The company may have been cooking the books for some time. Schröder continued:

"When the *Bundeskriminalamt* – the BKA – was formed in 1951 Lipzan was the subject of one of the first investigations. You know, at the end of the war many Nazis who were wanted for war crimes could not be found. Our people believed that this 'charity' was used to help them to escape from the country."

"And was it?"

"It was impossible to say. The payments appeared to be genuine. They were made to the estates of soldiers who were recorded as fallen. In 2030 there was another investigation because the company was suspected of avoiding tax and supporting right-wing organizations. Again it was unsuccessful and no charges were brought."

"But you think that's what they're doing?"

"Do you remember Hitler's Testament – how he hoped for the National-Socialist movement to rise again? We believe that the Charter was not so much a Charter but a contract, a contract intended to carry out Hitler's last wishes by establishing a new Reich."

I pointed at him. "So you're saying the drug company was a smart way both to launder Hitler's money and to perpetuate the Nazi dream."

He closed his eyes and nodded. "What is the name 'Lipzan' if you take out the L and the P?"

I visualized it. "It's 'Nazi', backwards. That's interesting. What about the L and the P?"

"I don't know. But it could be P for *Partei*, L for *lebt*."

"'The Nazi Party lives'?"

He shrugged. "This is a guess only. Of course they would not make it obvious."

I thought about what he was saying. "So a lucrative contract with the American military could result in a good deal of money going into right-wing organizations."

"Not just right-wing: far right. You are aware of the increase in neo-Nazi incidents in Europe: mosques bombed, synagogues burned, marches, assassinations?"

"Of course. And you think the company is responsible for those?"

"Perhaps not directly. We believe Lipzan works in more subtle ways. They feed on discontent: poverty, unemployment, foreigners, the spread of Islam, all such things. These are the objects of hate that can bring together right-wing parties, not just here in Germany but throughout Europe, perhaps even beyond Europe. And they are succeeding; these parties are winning more and more support. And with such parties comes the hooligan element that commits acts of violence."

"And you can't nail the cash flow?"

"No. The money path...ah..."

"Money trail?"

"Thank you, money trail, is very well hidden. Not even the parties who receive money know where it is coming from. Probably it goes into their books as 'anonymous donation'."

I was trying to share Schröder's vision of a small German pharmaceutical company reaching its tentacles into every European country, but it was a struggle. The whole thing, including the interpretation of the name Lipzan, smelled of paranoia. Maybe Schröder had a particular bee in his bonnet about it. When an idea dominates your thinking to that extent you can find yourself fitting all the evidence to it. I didn't want to make the same mistake.

"Herr Schröder, we're talking about something set up in 1947. Do you really think this has been going on for generations?"

Maybe my scepticism was showing, because he became even more intense, tapping a finger on the table again for emphasis. "Yes, we do. These people know very well that the time is not yet here for a revolution. But the goal is passed on from father to son like a sacred trust, a torch that must be kept burning until everything is ready, and then..." he opened the bunched fingers of both hands into the air, miming a Europe bursting into flames. He waited for a moment to make sure I'd grasped his meaning, and when I tilted my head in acknowledgement he relaxed back into his chair. "You see now, Colonel, why I wanted to talk to you. I wanted you to know this, before more American money goes to fund extremist politics that could destabilize all of Europe."

We sat in silence for a full minute. If they had solid evidence, they'd have moved against this company – or its charitable object – long ago. Schröder's case was flimsy, based on small indications, suggestions, suspicions, and inadequate material garnered during failed investigations. Over the years it probably amounted to a fat file and no doubt he was convinced by the sheer weight of paper. It wasn't enough for me, and it wouldn't be enough for a court of law. Any lawyer worth his salt could dismantle it and get it dismissed as a malicious and totally unjustified attack on a successful company that supported a reputable charity.

I took a deep breath. "Herr Schröder, I understand what you are saying but I can't see what I can do. If this new drug clears the FDA hurdles there'd be no good reason why the Army shouldn't approve adoption."

He spread his hands. "But someone like you should be able to influence the procurement committee…"

I was just about to deny any such influence, then I stopped to think. What if I *were* in a position to influence the procurement committee? Would Lipzan have an interest in me? You bet they would. I'd neglected to tell Owen Gracey about the flight to Berlin, but this wouldn't prolong the trip by much and I could report back to him after that.

"I must go." I got to my feet and he stood up smartly. We shook hands. "Thanks for your time, Herr Schröder. This has been an interesting conversation, very interesting. I'll see what I can do and I'll let you know where it goes."

"Thank you, Colonel. It has been a pleasure for me. In case you need more information, this is my card."

It was quite a while since I'd seen a business card – I'm used to swapping addresses between phones. I knew the Japanese still used cards; perhaps it was similar over here.

"Thank you." I put it in my billfold, then we shook hands. I held onto his hand a little longer. "By the way, Lipzan Pharmaceutica. Would you happen to have the contact details of the CEO? It might be helpful if I paid them a visit."

22

It was a one-hour flight from Berlin to Munich, and it was raining there as well, or maybe the storm was travelling with me. I took a cab to Taufkirchen.

Lipzan Pharmaceutica occupied a modern, two-storey building. Security was a lot lighter than at the GTAZ, and certainly less tight than you might expect from an organization dedicated to world – or at least European – domination. At the reception desk a security man took my name, picked up a phone, and hung up after a brief conversation.

He rolled his eyes up to me and said, *"Hier warten."*

I waited.

The bustling, heavy-breasted woman who came down to meet me was dressed in a navy business suit over a high blouse. She introduced herself in good, if accented, English.

"I am Frau Schenk, Herr Holle's Personal Assistant. Herr Holle asks if you would like a short tour before your meeting."

"Thank you. I would like that."

I accompanied her down a well-lit corridor. The walls were white, interrupted on the left by a series of doors with wire-reinforced glass panels. Inside I glimpsed white benches and glassware. She turned, gesturing to the doors.

"These are the laboratories. If you like to see inside please choose one for yourself."

I suppose my sensitivities had been raised by my conversation at GTAZ the previous day, because I read this as *We have nothing to hide*. I chose a door and we went in. I didn't expect to learn anything from looking at a lab, and I didn't. Except that this didn't look like synthetic chemistry to me; inverted microscopes, laminar flow hoods, racks with glass bottles rolling slowly inside a temperature-controlled cupboard – all these suggested activities based on large-scale cell culture. One of the white-coated staff looked up with only mild interest at what must have been a familiar intrusion. I was tempted to speak to him but decided it was unwise. I nodded to the PA and we went back to the corridor. She walked briskly to the end and turned right. Now there were doors on the right as well as the left and she opened each in turn: autoclave room, hot room, cold room, dark room with several fluorescent microscopes, and rooms with more specialized equipment like mass spectrometers, ultracentrifuges, and an electron microscope. It was the kind of stuff you'd expect to find in any well-resourced research establishment.

In the last of these rooms several young men were seated at monitor screens. There were cabinets behind them and I detected the quiet hum of cooling fans. Frau Schenk explained.

"Here is our computer facility. Franz?" She attracted the attention of one young man, who was sitting in front of a screen that displayed a rotating structure consisting of spiral coloured ribbons, folded back and forth on one another. He stood up and she spoke to him briefly in German.

He said, half to her, half to me, "Sure. What we're

doing right now is modelling molecular interactions between drugs and receptors. We do it in 2D here, and we have a dark room in back where we can set up a holodisplay to do it in 3D."

I said, "You sound like you've lived in the States."

He smiled. "Did my PhD at Stanford. Stayed on there a while."

I nodded, then gestured at the screens. "So are you doing this on line?" It was an innocent-sounding question but I already knew the answer; I'd heard the cooling fans.

"That's not secure. Any case it'd be too slow. We have our own mainframe. It runs fast, and the programs are pretty neat."

"Right, and all this is for molecular modelling?"

"No, other times we use computer models of metabolism and hormone interactions, stuff like that. We can do a lot of preliminary testing on those before we go full scale."

"I see. What about testing on animals? Do you do that here?"

He looked at Frau Schenk to provide the answer. Frau Schenk's eyes alighted on me for a moment, and I guessed she'd had to answer this question before. She was probably wondering if I was an animal rights activist. My uniform evidently suggested otherwise because she replied, "When this is necessary it is done at another, secure establishment."

I made a move towards the door and lifted a hand. "Okay, thanks, Franz."

"Sure, no problem."

We continued down the corridor and I followed as she turned right again. The corridor was evidently U-shaped, which meant we were heading back towards the entrance lobby.

"There are no production facilities in this building,

then?" I said.

"Oh no, this is a research establishment only."

Now we were in the lobby again and she led me up a flight of stairs and along another corridor. There wasn't any glass in these doors, just small panels carrying names and titles suggestive of senior administrative personnel. We paused outside the door at the end. She knocked, announced "Colonel Slater", and gestured me in with a "Please".

A tall, slim figure rose from behind his desk to shake hands. I took in ginger hair, bleaching at the temples. His suit was dark brown with a fine stripe. It looked expensive.

"Holle," he said. "Thank you so much for visiting us. I hope you have enjoyed your short tour of our facilities?"

I found myself looking into clear grey eyes behind gold-framed spectacles. "Thank you, Herr Holle. You have nice, modern laboratories. This building must be fairly new."

"Recently we have had a refurbishment. The original buildings are, of course, much older." He pointed out of a corner window. Across an area of grass, backed by trees, was a tall red-brick building that looked more in keeping with the 1947 foundation date.

"We use those buildings for conferences," he continued, "and to accommodate visiting staff."

I turned back from the window. "I gather you don't have any production facilities here."

"No, no. Here it is basically a research centre. Production is contracted out." He indicated a group of armchairs and I sat down, but he remained standing. "Now, Colonel," glancing at his watch, "it is the time for some coffee, I think. Will you join me?"

"Thank you."

He went over to his desk, buzzed the intercom, and spoke in German. Then he returned, sat down, and said, "I hope you like patisserie. We will have some from a maker in Vienna. They are very good."

We indulged in some light conversation about the weather at this time of year and how it compared with the United States. Minutes later the coffee arrived. The PA must have been on her starting blocks.

We continued to chat over coffee, strudel, apple cake, and other delicacies. I knew what he was up to. He'd had time since my call yesterday to confirm that I was who I said I was. If he was very smart, or well connected – and I suspected he was both – he would have learned that I was in close touch with General Harken at Washington, which wouldn't do my story any harm at all. Sitting here in my full uniform complete with all the campaign and medal ribbons I would fit the picture he'd already formed. Now he needed to extract a little more about me, what I knew and what I could do for them. I supplied neutral answers.

He tried again. "I have a confession to make, Colonel."

There was something disturbing about the way his spectacles caught the light. It gave him a slightly manic appearance which was at odds with the guilty hunching of the shoulders.

"Oh yes, what's that?"

"I looked you up before you came here. It was not hard. You attracted a good deal of media interest when you returned from Africa."

I closed my eyes and nodded slowly. "That was a while back."

"I visited Africa once. A wonderful country. Have you been back since?"

Interesting question. Surely he couldn't know? I played safe.

"Yeah, as it happens I was there not so long ago."

"No media interest this time?"

I huffed a short laugh. "When I was made full colonel

my role changed a good deal."

"For example now you are on the procurement committee."

It was next to impossible for any outsider to know who was on the procurement committee. For a start there was more than one committee. And because pharmas would love to lobby – or even bribe – the committee members deliberating over their particular drugs, their identity would be a closely guarded secret. I wasn't going to overstep the mark, but I was pleased that he'd taken the bait I'd dangled when I'd phoned him the day before.

"As I said yesterday, I'm not one of the committee members." I gave him a confidential smile. "Let's just say I'm in a position to advise them."

"And does this take much of your time?"

"Not a lot, no. They have other advisers. But I have a strong interest in anything that affects the welfare of our soldiers. It's a painful business when you go into an area to sort out a military problem and instead you lose men to disease. I speak from personal experience. Obviously I can't say more than that."

"Of course, I understand."

We had more coffee, and he persuaded me to take another small pastry.

He sat back. "I understand you are interested in our new product, Xylazib."

"I'm working up some background on it, yes."

"Xylazib is not simply an excellent choice for you, Colonel; it is the *only* choice. It is quite unique. As I'm sure you are aware, yellow fever is endemic in central Africa and South America, where your troops are operating at this time. The virus has many different genotypes, and the existing vaccine is not always effective. Xylazib is an enhancer: you still must use the vaccine, but Xylazib makes the immune system able to recognize the virus in all its forms. So the body resists the infection."

"And side effects?"

He spread his arms wide, his smile revealing small, even teeth. "I am glad to say we have seen no bad side effects. We expect to receive FDA approval at any time, and the way will then be clear for you."

I inclined my head. "You know, it would be very helpful if I could examine what you have so far from the clinical trials of that drug."

He cupped his hands together and looked pained. "I regret, Colonel, this will not be possible."

It was the answer I'd been expecting but I hadn't given up, not yet. This wasn't about neo-Nazi aspirations, whether I believed them or not. This was about a good soldier committing suicide and a close buddy being blown to bits by a drone.

"Let me put my cards on the table, sir. We have some concerns about your drug Prescaline, which we adopted a couple of years ago. Since that time several soldiers who were taking the drug became psychotic; some went rogue, killed a lot of people, civilians included. Your trials had to be conducted with a large cohort and I would have expected a side-effect such as that to show up."

His face came forward, the expression earnest. "I understand your concern. I assume you have not a direct link between Prescaline and these unfortunate cases."

"Not direct, no. Just highly suggestive."

"How many individuals are involved?"

"That information is classified. Let's just say more than single figures."

He nodded. "I am not a scientist, Colonel; my own background is in financial management. But this much I understand. In any large scientific experiment there will always be some unexpected results. Most of the time they have no rational explanation at all, and it must be concluded that they have occurred by pure chance. It would be misleading to include such results in the final analysis. It is a perfectly routine practice – statisticians call these results 'outliers'. My statisticians inform me that Prescaline is perfectly safe, but in a large clinical trial there will always be a few unexplained results. Unless they form some sort of consistent pattern they, too, will be considered 'outliers'."

"That's exactly my point. I'd like to have a look at your outliers. We want to know if the behaviour we're seeing follows the same pattern." I met his eyes. "And let me say this. We're real interested in Xylazib, but we need to be sure what we're giving to our soldiers is completely safe. That's why I'd like to see the raw data from the Prescaline trials, too."

"The Prescaline trials, too?" A slight tic pulled at the corner of his mouth, and I had the impression he was calculating furiously, weighing up the pros and cons. Then he smiled and opened his hands. "I did not make myself clear. Of course I am not unwilling to show you anything you wish to see. Normally not, of course – these matters are commercially sensitive – but because of your special interest I can make an exception. Nevertheless, as I have explained, this is a research facility. All commercial aspects – initial testing, production, packaging, marketing, clinical trials, data processing – all such things are given to more specialized subcontractors. It is a common practice, yes?"

"Outsourcing? Yes, it's common, but—"

"For me it is the only way." Again the lenses of his spectacles caught the light, and all I could see was the apologetic smile. "I do not have this expertise, so I must rely on people who do."

It's all too smooth. He's being evasive. I wonder what would happen if I rattled his cage a bit.

"Perhaps I could raise another point of concern. It's

the information I have that your company supports right-wing organizations."

He stiffened, and his lips tightened. "Really, Colonel, you are an intelligent man. You should not believe rumours put out by our competitors."

"So you deny your involvement with an organization called 'The Guardians of the Reich'?"

Again the lenses flashed. Had I gone too far?

"Why should I deny it? 'The Guardians' is a reputable charity. Colonel, history judges whether a war was right or wrong. But for me the soldiers who fight the battles are heroes, all of them. They are ready to give their lives for their country. And if they make that sacrifice they leave often families behind who are in need." His back straightened. If he'd been standing up I rather suspected he'd have clicked his heels. "We are not ashamed of these contributions. We help the families of heroes. We are proud that we do it."

It sounded to me like a prepared speech. I decided to let it go.

I waved my hand vaguely as if to dismiss the topic. "Okay, that's just incidental, really. Let's return to the real question: Xylazib and Prescaline. You're saying I can't inspect the clinical trial data?"

He leaned forward. "No, no, I did not say that." He leaned back again. "But for this you would have to visit the contract research organization that manages these things."

"Which is where?"

"It is located in North America."

North America, I noticed, not *the United States*. I frowned. "That far away?"

He smiled. "There are economic reasons. And in these days communication is easy, so distance is not important."

"Where exactly in North America?"

"Mexico."

23

Some people have romantic notions about Mexico and for all I know they're right. I probably have a different slant on the country, because for me the picture it brings to mind is one of guerrilla groups, drug cartels, corrupt police forces, vigilantes, and people trafficking. The company Holle directed me to was in the Mexican state of Chihuahua, which shares a long border with Texas and New Mexico. Being that close to the US border made me feel a little more comfortable.

I considered going back to Hereford first, but it would have been a waste of time, particularly as Holle was happy to leave me with fresh coffee and the remains of the patisserie while he went off to organize the visit. He even got Frau Schenk to make all my travel arrangements, which would be paid for by the company. In fact he seemed to be falling over himself in his anxiety to convince me that everything was above board. US Army contracts were obviously very profitable for them and he wanted to ensure my cooperation.

So I thanked him for his hospitality and one of his staff drove me through the rain back to Munich airport. I flew to Heathrow, where I changed for Dallas, and from there I caught a flight to the grandly named General Roberto Fierro Villalobos International Airport at Chihuahua city.

They'd booked me aisle seats on every leg of the journey so I couldn't see anything out of the window. Instead I took the time to think about how I was going to manage things after I got there, when the statisticians came out with the figures from the trials. We did quite a bit of statistics in my Geography degree, but that was twenty years ago, and it almost certainly didn't include the type of analysis they'd use in clinical trials. Still, I could look at the outliers and maybe even take some figures away for Harries – a lot depended on how guarded they were at this other company, and what Holle had told them they could and couldn't reveal. I needed to call Hereford to tell Owen Gracey where I'd gone, but I figured there'd be time enough to do that when I reached my destination. Which wouldn't be long now as the plane was coming in to land, buffeted by thermals. I'd been flying with the sun, so it was still Tuesday as I emerged into the arrivals hall.

I was met by a thick-set, unsmiling guy wearing wrap-around sunglasses, which he didn't take off, and a loose shirt outside his jeans. He wasn't my image of a company's front-end employee, but perhaps things were more casual out here and first impressions didn't count. He led me to the car park and over to an elderly sand-coloured Toyota all-terrain. Again it wasn't my idea of a company car, but this was presumably a low-budget outfit. The Toyota had, of course, been sitting in the broiling sun and the inside was like an oven. I took the front passenger seat and he got in behind the wheel. The radio came on with the engine but not, it seemed, with the air-con, which was either non-existent or didn't work. My ears were bombarded by two presenters laughing and chatting over each other in Spanish too rapid and confusing for me to follow. This gave way to a group featuring a bad singer and a thunderous drummer of the sort you could hear anywhere in the world. The driver made no move to turn it down. Before we left the city he stopped to fill the tank, so I figured we could be in for a long ride. While he was paying for the gas I took off my tunic and also surreptitiously turned the volume control down. By this time the heat had given me a raging thirst, and it was a relief when he came back with two opened cans of cold beer, one of which he passed to me.

"*Cerveza, señor.*"

I accepted the can. It was slippery with condensation. I lifted it to him in a slight toast.

"*Gracias. Está muy caliente.*"

I figured this might open him up a little but it didn't. The radio came on and he immediately turned the volume up again.

Within half and hour we were driving through undulating savanna, mainly coarse grass and low scrub with the occasional farm. The radio continued to blare but it was receding now, like it was coming from the end of a tunnel. Even with my sunglasses on everything seemed too bright, and I was having trouble focusing.

Must have been the long journey. Or was that beer stronger than I thought?

The last thing I remember before I closed my eyes was that I hadn't yet called Owen Gracey.

24

My eyes opened into an achingly white room. My head weighed a ton and it felt like my heart was beating right inside my skull and threatening to break out. I was in a semi-reclined position on a narrow bed. Freshly laundered sheets were tucked tightly round my middle. The air was warm and smelled faintly of cardboard and disinfectant. There were diffuser panels on the lights in the ceiling.

I'd awakened into a nightmare like this once before. Back then it was a military prison hospital. My breathing quickened.

Don't tell me I'm going through all that again!

I closed my eyes and tried to get some order into my thoughts. The last time it happened I'd been paralysed by a taser rifle. I moved my legs and arms, wiggled my fingers and toes. I wasn't paralysed. I tried lifting and turning my head to each side but the movement set off a fresh wave of pain behind my eyes and I fell back against the pillow.

Where am I and what in hell's name am I doing here?

The pain eased back to a throb again and I made another effort to concentrate. On the previous occasion I had no memory for events immediately before I lost consciousness. This was different: I had a clear memory of landing at the airport in Chihuahua city, being picked up by a thick-set guy in sunglasses, and driven off in an old Toyota. In a situation like that I'd normally be on maximum alert, looking out for landmarks, registering every turn, storing a mental map of the route, yet I must have fallen asleep—

I heard the door open and the way the sound played around the walls told me I was in a smallish room, not a ward. A nurse appeared at the bedside, took a look at me, and said something quickly in Spanish. The only word I caught was *cirujano*. What the hell did I want with a surgeon? It was no good, I couldn't get the words out in English, let alone Spanish. She went away and the door closed.

The guy who came in a few minutes later was wearing a white coat, unbuttoned. His face was pudgy, like it had been put together with plasticene, and the brown hair I could see was thinning. I put him in his early fifties. He looked cheerful, which he could afford to be. He didn't have a head on him like mine.

"Hi there, glad to see you're back in the land of the living! You're one lucky hombre."

His accent was faintly Texan. He wasn't Mexican – that was for sure.

I passed my tongue over dry lips and croaked, "Lucky?"

He smiled, but it was a one-sided smile that I didn't like. "Yeah, lucky we have a good clinic here. You rolled up with a bad case of cryptococcal meningitis. Been to Africa lately?"

Another croak. "Yes."

"That's where you must have picked it up. Your intracranial pressure was through the roof – that's why you passed out. We made a small hole in your skull to relieve the pressure. The infection's been treated, so you should be okay now. You'll have a sore head for a bit, is all."

"How long have I been out?"

"Twelve hours or so. You can get up when you feel like it, but take it slow and don't overdo it. We best keep you under observation a couple more days. Then you can get on with your business. Okay? Anything you need, the call button's right here."

He brought down a push-button switch on a lead, then left the room.

Cryptococcal meningitis? I withdrew an arm from under the sheets and lifted my hand to my head. My fingers encountered bandages. That's why my head felt so heavy. Shit.

It was all too much. I closed my eyes and went back to sleep.

*

When I woke up again bright sunlight was streaming into the room. The big clock on the wall said eleven-thirty. I hadn't slept like this in a long while. It must have been the after-effects of the anaesthetic. Or the infection.

What day is it?

If I turned my head carefully I could see the side table, and sure enough my watch was there, the familiar, old-fashioned Army-issue self-winder. I fumbled for it, put it on, and checked the date. Thursday morning.

Good God, I've been here for two days! What about these people I was meant to see? Are they wondering where I am? There's no way I can contact them, either – I didn't get the name of the company. I remember asking Holle but somehow the conversation got diverted. Maybe I'm here already – I *was* met at the airport and the surgeon said this was a clinic, not a hospital.

I turned back the sheets, sat up gingerly, and swung my legs over the side of the bed. Immediately my head started to pound again and I had to keep still for several minutes to let the room stop going round. Then I reached my feet to the floor. It was covered with a pale blue composite, slightly spongy to the touch and cool, but not uncomfortably so. I stood up carefully, winced at a fresh stab of pain, and went over to the window. There was nothing much to see: a sunbaked landscape with a sparse covering of tough grasses and the odd stunted tree, and in the background some mountains, floating in the heat haze. Then I noticed the fence. It was about twenty metres away and so flimsy as to appear pointless: just a row of posts with a single wire threaded between them. Perhaps it was electrified to keep out – to keep out what, exactly? Cows, horses, goats? No sign of those. Wild animals? I didn't know what wild animals they had in these parts. I didn't even know where I was.

I turned away from the window. I had my balance now, and I paced the room carefully for a bit. It was too small to do that comfortably, so I opened the door and explored the corridor outside. I walked slowly up and down but the door at each end was locked with a security pad. A row of windows provided a view along the frontage of a low, sand-coloured building. That meant I was in one wing. There was another wing sticking out and it was a lot shorter, because I could see past it to a third. Even here, in the very front of the building, no attempt had been made to cultivate the parched ground, which didn't look any different to the scrub landscape I'd viewed through the window in my room. As I scanned around I saw, about twenty metres away, the same fence I'd spotted earlier, so it presumably went right around the building. Just this much mental effort was making my head throb again. I went back to my room and crawled into bed.

The nurse woke me for lunch: a tray with salad, some sharp-tasting fruits, not all of which I'd seen before, and a bowl of baguette-style bread. There was water to drink;

coffee probably wasn't too good for me right now. I ate everything, surprised by my own appetite. I tried to think, but I felt tired and my mind just wouldn't stay there. I couldn't fight it, so I let myself drift off to sleep.

On the tray that evening was a spicy chicken dish, with guacomole and beans. When I'd finished, the nurse took away the dishes and then came back. She made a circular movement with her fingers and pointed to my head. Evidently she'd been told to take the bandages off. She detached the free end and began to unwind. There seemed to be yards of it. Her fingers were trembling. What was she so nervous about and why was she unwinding the damned thing? A skilled nurse would have dipped into her pocket for a pair of dressing scissors and cut straight through it. When she'd finished she stepped back and made a ball of the bandage. At that moment the surgeon came in.

He took my temperature and pulse, which again I would have thought was a job he could have left for a qualified nurse, had a look at my head, and gave a satisfied grunt.

"All healing nicely. If you're still okay in the morning we can transfer you to your own accommodation tomorrow afternoon."

He had that brisk manner some consultants adopt when they're impatient to move to the next bed, and he was out of the door before I could quizz him more closely about this mysterious infection.

I fingered my head. Within a shaved area I found a couple of stitches.

Cryptococcal meningitis, he'd said. I wasn't familiar with "cryptococcal" but I'd heard of meningitis all right. Could he really sock a meningitis infection with something so powerful it cleared it up in twelve hours? And shouldn't I have had the mother and father of headaches before all this, especially with my intracranial pressure going through the roof? I could remember quite a bit about the journey but I couldn't recall having a headache at any stage; I just fell asleep after the driver got me that beer—

I caught my breath.

I bet the bastard put something in that beer, something that knocked me for six. Why didn't I see that before? It must have been the drowsiness – I just wasn't thinking straight.

But I was thinking straight now, and they weren't nice thoughts.

Because if that driver did drug me, how much of this other stuff could I believe?

25

After lunch the following day the nurse brought in my clothes, my carry-on, and my possessions. I got up carefully, because my head was still throbbing, and dressed. Then I checked everything. Keys, fibrepoints, some tissues, a mixture of coins – cents and euros. I picked up my billfold and found my ID and all my credit tokens inside. There were several large denomination bills, both US and Mexican, because I'd changed some money in Munich. The amount looked about right. Perhaps my suspicions were ill-founded and these people were on the level after all. Cell phone?

Where's my cell phone?

I pressed the call button and after a minute or so the nurse came in.

I said, "*¿Dónde está mi teléfono celular?*"

She swallowed and shook her head. Did she not understand me?

I repeated the question slowly and clearly.

My Spanish isn't that bad, but again she shook her head. Her eyes darted this way and that, then she said something about the surgeon and hurried out.

He strolled in about ten minutes later. "Nurse says you have a problem."

"Yeah, where's my cell phone? Everything's been returned to me except that."

"Really? Okay, don't worry about it. We'll take a look around. Someone'll bring it to you when it shows up."

There was more I wanted to know – where was I, what was the name of this place? – but he was out of the door before I could even draw breath. I swore and sat down on the bed. Not having the cell phone was a damn nuisance. I wanted to call Owen Gracey, tell him what was happening.

I waited but no one showed up. There was nowhere I could go and nothing I could do, so I laid back on the bed and tried to think. It was useless; a train of thought would start but I couldn't hold on to it. After a couple of attempts to stay awake I surrendered and the shutters came down.

I was awoken by a single sharp knock on my door. I blinked and opened my eyes. The light entering through the window had faded somewhat and I registered vaguely that it must be late afternoon. Then, with a start, I realized someone was standing at the open door. I eased myself up. He was a tall guy in a white shirt and jeans and he had a holstered sidearm on his belt. Security man?

He took a couple of steps into the room, picked up my carry-on and jerked his head towards the door. Clearly an alumnus of the same charm school as the one who picked me up at the airport. I eased my feet to the floor and followed him. Presumably I was being taken to another room and perhaps they'd found my cell phone and put it in there for me.

Although my head still ached I was ready to pay plenty of attention to where we were going. He reached the door at the end of the corridor, placed his palm on the pad's reader, and we went through. It looked possible to continue through another security door directly opposite but instead we turned right and walked parallel with the front of the building. The corridor was wide and our footsteps were quiet, cushioned by the pale-blue composite flooring. Ahead of us a space opened up – the short wing I'd seen from outside the recovery room. It was the entrance lobby, with a desk, unmanned, and what looked like an office area. We crossed the space and continued in the main corridor beyond, the tall guy striding ahead without a backward glance. He turned left and I did likewise. This corridor was narrower. On the left was a row of doors; on the right there were windows, through which I could see another wing. In my head I now had a provisional map of the building. It was like two capital letters E, placed back to back: three wings to the front, the short central one being the entrance lobby, and three to the rear, of which we were in the central one now. We stopped outside a door with a number on it. He handed me my carry-on, said in Spanish "Your room", and walked off.

I watched him go, then tried the door. It opened and I went in. The room was simply furnished in low-end motel style, but it was a reasonable size. There was a double bed, a writing desk, a chair, an armchair, and a wardrobe with drawer units built into it. The flooring was the same composite I'd seen elsewhere, but the desk was standing on a rug with a primitive, presumably locally woven, design. There was no room phone and no sign of my cell phone. I looked for it in every drawer of the writing desk and every drawer in the wardrobe: they were all empty. Unless it was located I'd be cut off from the outside world. I didn't like that, I didn't like it at all.

I opened an internal door and saw a small en suite with a sink, toilet and shower stall. I returned to the room, went over to the window, and drew back the gauzy net curtain. There were no latches on the window; it was fixed double glazing. It looked out across a U-shaped space to a wing opposite. The windows I could see would belong to the corridor we passed by when we came out of the clinic. That one had a security pad on it, so entrance was restricted for some reason. In the open ground to the extreme right I could just make out the flimsy fence.

I lifted my bag onto the bed, unpacked my few things, and hung them in the wardrobe or put them in the drawer units. Then I went into the en suite and gave my face a quick splash in the sink. When I straightened up in front of the mirror I saw the shaven portion high up on the right side of my head. Stubble was already growing around the stitches in the skin. In addition there were four other sore spots on my head. I rubbed my fingertip lightly over them; they felt like small indentations, in fact I could just about see one of them through my buzz cut.

What were they doing there?

I grimaced, went back into the room, and tried to focus my thoughts. What was this place? The surgeon had mentioned a clinic, which seemed reasonable because no way was the rest of it a hospital. On the other hand it didn't feel much like a company building either. On the desk there were a few Spanish-language magazines and paperbacks. I leafed quickly through them, looking for a company brochure or other information but found nothing. I'd already checked the desk drawers, so I knew there were no clues there. Was there some sort of identification outside, lettering over the entrance, for example? After the clinic area I hadn't seen any more security doors so presumably I could go straight out through the entrance lobby.

I opened my door. There was no key on the outside or inside, so I just closed it, then retraced the route we'd taken minutes before.

The lobby was still empty. I walked up to the twin glass doors and tried one. Locked. Damn. For a few moments I stood there looking out. There was no road coming up to the entrance but there was a gap in that flimsy fence, so it clearly wasn't electrified.

If I could get past the locked doors it wouldn't be hard to leave, but where would I go? It was air-conditioned inside but it looked like it was baking hot outside, and all I could see from here was mile after mile of arid landscape. In any case I'd come here to ask questions about Prescaline. The need for answers hadn't gone away and I seemed to be in the right place to get them. I had to see this through.

I decided it was best to leave further exploration for the moment. Someone would probably be calling on me before long and I'd get some kind of briefing at last.

26

I was in my room, brushing up my Spanish with the magazines, when there was a knock on the door. I glanced at my watch – six-thirty – then got up and opened the door. A strange-looking guy was standing there.

"Hallo, mate. Heard you just blew in. If you fancy a bite I can take you for a spot of dinner. I'm Colin, by the way, Colin Osgood."

Colin Osgood was probably around my own age, but there any resemblance ceased. He was short and pear-shaped, narrow in the chest and round in the belly. His hair seemed to start too far back on his head, and it was brown, frizzy, and dry. His front teeth protruded at odd angles. He gave me a damp handshake.

I wasn't going to introduce myself as Colonel, and I didn't want him calling me Jim – not yet, at least.

"James Slater."

"Welcome aboard, James. This way, mate." The accent was pure South London.

He was wearing a short-sleeved shirt, so I left my uniform jacket in the wardrobe and closed the door behind me. I had a great many questions for this guy but I had no idea where he fitted into the hierarchy. I needed to proceed with caution.

At the main corridor he turned left and moments later we reached a T-junction. We must have arrived at the two wings at the far end. He turned into the wing on the left, opened a door on the right, and I was hit by warm spicy air and a loud buzz of conversation.

We'd entered a communal dining room. There were four small tables, separated but roughly lined up, with men already seated at three of them. Four longer tables were set at right angles to them a short distance away, and at a quick count there were forty places, all occupied by women. It was the first time I'd seen a dining-room segregated by sex.

The women were young – some not much more than teenagers. They were taking turns to get up and receive their meals from a serving table over on the far left. Colin didn't lead me down there, though; he indicated a chair, and we sat down opposite one another at the vacant table. There was room for four places but it was set for two: knives, forks, and spoons, a jug of water, tumblers, a bottle of beer each, and a bowl of that baguette-style bread, which I soon learned was called *bolillo*. It seemed that the men, unlike the women, would be served at table.

Colin had obviously noticed my puzzled expression. "The girls work in the factory," he said.

"Making…?"

"Clothes. Uniforms, actually." But before I could ask him who for he held up a hand. "Don't worry, Müller will explain everything to you."

"Müller?"

"Dr Erich Müller, he started this place and he runs it."

"What's the name of the company? I don't even know that much."

"Company? Not really a company, mate, more like a

commune. Pretty much self-contained. Has to be – nothing else for miles." His eyes settled on the beer. "Ah, the old *cerveza*." He didn't bother with a tumbler and when he set the bottle down again it was half empty.

"So what are you doing out here, Colin? Long way from – where was it? Brixton?"

"Spot on – you've got a good ear. Yeah, I'm an electronics engineer. Did my degree at Queen Mary's. Specialized in radio communications. Obvious choice for me, I was a radio ham in my teens. You're from the old country yourself, ain'tcha?"

"Originally, yes. But I've been in the States a long time."

A man in a white chef's jacket and trousers emerged from a door in the far left-hand corner carrying a tray. My eyes narrowed. The kitchen was through there. It probably extended to the end of this wing.

The man came over and served us with starters: a dressed salad of leaves and the sharp-tasting fruits I'd had before. With a "Dig in" Colin went to work on it with a will, following this by tearing off pieces of *bolillo* with his crooked teeth. It was hard to watch so I averted my eyes. I was wondering what use they had for a radio communications engineer in a uniform factory. Why did they recruit from abroad? Were there no qualified engineers in Mexico? Did he have to get a work visa? I kept the questions to myself and affected only a casual interest.

I helped myself to the bread and tore off a small piece with my fingers. "I didn't realise radio hams still existed."

He answered with his mouth full. "Ooh yes, very popular, it is. Just the ticket for me. Hated school, see? Shit time for me, that was. No good at sports, see – that's what the girls go for. Radio's much better; no one knows what you look like, you just chat, swap details about your kit, that kind of thing."

He must have noticed the shaven patch on my head by now, and the stitches, but he'd made no comment. That was odd. Perhaps he was just being polite, although I wouldn't have thought politeness was one of Colin Osgood's strong suits.

The chef or waiter removed our empty plates.

"And after your degree?"

"Couple of jobs. Second one was good: power transmission, right up my street. Then they bloody make me redundant, don't they? So I'm on the look-out for something and I see this advert. Great package, flights paid for, couldn't be better. I send in my CV and get the job. Been here ten years now."

The waiter was back. He placed a dish in front of each of us: rice, tortillas, and what looked like beef chilli. Colin attacked it all with gusto and conversation was at an end.

The meal was tasty and substantial. Colin noticed that my beer was untouched. He pointed. "Not drinking, James?"

"No, I don't drink." It wasn't true, of course, but I had to be at the top of my game. Colin needed no second invitation. He reached for the bottle.

"Don't mind me, then. Mustn't waste it, must we?"

The meal was rounded off with black coffee, Colombian, freshly ground. I pointed discreetly towards the men at the other tables. "Who are those guys?"

"I can introduce you, but not yet. First you need to know a bit more about the way things run around here."

"I wasn't planning on staying more than a couple of days."

He gave me a queasy smile. "We need to talk somewhere private. Your room or mine?"

I didn't hesitate. "Yours."

He got up, but before leaving said "Half a mo'" and

went over to one of the men. He handed him a small plastic disc and said something I couldn't hear what he said over the noise of other conversation. The man looked first at me, then glanced in the direction of the women's tables. Then he nodded at Colin. I heard "Cheers, mate" and he rejoined me. As he did so several of the men got up from their tables and all the conversation in the room seemed to die.

There was something peculiar about this set-up, something that made me feel very, very uncomfortable.

27

Colin's room was on the same corridor as mine but several doors further up. It was less tidy but otherwise identical. He took the armchair. I wasn't particularly enjoying his company, so I sat on the edge of the bed to maintain an acceptable distance.

"Dr Müller plans to see you tomorrow."

"Right. And where do I find him?"

"He's in the wing opposite the clinic. Someone'll have to take you there, 'cos the corridor's got a security lock on it."

"Yeah, I noticed."

"Müller likes to have people around who are useful to him. Take me, for example: I'm good on radiofrequency power transmission, just what he needs. You, well you got some pull with the US Army, I gather."

"I only came here—"

"Look, Müller asked me if I'd have a word before he sees you. Best thing is if I tell you what happened to *me* when I got here. Okay?"

I shifted my position a little. "All right."

"I told you I applied for this job and got it. So I fly out and they pick me up from the airport and take me to the clinic in that end wing. A guy is in there in a white coat, a doctor. Asks if I've been vaccinated against Q-fever. What the fuck do I know about Q-fever? He says there's been an epidemic round here, not the normal form, neither, much nastier. They have a stock of the vaccine, he says, and he can do it right away. Sounds good to me so I roll up my sleeve. Next thing I know I'm waking up in bed with a head full of bandages."

My skin began to crawl. He went on:

"I get a visitor, same guy. Says unfortunately I had a serious reaction to the vaccine, Anna-something-or-other."

"Anaphylactic shock?"

He pointed a finger at me. "'At's it! Put the pressure up inside my skull. They had to make a hole to let some fluid out. That's why a bit of hair's missing when they take the bandages off. This starting to ring a bell, is it?"

I reached up and rubbed gently at the stitches.

"Yes, mate," he said. "I'm afraid they did it to you an' all."

I ground my teeth. "Go on."

"Well, it's a load of old cobblers, innit? What they done was, they put this little implant inside my skull."

I gave him a tired look. "You're not going to start telling me this Dr Müller can now control our brains. That's science fiction."

"No, no, mate, much simpler than that! See, there's a couple of leads going down into something called the thalamus. I looked it up after. It's some sort of pain centre."

"I know what it is."

When I recovered from my brain transplant I wanted to understand exactly what had been done to me, so I read as much as I could about brain anatomy. I learned that the thalamus was about the shape and size of a walnut, and that it lay deep inside the brain. It acted like a telephone exchange, receiving signals from the body and directing them to the right part of the cortex. And those signals did include pain.

A wave of anger swept through me. I leapt to my feet and paced back and forth in the small space. Someone had been inside my head! As if I my brain hadn't been abused enough in the past, someone had done it again, probing around without my knowledge, without my permission, violating my human rights – not just my rights but the proprietorial rights any individual had over their own body. The anger was washed away by nausea. I started to overbreath. I put my fingers to the scar, trying to feel what had been done to me, but of course this was just a couple of skin sutures; whatever damage there was, it was deep inside my head. I ran my tongue round my lips. I was shaking.

Colin was watching me with a bemused expression, baffled perhaps at the strength of my reaction. But how could he know – how could he possibly know – what I'd been through, and what this additional insult meant to me?

"Sorry," he said, with that uneasy smile. "Bit of a shock, I know. But you're having it easy compared to me. Sit down a mo' and I'll tell you why."

Reluctantly I perched on the edge of the bed again and made an effort to control my breathing.

"When I come out the clinic I'm innocent as a new-born babe. I don't know nothin' about thalamus or implants, nothin' at all. They take me to see Müller and he explains it to me. This whole place is wired. Behind his office – end of that wing – there's a room with a radio transmitter, a fucking powerful one. The antennas are in the ceilings all over the building and there's one buried around the outside, where that ropey-looking fence is. And it's controlled from several places, including this panel in front of him. You won't get close enough but I know all about it. It's a modified sound studio deck, with a touchscreen and a load of sliders. So I'm standing there listening to him and he says he's going to give me a demo. He pushes up one of those sliders, and – Jesus Christ, I never knew pain like it! I'm telling you, if the worst toothache and earache you ever had was like ten on the scale, this would be a hundred. It was so bad I must have passed out, 'cos next thing I knew I was on the floor. The pain had gone, just like that, only a weird kind of memory of it hanging on. I picked myself up. I couldn't think straight. I felt sick and my mind was all over the shop.

"After that I hardly spoke to him. I had to cooperate, I knew that, but I dragged my feet, answered yes, no, froze him out – know what I mean? He knew he'd dropped a big clanger, doing that to me. So after a while he says he's sorry and he'll make it up to me and he does, he really does. So I loosen up a bit. We get on all right now. He prefers it this way, says it's 'more efficient'. Very big on 'efficiency' is Dr Müller. Well, all these Germans are, aren't they?"

I said nothing. I wasn't fond of stereotyping, whether it was by religion, race, tribe, or nationality; it led people into some very dark places. In any case, having a German name didn't mean he *was* German. Most of the Olssons living in the USA had never been near Scandinavia.

The lack of a chummy reply about Germans didn't seem to worry Colin. He leaned forward. "Thing is, he's learned his lesson. He won't do a full-on demo with people like you and me any more, 'cos he's after your cooperation. So you're lucky."

It was the second time in a couple of days I'd been told I was lucky. I wasn't feeling lucky. Angry, yes. Sick to my stomach, yes. Lucky, no.

He sat back again. "What I mean to say is, play your cards right, and don't for fuck's sake get on the wrong side of Müller – not worth it, believe me. And don't try to leave this place. You try to cross that perimeter fence and you'll die in agony, full stop."

"I'm a prisoner, then?"

"Yeah, well he'd say you're an honoured guest." He laughed.

I was tempted to ask Colin what his cooperation with this man Müller involved, but my mind was too full to pursue it right now.

I stood up. "Thanks, Colin. Got a lot to think about. Need some time, okay?"

"Sure, we'll talk some more when you're ready."

At the door I paused and turned round. "By the way, what was that plastic disc you gave to the guy at the table?"

He chuckled. "Another time."

*

I walked quickly back to my room, adrenaline coursing through my veins. Any trace of the earlier drowsiness had vanished and the throbbing in my head was all but forgotten. I pulled out the chair by the desk, dropped into it, and rubbed my fingers over the stitches and the small dents on my scalp, which had begun to itch. I tried to shepherd my scattered thoughts.

First question: could I believe what Colin had told me? Yes, I could, because it explained the four indentations. I'd wondered about them and now I remembered. For precise procedures on the brain, surgeons used something called a stereotactic frame. It fixed the head at four points. They wouldn't use it just to drill an arbitrary hole, so that agreed with Colin's account.

Second question: was it feasible? That harder because I was no electronic engineer. On the other hand I'd picked up a certain amount from the need to understand weapons systems and computer technology. What was the nearest thing I'd come across? I pondered this for a bit, then I homed in on the pencil mines we used in the operation in Northern Tanzania[3]. We placed them in the ground with an auger and the only thing you could see was the antenna, which looked like a blade of grass. They were designed to be remotely triggered; the digital signal you sent out contained the address of one particular mine and only that one exploded. All it took was a tiny microprocessor, and something that size could easily be accommodated in an implant. It sounded pretty similar in principle. The sender – Müller, presumably – would enter an address and then he could activate the implant in one individual without affecting anyone else. Colin said the transmitter was really powerful, so the devices were probably powered inductively, too. That would avoid the need for a battery, cutting the size of the implant still further and giving it an effectively unlimited operating life. The signal at the perimeter fence didn't need to contain an address; it would whack anyone stupid enough to stray too near. So yes, it all sounded quite feasible.

Third question: the thalamus was a small target and, as I remembered it, the part involved with pain was near the front. How confident could they be about getting the electrodes in exactly the right place? That one would have to wait for an answer.

Final question: I was a captive in a cage without bars, at the mercy of a man called Müller, pretending I could get a procurement committee to give their approval to the adoption of a drug, which I couldn't. How was I going to get out of this?

The answer to that was: I hadn't the faintest idea.

---

[3] See 'Counterfeit' by this author.

28

The following morning I had an early breakfast in the place that had served dinner the previous evening, then returned to my room. I'd been thinking most of the night about what I could do. One thing was certain: right now this man Müller, who I'd be meeting this morning, held all the cards. Although I'd happily wring the man's neck I needed to control my anger because at this stage it would be foolish to challenge him. What I needed was information, information about the set-up, what it was for, who was involved, how it connected with Lipzan Pharmaceutica, why they'd gone to such lengths to keep me here, and above all whether there were weaknesses I could exploit to defeat them. The best way to gain that information was to start with polite indignation, progress to interest, and then to apparent cooperation. Müller, for one, needed to think he could trust me.

I didn't have long to wait. There was a knock at the door and when I opened it I saw a young man in a plain white shirt and jeans. He wasn't the tall one who'd shown me to my room the previous day, but he looked to be from the same stable. Like the other one, he was armed and, like the other one, he didn't waste time on pleasantries. To my regret, the burly guy who'd picked me up from the airport and drugged my beer hadn't made an appearance since I woke up in the recovery room. I had a score to settle with him.

White-shirt-and-jeans said he'd take me to Dr Müller and I told him to lead on. We went down to the secure wing. The so-called clinic was on the left but, as I'd anticipated, he turned to the right and placed his palm on the reader. We entered a corridor similar to mine, except I could see only four doors on the left, with a fifth – another security door – closing the corridor at the far end. It would be good to get past that; it was where the radiofrequency transmitter was housed. We had, however, stopped at the first door. He pressed a button and spoke in Spanish to a box on the wall.

"I have Colonel Slater with me."

"Entrar" came from the box, and he showed me in.

I was expecting to enter a comfortably furnished executive office: curtains, carpet, perhaps some wood panelling, desk, bookshelves. What confronted me was a complete surprise. The room was large, at least four times the size of the room I'd been given, brightly lit and almost featureless. The walls were plain white and uninterrupted by pictures or hangings of any sort. There were no windows; strong illumination came from glow panels in the ceiling. The floor was covered with the same pale-blue composite I'd seen everywhere else.

We'd entered from the side, and the man seated on my right was presumably Müller. He was behind what looked like a low laboratory bench, also white. My escort led me to a white plastic chair about ten feet in front of the bench and I sat down, isolated more or less in the centre of the free space. Without another word my escort left, and as he pulled the door shut behind him I noticed from the dull click how dead the acoustic was. I had the sensation of having been planted in the middle of a sterile, soundproofed interrogation room. It was unpleasant, but I wasn't going to be intimidated. I crossed my legs and waited.

Müller was about sixty. He had silver hair, cropped closely above the ears. The skin of his face appeared to have slipped, drawing tight over pale, hollow cheeks, the slack folding over his shirt collar. His ears didn't protrude but they were large, and the pendulous lobes reinforced the impression that his face was altogether too long for his body. In front of him was a panel like a sound studio deck, confirming Colin's account. Müller turned pale eyes on me and spoke without rising.

"You must forgive the unconventional welcome, Colonel. I trust Colin has given you some explanation."

"I came here to examine some clinical trials, Dr Müller. I wasn't expecting to be… detained."

Thin lips curled into a smile. "Of course not, and at the moment this is an imposition for you. I must confess that for me, on the other hand, it is a pleasure to meet someone of such wide experience. I regret I have never been in a combat situation myself but I admire those, like yourself, who have. And I have read the media reports of your exploit in Africa. A triumph, if I may say so. You started with so little, yet you unravelled the whole operation."

I kept my tone stiff. "Is that why you brought me here? You thought I was getting too close to your operation?"

"In part, yes, but there were other reasons. You know, we have been lacking the sort of connections that you may be able to offer us. In time all will become clear; I assure you that your patience will be well rewarded."

I frowned. What else did he want from me? And ell rewarded how?

"And after that?"

Again the bleak smile. "None of us can see into the

future, Colonel. Let us not think about it at this early stage."

"What about the clinical trials?"

"Oh, you may discuss those quite freely with our people. Josef Baer and Klaus Tilmann are in charge of these matters, and they have a couple of assistants. Josef would probably be the best one to talk to."

"But my cell phone hasn't been returned to me. I won't be able to report my findings."

He inclined his head. "That is true, I'm afraid. The very nature of this operation prohibits outside communication."

Goodbye to my cell phone, then. That bloody surgeon knew it all along – something more he lied about. *We'll take a look around. Someone'll bring it to you when it shows up.* Yeah, in a pig's eye.

The situation in this office was bizarre. I couldn't move for fear that he'd push one of those sliders up, and he couldn't move because he couldn't afford to be out of reach of the panel. The two of us were frozen in a kind of tableau, with only this conversation bridging the still air between us.

I gave a short sniff, as if drawing a temporary line under that topic. "I must say your English is excellent, Dr Müller."

"Thank you. It is important to know an international language, and there is none more international than English."

"But surely your native tongue is Spanish."

"Spanish and German. We always spoke German within the family – and English because it would equip us for life. But I grew up with Spanish, too. One has friends, one goes to school, later one has to deal with local bureaucracy. I have been reading, writing, and speaking in German, Spanish, and English ever since I was a child."

I felt a grudging admiration. I could say a few things in several languages, but Spanish was the only one I could really speak, and even then I wouldn't have said I was completely fluent.

I looked around me. "Languages and engineering. Colin tells me this building is networked in a most interesting way."

"Yes, it was my idea and my creation."

"But here? Why here? You're in the middle of nowhere."

He smiled, but there was no warmth in the smile. "It is true we are isolated. I have lived in some wonderful cities and I miss the amenities: the libraries, the museums, the theatre, the opera – I love opera, especially the operas of Wagner. I can watch holorecordings, of course, but it is no substitute for the live performance." He sighed, then shrugged. "Some things, however, must be sacrificed."

"Why?"

He looked at me for a few moments before he answered. "Tell me, Colonel: what does a person desire most in this life?"

"I don't know. Money?"

"Money!" He flapped a hand away. "Money is merely a means to an end."

"Power, then."

"Closer. Come now, Colonel, what would give you the ultimate satisfaction?"

I thought about it. Seeing my men return unharmed from a successful mission. Earning the praise of superiors, perhaps, for a well-planned operation. I knew I was trying to steer away from what was uppermost in my mind. Twice in my life I'd loved, and had the love of, a woman. No feeling could compare with that. Those loves were gone but the warmth of the memories still lingered. Such things were sacred; I wouldn't allow this man to defile them. Instead I offered:

"Respect."

He pursed his lips. "Not really. Respect is a voluntary tribute and one must struggle always to deserve it. But obedience, absolute obedience to your every command, your every whim – can anything compare to that?"

"And that's what you've achieved here?"

"Yes!" He hissed the word like a cobra striking, jerking his head forward, so that the loose folds of flesh at his neck shuddered with the movement. As he sat back again he said:

"Would you care to know the background to this establishment?"

"I certainly would."

He tapped his fingertips together. "I think it will interest you, Colonel, because the full history has never been revealed. Have you heard of Dachau?"

29

"Dachau? The death camp run by the Nazis during the Second World War?"

Müller's nose wrinkled in distaste. "You can call it that. I prefer to think of it as a way-station in the elimination of undesirable elements: political prisoners, criminals, foreigners, and racially inferior peoples."

My gorge rose but I kept quiet.

"Some were used as a labour force," he continued, then that same dismissive gesture, "but all this is well known. I wish to tell you about something that is less well known. At Dachau a group of cells in the punishment block was assigned for use by the local Gestapo, equipped specially for the interrogation of members of the resistance and suspected spies. You will be familiar with this kind of thing, of course; both the US Army and the CIA have used such methods to combat terrorism."

I gritted my teeth. "Torturing captives is contrary to international law."

"Hah!" It was a short, ironic laugh. "It takes place nonetheless. But let us continue. During the Second World

War these activities were an essential part of the conflict and they were tolerably successful. The tools of the Gestapo were crude but effective: the pliers, the electrodes, the rubber truncheon, the genital vice, the soldering iron, and so on. Unfortunately these methods often brought the subjects close to death. It called for medical attention to revive them for further rounds of interrogation." His chest seemed to swell. "At Dachau that treatment was administered by my grandfather, Dr Bruno Müller, who served in the SS Medical Corps with the rank of Haupsturmführer."

He paused, perhaps allowing me a moment to be suitably impressed.

"Some prisoners were beyond his help and died without revealing their secrets – or perhaps had no secrets to reveal. My grandfather thought this was unsatisfactory. He wished to devise a better way of conducting the interrogations. From his medical training he knew that the perception of pain, its aversive quality, the location of where in the body it is coming from, and its emotional associations, are all processed in different parts of the brain. They travel, however, via a common pathway: the thalamus. Stimulating the correct part of the thalamus should produce all the sensations of severe pain without the risk of the patient dying from actual physical injury. You understand?"

He was waiting for confirmation. I moistened my lips, swallowed my disgust, and went one better. "Yes, I can see that would be more targeted, more efficient."

His face lit up as I thought it might. "Targeted – exactly! And far more efficient, yes! He commenced experiments immediately using some of the ordinary inmates as subjects."

"These people weren't anaesthetized?"

"Restrained but not anaesthetized – naturally – the

subject would not be able to describe what he or she felt if they were not conscious. There was no need to take sterile precautions either, because these parasites were due for extermination anyway. My grandfather simply gave them the opportunity to contribute something to science before they were—"

A buzz sounded from his panel, and a flash of annoyance crossed his face. He pressed a switch.

"*Ja?*"

There followed a conversation in German. Who was he speaking to? Whoever it was, the interruption gave me a brief opportunity to collect my thoughts.

This man Müller is even more dangerous than I thought. He's put himself in a position of absolute power – he could destroy me just by extending a fingertip. I'll have to be very careful how I play this. Above all I mustn't show him what I really think of his warped ideology.

He clicked off the intercom and looked up. "Now, where was I?"

I prompted him. "Did your grandfather go on to use this technique to interrogate prisoners?"

"No, there was not the opportunity for that. By the time he was ready it was 1945. The English and the Americans were fighting their way deep into Germany. So he took his family into hiding. After a few months they succeeded in crossing the border into Switzerland. He made contact with an organization there which helped to get him out of Europe."

"The Guardians of the Reich?"

He gave me a searching look, followed by a small smile. "Yes, the Guardians helped him. They were prepared for this: homes had been built for the purpose in the Misiones Province of northeastern Argentina, and initially Bruno Müller settled there with his wife and baby. The baby was Friedrich, my father."

Schröder would be delighted. Here was Müller confirming all the suspicions German intelligence had about The Guardians of the Reich. Evidently it existed in some covert form even before Lipzan gave it a spurious respectability. Of course, Müller could afford to be open with me; I had no way of escaping or communicating with the outside world. And no doubt it satisfied something in him to share this history with me, which was why he was doing it.

"It was a temporary hideout, and not really necessary. Argentina's leader, Juan Peron, was happy to welcome them and many of their compatriots to his country. In time my grandfather developed business interests in Venezuela and the family moved there. But," he held up a forefinger, "with great foresight, Dr Bruno Müller had brought with him the records of his experiments. These he left to my father, and my father left them to me. I alone knew what to do with them." He sniffed. "Colin has helped to maintain and update the system since he joined us but the basic installation was my own work."

His satisfaction was evident.

"Your doctorate is in…"

"Engineering Sciences. At Cambridge, in England."

I decided to feed that monstrous ego – and his admiration for his appalling grandfather – to learn more.

"Those experiments – it was more than a hundred years ago. No magnetic resonance imaging, no computed tomography, no medical ultrasonography, nothing to guide the investigator to that part of the brain. Your grandfather must have been extraordinarily skilful to place the electrodes so accurately."

Müller looked pleased. "Yes, he was. Initially, of course, the records show there was some trial and error, and a number of experimental subjects were wasted, but he was soon able to place the electrodes very precisely."

"And you use the same technique here?"

"Yes, my two surgeons have practised it for a long time and they are invariably successful."

My heart was thumping. I had the glimmer of an idea, and I filed away the nugget of information as if it were pure gold, which in a sense it could be. Still, there was much more I needed to know.

"I don't entirely understand. The driver who collected me from the airport, he was outside of your radiofrequency field. He didn't have to obey your orders."

"He is different. Like the man who showed you in here, they are on rotation from the local militia. We have an arrangement, you see. They provide services, supply us with such things as meat, vegetables, clothing. Our little factory produces uniforms for them. Any they cannot use they sell to their comrades-in-arms."

"Does it have a name, this militia?"

"They call themselves the LRA. It is short for *Los Revolucionarios Ardientes*."

The burning revolutionaries. Not bad. "And their comrades-in-arms?"

"Other armed groups, also set up in opposition to the government. For some time they have recognized the futility of working in isolation, so they have joined forces."

I knew something about South American militias and this didn't ring true. "I'm not aware of any combined operations mounted by these groups."

"Oh, you are quite right, Colonel. It would have been more accurate to say they have entered into 'logistical cooperation'. There is a continuous traffic of intelligence, food, supplies, armaments in both directions, from Columbia and Venezuela through Nicaragua, Honduras, Guatemala, to Mexico." Abruptly he straightened up. "It is enough for the moment, I have things to attend to. We will talk again, perhaps tomorrow. You will find the militia man is waiting for you outside."

I got to my feet and nodded. "Until then."

As soon as white-shirt-and-jeans had taken me through the security door I told him I could find my own way back. He shrugged and left me to it. I walked towards my room.

The meeting with Müller had been a wake-up call for me. What Viktor Schröder had referred to as extreme right-wing wasn't just a political label; it was a state of mind I'd hoped never to encounter. I knew what the Nazis had got up to during the Second World War – I could still remember my incredulity when I first read accounts of the Holocaust. In my mind, though, I'd assigned that savage disregard for human life and dignity to another era, as primitive in its way as the Spanish Inquisition or the Salem Witch Trials. But it wasn't in another era; it was right here at this time in this building, in an apparently cultured and highly educated individual who actually applauded those deeds and embraced the odious doctrine behind them.

I reached my room, closed the door behind me, and sat on the bed, still thinking.

I really needed to get out of here with what I knew. I'd been foolish not to keep Owen Gracey informed of my movements at every stage. He'd probably reported me missing by now, but where would they look? Alan Wicklow must have told him about my interest in Lipzan Pharaceutica, so that would be the obvious place to start. Holle would no doubt confirm that I'd visited him but he'd say he had no idea where I was going next. If they accessed airline records they would see I was a passenger on a flight out of Munich, but it went to Heathrow, so it would look like I was returning to base. If they were really on the ball they'd pick up my subsequent flights to Dallas and from there to Chihuahua city. Based on the slender possibility they could trace me that far, what then? What were they going to do: search the whole of Mexico? It was hopeless. No one was going to rescue me. The only way I'd get out of here was if I did it myself.

My thoughts returned to Müller. Despite his show of disdain for money, money was involved here – no doubt about it. It took money for his father to send him to Cambridge. It took money to put this building up and equip it in the way he had. It took money to keep that local militia sweet. I imagined the food would cost them nothing: they'd loot it from farmers who were too terrified to report it. But it would need more than a supply of uniforms to sustain a partnership of that sort.

So where did the money come from? I was missing a big piece of the jigsaw. Would it help to find out what it was? I had no idea. I only knew that in a situation like this, knowledge was power, and I was still in the early stages of acquiring it.

30

In the evening I went to dinner with Colin again. I disliked the man, and in any other circumstances he was the last person I'd choose as a dinner companion, but I needed to cultivate him because he knew things I didn't. I wasn't very forthcoming myself but he was happy to talk enough for both of us. Eventually he asked:

"Seen Müller today?"

"Yes. He explained a few things. We may speak again tomorrow."

The coffee came, hot and strong like the previous day.

After a couple of sips I inclined my head towards the men at the other tables. "Which of those guys is Josef Baer? I need to talk to him."

Colin turned his head. "Next table. See the sad-looking bloke, my side? That's him."

"I'll just have a quick word."

The men stopped talking and looked up as I approached. The one I wanted to see was only in his forties and he had a full head of black, oily hair. Colin was right, though, he was sad-looking: a down-turned mouth and dull, heavily lidded eyes. The two men at the table beyond him also looked up. One was the surgeon who'd conned me about the operation. Maybe one day I'd get the chance to flatten him – I'd certainly look forward to that. For the moment I just ignored him and turned to the man Colin had identified.

"Josef Baer?"

"*Ja.*"

"I'm James Slater."

"Oh yes. Dr Müller said you wished to speak to me."

"That's right. Could we have a few moments this evening, say around eight o'clock?"

"Yes, we can talk in the office. I will meet you in the entrance lobby."

I went back to Colin and sat down, watching as the waiter topped up the coffee cups. I said nothing until he withdrew.

"Colin, Müller told me you've been helping him maintain and upgrade the installation here. I don't get it. This place is a prison. It's like locking the door to your own cell. Don't you want to get out?"

"Me? No, why should I? I like my work, I get a nice room, no cleaning or cooking to do – all done for me. No washing, just drop your stuff on the floor in the room and it's back next day."

Evidently not all the girls worked in the factory; some were cleaners, and there was a laundry somewhere around with a few working in there.

"And the food's great," he went on, "if you like South American, which it so happens I do. What's not to like?"

"But you have no freedom. You don't get any news, any television, any interactions outside the group you're with—"

"After a bit you don't miss any of that. Television? I never was one for game shows and football, and the news is always depressing, so what the fuck? We've got a few books here, so I do a bit of reading if I'm bored."

I looked at him, holding his gaze until he began to fidget. "There's something more keeping you here, isn't there?"

He gave me a sheepish grin. "Yeah, there is. My room?"

We went to his room and sat down as before, me perched on the side of the bed, Colin in the armchair. He hooked the upright chair with the toe of his shoe, dragged it towards him and put his feet up, ankles crossed.

"You asked what keeps me here, James. In a word, bedtime. You noticed anything about the factory girls? Young, slim, nice-looking?"

Something cold contracted inside my stomach, because I could see what was coming. I'd only suspected it up to now; I'd been hoping I was wrong. He went on:

"It went quiet around the time we left last night, didn't it?"

"Yes."

"That's when the white plastic discs come out. The one you saw me hand over, it's got my room number on it. When we finish dinner I put it in front of the girl I fancy spending the night with and she comes to my room. We all do it. You'll get one, too. 'Course, you'll have to behave yourself."

So that was what Müller had meant by *Your patience will be well rewarded*. This wasn't just a prison; it was—

But Colin had barely paused. "Müller calls it 'privileges'. It's a way of keeping his people happy."

"His people," I repeated. "You mean everyone but the girls."

He blinked at me and pursed his lips, and for a moment I thought he was actually considering the possibility that this arrangement might be less than appealing to the girls. Then his face cleared and he grinned. "Look at this way, mate: they get a bit of variety, too."

So much for that. Did Colin have any redeeming features at all? If so I had yet to stumble across them. But I'd seen an opportunity.

"What if they don't cooperate?"

"Oh, if they don't want to play ball Müller gives 'em a reminder – you know how."

I fed him the subtle prompt. "Toothache and earache."

"Ooh no, not always. The pain turns up in different places for different people. I've asked 'em about that. One of the girls says to me, a man wouldn't understand. So I say, go on, try me. So she says when she was about twelve and her tits were developing, some kid gets fresh with her, and he helps himself to a handful, gives 'em a good ol' squeeze. It hurts a whole lot. It was like that, she says, but worse." He shrugged. "Right enough, I didn't have a clue what she was on about. Other girls say it was like period pains, or they got it in the back or the guts. Like I say, it varies. One thing's always the same, though: they don't want it again. So they behave theirselves."

It was just the confirmation I was looking for. But Colin hadn't quite finished.

"If they're really difficult Müller sometimes gives 'em to the LRA."

"The local militia."

"Yeah, they get a much harder time there."

He'd surely seen the look on my face, because he added quickly, "Look, I know what you're thinking. But a nice-looking bloke like you, tall, good build, blond hair, cleft chin, you never had any problems pulling, right?"

I was reluctant to contradict him, so I just said "Right".

"Look at me. I'm no oil painting, I know that."

I saw protruding teeth, a face pocked from a pimply adolescence, a pigeon chest and a pot belly, and I couldn't disagree.

"Back home girls wouldn't give me the time of day. Here I do all right. There's about forty of 'em in there. I can have a different one every night of the week if I'm up to it. Well, I say forty. Some are off limits."

"You mean menstruating?"

"Nah, the kids don't cycle because of the contraceptive pills they take. I'm talking about Müller. He likes girls but he gets tired of 'em quickly. Any that come in new, he gets first crack, while they're fresh, if you know what I mean. We give those ones a wide berth, otherwise there'd be hell to pay. It's his way of staying in control. You move in, he'd see that as rebellion."

"Suppose a girl doesn't take the pills? Suppose she gets pregnant?"

"She wouldn't take the chance, mate. If Müller found out she was in the club he'd definitely give her to the soldiers."

I took a deep breath. "So Müller uses them, then puts them into general circulation."

"That's right. And this," he filched in a pocket and brought out the white plastic disc, "is your ticket to paradise, chum." He kissed it. Then he looked at it and blinked eyes that were devoid of lashes. "Which reminds me." He pulled his legs in and laughed. "Sorry, I need to book my bird now before they all fly away."

We walked together down to the main corridor. There Colin hurried off with his precious plastic disc, his feet flapping on the composite flooring. I sucked a breath between my teeth as I watched him go. From what I knew, this place was a prison for everyone except for Müller, the surgeons, and the militia men. But Colin was in a unique position. Colin had earned the trust of Müller. He alone had the skills and the access to shut down the transmitter and fling the doors wide open. Only he'd never do it because he was having far too much fun. Tonight, as every night, he'd plonk that plastic disc in front of some unwilling, unfortunate girl and force himself on her.

It was a pity about Colin; it would have been easier to destroy this place with his willing assistance. I would just have to settle for his unwitting assistance.

I checked my watch. It was two minutes to eight and I had an appointment to keep.

31

Josef Baer was waiting for me in the entrance lobby. He dipped his head in the Germanic style as we shook hands, then he led the way to the end of the main corridor. To the right was the corridor where I'd met Müller, but he turned to the left, palmed the reader, and I followed him through.

He opened the third door. Before he went in I said, "What are the rooms we just passed?"

"Those two? Oh, they are for the soldiers."

"The LRA men?"

"Yes."

I pointed to the next door. "That was my recovery room – what about the rest?"

"Another recovery room, then the rooms for the surgeons."

"What about the nurse?"

"She is just one of the factory girls. They bring one here any time we have a new arrival and put her in a uniform. She is not really a nurse."

I nodded. That explained a lot.

"And the door across the end of the corridor, that'll be the surgical theatre."

"Yes. They call it the clinic."

I gave him a rueful smile. "I know."

"Of course you can not get into this corridor or the one opposite without an escort."

"What about the entrance door? Is that always locked?"

"No, only when there is someone new here who has not been told about the fence."

That made sense, too. They wouldn't want people like me destroying themselves because we didn't yet know what was inside our heads.

We entered his office. The louvred blinds on the windows were closed and he switched on concealed ceiling lights. I saw four desks, each with a computer terminal, and a table with a multi-function office printer. My heart leapt. Was this place networked? Could I contact Gracey or Harken from here? I held myself back. I would need to proceed carefully.

He pointed me to a chair and sat down side-on to the desk, his hands in his lap.

He opened the conversation. "Dr Müller said you are a Colonel in the United States Army."

"That's right."

"I am sorry you find yourself here, Colonel."

"James."

He nodded. "I am Josef."

"Well, Josef, I'm not altogether delighted about it myself. But there are two ways of looking at a situation. It can be the end of the road – or the beginning."

He rolled those heavily lidded eyes towards me. What I saw there was only the end of the road.

"How long have you worked in this place?" I asked him.

"About four years."

"And before that, Taufkirchen?"

"Yes, but in fact I still work for Lipzan Pharmaceutica."

"Josef, I'll come straight to the point. The US Army is

giving Lipzan's drug Prescaline to our forces when they're posted to tropical regions. I'm a bit concerned about unrecorded side-effects. We've had a few incidents of soldiers going wild, killing people. Did you see anything like that during the trials?"

There was a long silence. He looked very uncomfortable. Eventually he swallowed, and said, "You know you cannot leave this place? And there is no communication with the world outside."

I glanced at the computers but said, "Yes, it certainly looks that way."

"So what I tell you, you can never tell anyone else."

"See here, I've spent a bit of time on this, and I'd still like to know the answer. For my own satisfaction."

He avoided my eyes, looked at his hands. "You have met Holle?"

"Yes."

"I had disagreements with him."

"Over the trials?"

"Yes." He took a deep breath. "Do you know anything about drug development?"

"I know it's an expensive business."

"Very expensive. Prescaline went through Phase I and Phase II trials without any problems. But Phase III was much larger, about four thousand subjects. We started to see some bad effects."

I felt a thrill and my pulse was racing. "What kind of effects?"

"Mostly headaches and nausea. But a few subjects developed severe paranoid tendencies. They became very violent." He swallowed. "They attacked people."

Poor Scottie, I was right all the time. "Go on."

He looked up. "I am an honest man, James. The correct procedure was to include these incidents in the final report. Holle would not hear of it. He said these people had been psychotic to start with; it was nothing to do with the drug, and it would be misleading to include them in the trial." He shrugged. "You can see it from his point of view. He is a businessman, not a scientist. By the time Prescaline cleared the Phase I and Phase II trials the company had already spent millions of dollars. Phase III added a huge amount to that. It was essential to have FDA approval if the company was to recover its investment. And it is not a large company – failure could have resulted in bankrupcy. I knew all that but I stood my ground."

"So Holle sent you here."

"He tricked me. After a while he said I was right, the reputation of the company was at stake. And now I should have a holiday, because I had earned it. That was not unusual – he would sometimes send a favoured senior colleague here for short holidays."

I could see how they might enjoy that but I said nothing, just let him continue.

"I was happy that our differences had been settled in such a friendly way, so I was eager to come here for my short holiday. But it was not a holiday. I woke up in a recovery room. The rest you know."

"Did you leave family behind?"

He gave a short, humourless laugh. "I am divorced, and my ex-wife is still trying to squeeze more money out of me. It seemed like a good escape – at first." He shook his head.

"And then Müller explains that you will have to remove the 'outliers' and write the report the way Holle wants it. Or else."

He looked away again. "I have seen what Müller can do to people, people with this in their heads." He tapped his skull. "I had no choice. It took about eighteen months for the FDA to give their approval. The United States Army adopted Prescaline soon afterwards."

"What about Xylazib, Josef? Does that have side effects, too?"

"Xylazib is a different compound. But I have noticed that some subjects developed a disorder of the blood."

"And you'll have to leave those out of the report."

"Of course."

I was still thinking about those computers. "Something I don't understand. Mr Holle referred to this place as a contract research organization, running the trials, collecting and analysing the data, and sending in the reports. How can you do that when you have no communication?"

Baer was shaking his head. "It is not true. Holle has complete control over the trials. Lipzan's sales force recruits doctors into the trials and the doctors recruit the patients. There are financial rewards for both doctors and patients. A lot of the subjects come from poor areas of South America, so you can imagine there are plenty of people willing to take part. The figures are collected by Lipzan and finally sent to Müller. Only the analysis is done here. That is my job, and I have to write the reports just the way he wants them. Then he transmits the reports back to Lipzan for them to submit."

"Oh, so you're not networked in this building."

"No. Only Müller is connected to the outside world."

My ballooning hopes deflated abruptly. To cover my disappointment I said quickly, "The doctors who take part in the trial – I suppose they never see the whole picture."

"No, they may be sent a summary but by that time, of course, any negative results have been removed. It is a clumsy system, but in this way Holle can be assured of a market for every single drug Lipzan makes." His voice began to quiver. "I do not like what I do, James. I am sorry for your soldiers and the people they killed. It should not have happened."

He blinked rapidly. I reached out and put a hand on his arm. "It's okay, Josef, it's okay. I can see you had no choice."

We sat in silence for a while. Then I said, "You're obviously unhappy here. Have you thought about escaping?"

"Escape?" He raised his eyebrows. "Impossible. Here we are a long way from any help. And there is the electric field all around this building. It would kill me if I tried."

I nodded, my lips tight.

He tilted his head wistfully. "Sometimes I have thought about doing that – ending my life by deliberately walking past that fence. But it would be a dreadful way to die."

"Your colleague, Klaus Tilmann. Did the same thing happen to him?"

"Klaus is young, single. He had no disagreements with Holle, but it is a lot of work to analyse the trial data and Holle thought I needed some help."

I paused for a moment then said, as gently as I could, "Josef, do you have a white plastic disc with your room number on it?"

A crimson flush spread over his pale cheeks. For a while he said nothing. Then he swallowed hard. "They are nice girls and I am sorry for them, but I have a bad life, too. What else is there for me? I know it is wrong, but all I want is a little comfort." He fixed moist, red-rimmed eyes on mine in mute appeal.

Sad-looking was right. This guy was seriously depressed. I didn't want to sound judgemental, so I kept my tone neutral. "Do you talk to the girls? Where do they come from?"

The tip of his tongue travelled over his lips. "Yes, I talk to them, always. Some do not wish to talk. Others do. They come from many places: Nicaragua, Honduras, Guatemala, Venezuela, one or two from Brazil."

"Do they say how they were brought here?"

"Some were kidnapped, taken off the street. Others were offered jobs, good jobs, in Mexico City, even in the United States. Then they were passed to the soldiers. The soldiers bring them here."

I got up. "Thanks, Josef. I'm sure we'll talk again."

He looked up and nodded resignedly. "I will let you out."

As we walked to the security door I said, "Those soldiers: how often do they change over?"

"Every week. They come here two at a time. There is quite a demand to be on duty here."

I'll just bet there is.

He opened the door and I left him there.

On the way back to my room I paused in the entrance lobby. It was deserted. Beyond the glass doors the landscape was in total darkness. I imagined those frightened girls reaching this isolated place at the end of their long journey. What was it Baer had said?

They come from many places: Nicaragua, Honduras, Guatemala, Venezuela, one or two from Brazil.

The logistical link-up between the rebel groups would provide the perfect conduit for transporting the girls. But what was in it for the militia men? It would have to be a lot more than a few uniforms. Was something else travelling in that conduit?

Drugs! A transport link like that would be a godsend to the cartels at each end of the chain: they could ferry cocaine along it from Colombia and Venezuela through Mexico and into the United States.

I felt sure that was it, but where did Müller and his establishment fit in?

I went back to my room and paced around for minutes on end. Then it hit me. I looked up at the darkened window, seeing beyond it the whole scheme.

The drug trade generated a lot of money, and that money had to be laundered. Enter the Guardians of the Reich. With their established network for the secret distribution of funds all over Europe it was an ideal partnership, and the Müllers had all the connections to make it happen. Laundered money went back to the cartels and the Müllers took a generous cut.

I allowed myself a moment of grim satisfaction. At last I knew where the money came from.

Who started it? The Nazi grandfather, Dr Bruno Müller? Were these his "business interests"? Probably. It was certainly developed further by his son Friedrich. The ingredients were all there.

The man I'd seen this morning, second-generation Dr Erich Müller, must have been realistic enough to accept that the dream of world domination wasn't attainable in his lifetime, so he created a small Reich of his own, of which he was the supreme ruler. He developed the technology and built this place, and populated it with girls trafficked via the same route as the drugs. Whatever the uniform factory produced was peanuts in comparison to all this. It may have been an afterthought, a way of occupying the girls during the day, making something useful for the LRA. There was no problem about occupying the girls at night.

32

I'd just about finished breakfast next morning when I sensed a presence at my right shoulder. I looked up into the unsmiling face of white-shirt-and-jeans. He said in Spanish:

"Dr Müller wants to see you."

"*Ahora?*"

"*Sí, ahora.*"

I got up and followed him.

As I entered Müller's office I saw that he was seated, as before, in front of that modified sound studio deck with its row of slider controls. The chair that had been placed for me was at about the same distance from Müller, but for some reason it had been offset to the left. He waited until I'd sat down and the soldier had left.

"Good morning, Colonel. You have had the opportunity to talk to Mr Baer?"

"Yes, it was very helpful."

"Good. Mr Baer is not a well man, I think. It may be necessary to dispense with his services."

I felt a jolt of alarm. "My impression was that he's doing a good job under difficult circumstances. If he gets a little depressed from time to time it's understandable."

He looked at me for a while, then said, "Well, well, that

is not why I brought you here. We have a new recruit for the factory."

For your bloody harem, you mean.

"And?"

"And I thought you would like to observe her induction."

"I'm not sure why you—"

"Really, Colonel," he said firmly, "I think you should. It will demonstrate for you the technology that underlies our enterprise with a clarity that should ensure your future cooperation."

I opened my mouth to speak but he held up a hand. "Do not move, stand or speak at any stage. I must insist on this. Do you understand?"

The blood was hot in my face, but I replied quietly, "Yes."

"Good." He pressed a button and spoke into a microphone. The door opened and I glanced to my right as they came in. My interest quickened. The girl was tall, slightly taller than the young soldier who was holding her too firmly by the upper arm. Her plain pale green dress set off auburn, shoulder-length hair. She glanced quickly around and I noticed the bare patch high up on the side of her head. I also noticed that she had green eyes and a figure that would certainly get your attention if you ever saw her in a crowd. The man led her right up to Müller's desk, and the moment he relaxed his grip she shook off his hand with a clear show of annoyance.

Before the soldier had even left the room she was telling Müller just what she thought of this treatment. The Spanish was very rapid, but I caught phrases, and I followed the subsequent conversation all too clearly.

"This is an outrage! Why have I been kidnapped by your thugs? What have you done to me?" here she stabbed a finger at the shaven patch on her head. "It is disgraceful,

I demand to be released immediately—"

"Be quiet!" Müller thundered. Then in a quiet, level tone, "What is your name?"

She drew herself up. "I am Delfina Rosa Antonia Teresa Santos."

"Delfina, you will not ask questions or make demands. I will make the demands and you will obey them without hesitation."

She held her head high and huffed derisively. "You're out of your mind."

He sighed. "Take off your dress."

I tensed, scarcely able to believe what I'd just heard. She recoiled but recovered quickly, gathered herself, then spat in his face.

"*Cochino!*"

Almost simultaneously she kicked off a shoe and reached down. I thought she was about to brain him with it but she never got that far. As she bent over he advanced a slider and her body went rigid. With a gasp she reached a hand to her lower abdomen. Müller left the slider there as he took a tissue from his pocket and slowly wiped the saliva from his face. He was white with rage. He threw the tissue aside and I could see his fingers as he pushed the slider further. A low moan escaped from her. Now she was clutching her abdomen with both hands, bent double, breathing hard through her mouth. He played with the slider, jerking it forward and back, eliciting a loud cry on each movement, and then he drew it back. She collapsed to the floor, gasping.

I drew in my feet, about to rise from my chair and yell "Stop this, stop it at once!" but Müller seemed to have anticipated my reaction. Without even looking at me he held up a warning hand. I remembered that I was supposed to be an interested observer here, nothing more. In fact it would probably give the man even more satisfaction if he saw how appalled I was, so I did my best to appear impassive. Inside I was seething.

"Get up!" he shouted at her.

Slowly she gathered herself together and stood facing him again, still bent slightly, still breathing hard.

"If you do not obey me," he said, "you will suffer. I can make you suffer a great deal. Now take off your dress."

She hesitated. He responded by stabbing at the slider. Her head jerked back, mouth open, and my ears rang with the scream. He returned the slider.

Now all my instincts were compelling me to leap into action. Two, three strides and a strike to the throat is all it would take – except I wouldn't make it that far. I was quite sure my address was already entered on that panel and all he had to do was move one finger and I'd be stopped in my tracks. After that any prospect of getting out of here and of dismantling this ghastly setup would be gone. My muscles were rigid with the effort of maintaining self-control.

She lowered her head and looked at him. Then she reached behind her neck to unfasten the hook and eye at the top, then behind her back to draw down the zip. The dress came off in one smooth motion and dropped to the floor.

But Müller hadn't finished.

"Now take off the rest."

Her voice was hoarse, but the stream of Spanish she loosed at him was like automatic gunfire. He shrugged and pushed the slider, and this time it went further forward than ever. She clasped herself and dropped to her knees with a shout of agony, then she fell to one side, wailing and spasming.

Her cries echoed inside my head and my eyes pricked with tears. Images floated in front of me: Sally Kent, biting back the pain from a shattered femur, David van der Loos, delirious from malaria, Abby Moore, shot in the spine – I'd served with them all and felt their pain, as I was now feeling Delfina's.

You bastard, you irredeemable, sonofabitching bastard. I'll get you for this if it's the last thing I do.

He pulled the slider back. For a while nothing happened. The only sound was the low sobbing coming from Delfina. She dragged herself to her hands and knees and stayed there. Her mouth was open, and saliva trickled from it in a thin, clear stream.

"Get up," Müller snapped, "or do you want it all over again?"

She rose unsteadily to her feet and wiped the back of a hand across her mouth.

"Now do what I said."

She paused, still breathing hard. Then she unhitched the bra, slipped the thin white straps over her shoulders, and shrugged it off. It landed at her feet.

Müller's tongue flickered over his loose lower lip. "*Schnell!*" he shouted, lapsing into his native tongue for a moment. Then back into Spanish, "*Rápido! Todo!*"

She hesitated, and he reached for the slider again, but she quickly complied, hooking her thumbs into the waistband of her knickers, pushing them down below her knees, and stepping out of them as they fell to the floor. She straightened up again, but the dignified bearing had gone; she looked somehow diminished, head bent forward, arms hanging loosely at her sides.

Müller nodded. "That's better. Now turn, and show yourself to the Colonel."

So far she hadn't seemed to register my presence, but now she lifted her head a little and turned. I was vaguely aware of her breasts, of the dark flame of pubic hair, but that was only in my peripheral vision because her contemptuous gaze swept the room and rested on me, and

I shrivelled in the heat of her loathing. My cheeks burned – with embarrassment for me and for her.

Müller got to his feet. His voice was matter-of-fact as he switched to English. "You may leave us now, Colonel. I have some unfinished business with this young lady."

I set my jaw and got stiffly to my feet. My voice was as steady as I could make it. "Thank you, Herr Doktor. Very impressive."

33

I didn't want to see anybody. I hurried back to my room and paced around. My guts were turning over. I'd just witnessed a proud, beautiful woman being utterly degraded, and Müller had shamed me along with her. I was pretty sure no one had told her what that small wound in her head was about, so the pain of her ordeal would have been amplified by shock and disbelief. I criss-crossed the room, clenching and unclenching my fists. I couldn't get the images out of my mind: Delfina writhing in agony on the floor, arms wrapped around her body, and finally, head bowed, her resistance broken, standing naked before her torturer. I didn't even want to think about what Müller was doing to her now. I wished to heaven I could get her out of here. But she wasn't alone: every girl in that factory must have been subjected to similar treatment. Now, with the memory of that intense pain burned into their minds, they would submit night after night to whoever placed a white plastic disc in front of them. I stopped at the window. I had to go outside, to get some air and try to rid myself of the sour taste in my mouth.

Would the entrance door be locked? Probably not. Unlike me, Delfina and the other girls would have been marched straight from the clinic to see Müller, and no doubt he'd take some satisfaction in telling them about the fence himself.

Unsmiling white-shirt-and-jeans was hanging around at the front entrance. He stiffened as I approached.

"Where are you going?"

I'd had enough of this. I didn't even bother to use Spanish.

"I'm going to stretch my legs. You have a problem with that?"

Go on, take a crack at me. I'd be delighted.

His eyes roved over me, sizing me up. Then he said, again in Spanish, "Stay inside the fence."

I ignored him and pushed through the door. It breathed shut on the air-conditioning and the heat hit me right away, drilling out of a clear blue sky and coming back at me off the ground. Vehicles had worn a path to the front entrance and I strode out along it as far as the fence, which was every bit as flimsy as it looked from my room. There was the wide gap I'd seen before – clearly there to let vehicles through – but I wasn't daft enough to walk through it; the cable would be continuous underground and there was no slider controlling that field, it was running at full whack.

I squatted to examine the path more closely. To judge from my own experience, Delfina would have arrived two, maybe three, days ago. These tyre tracks weren't old, but they weren't as recent as that, so where had she been brought in? I thought about it. She'd been kidnapped and handed over to the soldiers. Müller said the LRA made food deliveries, and that wouldn't be at the front here, it would be to the kitchen, adjacent to the dining area at the back. They must have used the same route to deliver Delfina.

I brushed my fingers across the most recent tracks.

They were probably from the old Toyota that I came in. I straightened up. Come to think of it, where was the Toyota?

I turned round and looked at the building but I could see no sign of either the vehicle or a garage, so the question remained unanswered. Still, it seemed like a good opportunity to confirm and extend the picture of the place that I'd built up from the inside.

The building was faced with a pale reddish-brown plasticrete, and they probably had solar panels the same colour on the roof. It wouldn't be that easy to spot from the air, although in low sun the shadow would be a giveaway. In front of me was the short wing with the entrance lobby. To my left was the secure wing where I woke up three days ago with a thumping headache. The so-called clinic would be at the end, then the rooms for the surgeons, the recovering patients, Baer's office, and the visiting soldiers. What was in the wing to my right?

I moved off in that direction. The noise of machinery came to my ears and got louder as I approached, the smooth chatter of many sewing machines, like a Far Eastern sweat shop. The uniform factory. It had windows but they were obscured by louvred blinds. I skirted the wing. There were no windows on this side of the building. I walked along it, pacing out in my mind the length of the factory, then the dining room, and finally the kitchen. On turning the corner I saw a door at the back, tyre tracks leading right up to it. It was just what I'd suspected: the door led into the kitchen, and the deliveries from the LRA camp came from this side. The tyre tracks were more numerous and more recent than the ones at the front, and they were heavy duty, made by something bigger than the Toyota.

I looked up in the direction travelled by the vehicles, a path of packed sand, dirt and scattered white stones denuded of the tough grass that grew everywhere else. It led through another gap in the fence, then disappeared into the savanna. Beyond it, swimming in the heat, were low mountains clothed in scrub and trees. From the position of the sun the building faced south-west. It would be good to have the precise coordinates, but that was another reason Müller wasn't giving me back my phone.

I scanned the horizon from end to end. I could almost see the strands of the web of evil that stretched across this continent. And sitting at the centre of the web, like a venomous spider, was Erich Müller. Where did Holle fit in? I closed my eyes. Of course! The Guardians of the Reich wasn't a charity supported by Lipzan Pharmaceutica at all: it was the organization itself. The Guardians provided the conduit for the money flowing from Mexico, and Lipzan gave it an apparently legitimate front. To keep up the deception the company would put on the books the requisite donations to the so-called charity. They could well afford to do that. Their own profitability was assured, because they could transport people like Baer here and coerce them into fudging statistics and writing false reports that secured one hundred per cent market success for every new product. No wonder Schröder and his predecessors hadn't been able to nail them. The company's finances would be irreproachable, and the rest was well concealed.

I shook my head. It was all very well to know this, but so long as I was trapped in this place I couldn't do a damned thing about it.

I resumed my walk, past the central wing with my room somewhere in the middle of it, and past the windowless end of the far wing that housed the radiofrequency transmitter.

As I rounded the far corner I got a surprise. There, beyond the fence, was another structure: low, sand-coloured like the main building, with a pair of large doors. That would be where the Toyota was kept. And it was big enough to take at least one more vehicle. I stood looking at it.

Why put it all the way over there?

I had no idea so I walked round to the front and passed through the cool entrance lobby, ignoring the guy still hovering there.

Even the brief exposure to the fierce sun outside had brought me out in a prickly sweat, so back in my room I stripped and had a shower. Then I patted myself dry, washed out my shirt, and hung it in the cubicle.

The far wing with the radiofrequency transmitter – that was the nerve centre; destroy it and this place would be thrown wide open. First I needed to find out what was inside it, but how? The corridor had a security door and whenever I was taken through it to see Müller I was escorted by one of the soldiers. I needed to find another way.

*

As usual I went into dinner with Colin. After Müller's demonstration that morning his company was especially irksome.

"Caught sight of the new bird today," he said. "Delfina, her name is. Müller should let her go soon. He doesn't keep 'em long."

"Is she all right?"

"I should say. Fuck me, the tits on her! Can't wait to get a piece of that."

I suppressed a strong desire to straighten his crooked teeth with my fist. "I meant has she recovered? I was there when she came in. Müller gave her one hell of a pasting."

"Dunno about that. I mean, you don't expect 'em to look happy, do you?"

What a caring individual you are, Colin.

He turned his head. "'Allo, 'allo, here she comes now. That's Maria with her. She's kind of a supervisor in the factory."

I looked up to see Delfina being led in by the woman he called Maria. Maria was a comely, smooth-complexioned woman. She was more heavily built than the younger girls, which gave her a maternal look. Her arm was draped gently around Delfina, who was staring ahead with haunted eyes, like a person in a trance. Maria said something as she sat down, and one of the other girls went to the counter and came back with a starter, which she set in front of Delfina. So far as I could see it remained there, untouched.

I glanced along the men's tables. Conversation had ceased. They were all eyeing Delfina.

If Müller was about to release her into general circulation she'd be up for grabs. These men would be climbing over each other to get at her, but I had a feeling it would be Colin at the head of the queue.

Could I really stand by and let that happen?

34

I was still thinking about it the following morning when Josef Baer and I were summoned to Müller's office. With yesterday's demonstration still fresh in my mind I could think of a variety of words better than "office" to describe that room. This time, at least, there was a more business-like air to the meeting, and we were allowed to sit close to his desk.

He came straight to the point, speaking English for my benefit. "Mr Holle called me this morning. Xylazib has obtained FDA approval. The next step is sell it to the United States Army, and he wants to do that as soon as possible. We must make the application. Baer, you have analysed the data. You have all the figures?"

"Yes, Dr Müller, the statistical analysis is complete and the tables prepared."

"So, Colonel. With this information you can now write the application."

My pulse raced. I'd never written such an application in my life. Josef could probably show me the type of thing they'd done in the past, but that wasn't the point. Xylazib wasn't safe. I didn't want the Army to be using it. And I needed more time to prepare an escape. I thought quickly and something came to mind, something Josef had said to me when I was asking how the trials were conducted.

A lot of the subjects come from poor areas of South America.

I turned to him.

"Mr Baer, have you analysed the distribution of the trial subjects by age, gender, ethnicity, and country?"

He blinked. "Why do you ask?"

"The United States Army is a mixed bag, like the population: whites, blacks, Hispanics, and so on. The Army needs to be sure they're all going to respond to the drug the same way. If, for argument's sake, most of your subjects came from South America that wouldn't be representative."

Baer nodded. "It is true there were many from South America but other nationalities were included. We were able to analyse all these things."

Well, that hadn't worked. I was kicking myself for even raising it. The drug probably wouldn't have got past the FDA without data like that.

Müller said testily, "Really, Colonel, you are not dealing with amateurs here."

I hastened to retrieve my position. "No, of course not. What I mean is, the procurement committee likes this kind of information presented graphically, in pie charts and column charts as well as tables. It's easier to absorb."

Müller scowled. "We did not have a problem with Prescaline, Baer?"

"No, Dr Müller, but…"

I held my breath. I'd been winging it, and my credibility was on the line.

"But," he continued, "it did take a long time. Perhaps this was the reason."

I breathed out. Did Baer see what I was trying to do? Probably not; he just didn't want to contradict me openly.

"There you go," I said, looking at Müller. "So before

we do anything else I should take a look at the analysis and the presentation to make sure it's in the right form. That's why you wanted me here, isn't it?"

Müller said impatiently, "Yes, yes, that's true. How long is this going to take?"

I pursed my lips. "Hard to say without looking at the data. But it's worth doing. Always quickest to provide them with everything up front. 'Course," I added, "I'll need Mr Baer's expert help."

Baer glanced my way and there was gratitude in his eyes.

Müller ruminated for a moment, then said, "All right. You had better work on this together. I want it done as quickly as possible."

We got up. Josef dipped his head in his usual fashion and left the room, but I waited behind. Müller raised his eyebrows.

"A private matter I wanted to talk to you about, doctor. A kind of sensitive one." I shifted my feet a little so as to look ill at ease.

"Go on."

"That girl, Delfina, the one we saw yesterday. I was wondering whether... er, when you've finished... entertaining her, she could, um, come to my room in the evening."

He looked at me, his lips curved in a mocking smile. He held that look for several long seconds, then said:

"She does not please me. I was planning to send her into the factory today. I will give you a disk and you can exercise your 'privileges'."

"Er, but you see, this girl, she's very attractive. There'll be a lot of competition for her. I was hoping you could... erm, assign her to me yourself. It's entirely in your hands, of course, but I'd consider it a personal favour."

The smile was more crooked than ever. "This is not a

problem, Colonel. You can have her tonight."

"Thank you. Look, I don't want to cause any ill-feeling among the others. I'm new here and they could see this as jumping the queue."

He shrugged. "I will tell her to say that Dr Müller has not yet finished with her." He met my eyes. "She will, of course, do as she's told, in this and every other way."

"That's great. Thank you."

I couldn't help all the girls but at least I could try to alleviate the suffering of this one.

*

It wasn't hard to keep what I'd done from Colin at dinner that evening, because he more than compensated for any taciturnity on my part. Now that I was fully in the picture, he was keen to parade his extensive and intimate knowledge of the girls, which he did between courses.

"Take this table here," he said. "On the end, the skinny dark-haired one with the plaits, that's Camila."

I glanced up. The girl didn't look old enough to be out of school.

"Too bony to be a great fuck, but she does a decent blow job. Next to her, is Rita…"

And so he went on. I registered the names and ignored the rest: Beatriz, Sandra, Genoveva, Victoria, Eugenia, Francisca…"

I was so used to attaching names to faces that I did it automatically now. It was harder in the Force when you were out on an operation with the guys all camo'd up. Sometimes you only knew who they were from the way they walked or the type of weapon they were carrying. By comparison this was easy.

"Now Dorotea…"

This was getting tiresome. "Colin, can I stop you there? It's too much to take on in one sitting."

"Oh." His face registered disappointment. "Right."

There was a lull in our conversation, and as a result I became more aware of the steady buzz of background conversation. That was probably why I noticed how suddenly it faded. I looked round to see one of the soldiers coming in. He bent down to speak to a girl at the first table, and she pointed to the second table. He went over and said something to a pretty teenager with short brown hair. Then he left. I saw the girl opposite put her hand to her mouth. The girl he'd spoken to slumped, and several others came round to hug her.

Colin followed my gaze. "That's Daniella."

"She seems to have got some bad news."

"You could say that. Not hard to guess. Mrs Müller's asked for her."

I felt a stab of surprise. "Mrs Müller? The guy's surely not married?"

"Oh, he's married all right. Lot of German families in South America. Mrs Müller came from one of those."

"And she doesn't mind what he does with the girls?"

"Her?" He laughed. "Oh no. Her tastes are different. She likes the girlies, too."

"So she gets them after him and then they go into circulation?"

"No, the girls aren't good for much when she's finished with them, not for a while anyway. One told me about it. The woman has a whole tool kit of goodies in there. The more they scream the more she loves it. She gets off on it, see?"

"Good God." I shook my head. "So this girl, Daniella, has to go to Mrs Müller tonight?"

"Straight after dinner. He's waiting to take her along there now." He pointed and I saw the soldier lounging at the entrance. Colin pinched his lower lip together. "Daniella... As I recall she's been there once already, so she knows what she's in for. That's a bit rough. Well, you won't be seeing her for a while."

I hardly touched the rest of the meal. Daniella got up, and her friends gave her farewell hugs and pats and made reassuring noises. Then she left the dining room, head bowed, tears running down her cheeks.

A surge of anger sent the blood to my head. Mrs Müller just joined her husband at the top of my hit list.

*

At ten o'clock there was a knock at my door. I opened it and saw Delfina standing there. She'd come barefoot, wearing a simple nightdress. The figure inside it was a curvaceous shadow, backlit from the corridor.

In Spanish I said, "Come in, Delfina."

She entered the room, staring blankly past me, her face tight with resolve. By the time I'd closed the door she'd taken off the nightdress and dropped it to the floor. Now completely naked, she got onto the bed and lay on her back with her thighs parted. The open invitation to make use of her body was both submissive and insolent.

I picked up the nightdress from the floor and held it out to her. Speaking quietly in Spanish I said, "You can put this on. I didn't ask you to come here for that."

She rose on one elbow, snatched the nightdress with her other hand, and held it to her chest. Then she looked at me and her green eyes narrowed. "What then? What else do you want me to do to you?"

"Delfina, I'm not what you think. You must know the effect you have on men. Did you see them in the dining room tonight? They all want you in their beds. You'd probably end up with Colin."

Blood drained from her face. "The engineer? With the teeth?"

"Yes. I asked Müller to send you to me because I want to protect you. You can stay here tonight. I won't touch you."

"I don't believe you."

"There's no choice. You have to believe me."

She frowned. "Maybe you don't like sex with *women*."

I caught the emphasis.

"Oh I like it, all right – when the partner is willing. Otherwise it's not sex, it's rape. Now put on your nightdress while I change in the bathroom. I'll sleep next to you, but you have nothing to fear from me."

In the bathroom I took off my clothes and put on boxer shorts. I don't like the restriction 1§of anything more, even in cooler climates than this. When I returned to the bedroom she was under the sheets. I slipped in beside her, aware of the way she froze at my presence.

It wasn't a large bed and as we lay side by side I could feel the warmth of her body through that thin nightdress. It comforted rather than aroused me. The mere notion of taking advantage of an abused, defenceless woman repelled me and banished any more primitive instincts I may have had.

I wasn't aware of dropping off to sleep, but I woke up realizing I'd been disturbed by a slight jolting of the bed. I opened my eyes just enough to register that the room was still dark. My mental clock told me we were still in the early hours of the morning. I sighed and I was just settling back again when I heard a stifled sob. This time my eyes flew wide open.

"Delfina?"

The crying, suppressed until this moment, now broke its bounds.

"Delfina, Delfina…" I reached out to put an arm around her and she shrank from the touch. "It's all right, it's all right. I won't hurt you."

Still barely awake I forgot I was speaking in English, but my tone of voice seemed to achieve the desired effect. She heaved a huge sob and rolled against me, her head in the hollow of my shoulder. I felt the softness of her hair under my cheek, the cool of her tear-stained face against my skin.

I felt both sorrow and anger. With Dr Bruno Müller's help, the Gestapo would have rendered this beautiful woman unrecognisable. Thanks to his loathsome experiments his grandson now had a more efficient way of securing her cooperation, but it wasn't at zero cost. The damage she'd suffered was within: her self-esteem had gone, the spirit that was her driving force vanquished. Müller saw her as a worthless object and he'd made her see herself the same way.

"Listen to me, Delfina," I said softly, in Spanish now. "You can survive this. Inside, you are the same person as you were before. Try to pretend the rest is happening to somebody else."

The sobs continued, but gradually they subsided. I'd secured her trust at last, and she'd gone to sleep in my arms.

*

We awoke early. She jerked back in apparent surprise at finding herself with a man. Then she relaxed and fixed those lovely eyes on me.

"What is your name?" she asked.

"Jim."

"Thank you, Jim."

I got out of bed.

"Come here again tonight. If anyone puts a plastic disc in front of you, tell them the same thing: Dr Müller hasn't finished with you. Okay?"

She nodded. "Okay."

I smiled, jerked my head towards the door, and said in English, "Off you go, then."

She shuffled across the bed, stood up, and padded quickly over to the door. It closed softly behind her.

220

35

I didn't go back to bed. The entrance lobby was deserted when I went out to jog half a dozen times around the complex. After that I came back to my room and did press-ups and crunches in my room before taking a shower. An hour later I was sitting down to breakfast with Colin.

Back at Fort Piper I normally had a substantial breakfast – I needed the fuel on board when I was training with the men. The exercise I was doing here wasn't really enough for me, and it was boring compared to the circuit training, the assault course, the unarmed combat, the 10-k run, fully loaded. I didn't want to put on weight so I watched what I ate and breakfast for me was a coffee and some fruit. Colin had no such inhibitions; he was busy demolishing a plateful of bacon, egg, hash-browns, and some kind of sausage. The smell of it was almost overwhelming. I didn't mind. It wasn't a particularly worthy thought, but I got a sort of smug satisfaction out of watching all that greasy food going into him rather than into me. Normally I'd contrive not to be around Colin at breakfast, but there was still a lot to learn about this place and especially about that radiofrequency installation. As usual I led into the conversation obliquely.

"Colin," I said, "you were saying the other day you really enjoyed your work. What exactly do you do?"

He brightened. "Mainly keep the transmitter in good trim. Some of the units in there are pretty old. Don't get me wrong, it's great stuff, but it needs tuning and tweaking from time to time."

"How old is 'old'?"

"More than a hundred years, mate."

For a moment I thought I'd misheard him. "As old as that?"

He loaded up a fork. "Yeah, just after the Second World War. It was pretty much chaos around then. The big stuff we've got was used in radar. In those days it was all vacuum tube technology. It's interfaced with computers now, but we still use the tubes to drive the antennae. I've got a 20 kV power supply in there, water-cooled anodes, thyratron switching. Beautiful gear – well, the Jerries made things to last, didn't they?"

"So who brought them here?"

"Dunno. I s'pose it was Grandpa Müller. Could have pretended it was for an air defence system or something. Right then it was war surplus. They were glad to get rid of the stuff."

I thought about that. "So he already had ideas about making a set-up like this?"

"Maybe. But he was a medic – wasn't he? – not an engineer. And even if he'd got the transmitter going it wouldn't have been much use to him."

"Why?"

Colin stabbed a pudgy finger on the table as he was chewing a mouthful of bacon and egg. I tried to maintain an interested posture while distancing myself from the odour issuing from his mouth. He swallowed the mouthful noisily. "Two reasons. First, you couldn't make an implant like that small enough, not with what was around back then. Second, you wouldn't know how to coat it."

"You mean it could have set up some sort of reaction?"

"That, yeah, but it'd probably pack up even before. Fluid gets in and buggers everything up, see?"

As I had one of these things in my own head I felt far from comfortable. "Have those problems been solved now?"

"Oh yeah. Some of us have had one in for years. No problem."

Time to be direct.

"Sounds really interesting. Would you like to show me the installation?"

His eyebrows shot up. "Show you? Ooh, no, I couldn't take you in there. Müller would do his nut."

"I don't have to go in; I could look through a door or something like that. I'd really like to see the sort of thing you do."

"Yeah, well… " He picked his teeth with a fingernail. "When?"

"I have to do some work with Baer this morning. How about this afternoon?"

"All right, tell you what, we can go there after lunch. Should be able to give you a peek in, at least."

"Great. Thanks."

*

After my session with Baer I lunched with Colin, then followed him down the main corridor to the end wing. He placed his hand on the reader to open the security door on the right and we walked past Müller's office and along the corridor to the end, where he opened the other security door. I felt a frisson of anticipation as we went through.

Immediately in front of us was yet another door, this one with a wire-reinforced window. I could hear a faint noise.

Colin turned. "You stay here and look through and I'll tell you what you're looking at."

I nodded. The hum of machinery rose as the door opened, then fell as it closed behind him. Colin started to give me the guided tour from inside. I opened the door a crack.

"Can't hear you properly, Colin. All right if I keep the door open a bit?"

"Yeah, okay."

"What's that noise, anyway?" I said.

"Diffusion pump, maintains the vacuums. There's a back-up in case it needs servicing."

With the door slightly open I had a much better view. My eyes were darting all over the installation, looking for potential weaknesses. The room seemed smaller than Müller's office, but it was hard to tell because the centre was occupied by a copper-mesh cage, a sort of room within a room. It was hard to see what was inside it.

Colin anticipated me. "Hang on on a bit," he said, and switched a light on inside the cage. This revealed a line of metal columns behind a steel cabinet. He pointed. "Those tubes drive the antennas. Four of them. Only one on all the time, and that's the one that drives the antenna under the boundary fence. I rotate that job to each of them in turn, but I don't really need to. Like I said, built to last."

When he'd talked about tubes I'd envisaged ones with glass envelopes like I'd seen in science museums when I was a kid. The metal columns in that cage were nothing of that sort. Presumably they were there to protect glass tubes inside them. Would they withstand a good charge if it went off in here? The shock wave would be contained by the walls, concentrating its effect, even though it would blow the room door out. The walls of the copper cage were thin, so they'd rupture easily enough, but how robust were those columns? This stuff wasn't intended to be bomb-proof – the radar installation would have been housed inside a reinforced concrete bunker. Even so, cost wasn't an issue when that equipment was made, and they'd have been engineered to a high standard. From what Colin had just said, any one of them could be driving the antenna under that flimsy fence.

I glanced around. The diffusion pump might be a better target; it would be connected via a vacuum line. Destroy the vacuum and you've destroyed all the tubes at once. But where was it?

"I don't see the diffusion pump, Colin," I said.

He pointed to the steel cabinet under the columns. "Inside there. The backup's in there as well."

Not so good. The steel cabinet looked strong, and there was a lock securing the twin doors.

"Those," he said, pointing upwards, "are the EHT cables, 20 kV."

I looked up. The cables would have been a good target, too, but they were armoured with flexible metal sheaths. That was nothing to do with security; extra high tension cables were often clad like that.

I let him continue. He'd gone over to an open rack, which he indicated with evident pride.

"Switching circuitry in here, used to be thyratrons, I changed them to thyristors, updated all the control circuits to solid state. Computer motherboard to handle all the addresses…"

I was less worried about the solid state circuitry. That would be blown apart or fried in the intense heat of an explosion. But from what he said it was there to address the radiofrequency signal to individuals. The tube driving the field under the fence would be on all the time, so knocking out the control circuitry wouldn't necessarily help. It would be nice to know that for sure, but just asking the question would be far too revealing.

He rested a hand on the copper cage. "I put this in as well. Nice job, innit? Soldered all the joints myself, copper spring seals on the door and the hinges."

"Why do you need it?"

"Heard of a Faraday Cage?"

"Vaguely." Of course I had. I remembered it from physics.

"Well that's exactly what it is. High-frequency fields can't get past the mesh, so if they're inside they can't get out, and if they're outside they can't get in. The antenna system's complicated in this place and you can get a bit of reflection. The copper mesh keeps me safe, screens me from any radiofrequency leakage inside." He chuckled. "Last thing I want is toothache and earache if I'm working in here."

"Wouldn't solid metal sheet be better?"

"But then you couldn't see inside. If the mesh is fine enough it works the same. Seen enough?"

"Yeah, thanks a lot. Very interesting."

He gave me a suspicous look. "Why d'you want to know all this, anyway?"

In his enthusiasm he'd clearly revealed more than he intended.

"Just interested in what you do over here," I said casually. "And I thought you'd like to show it to me."

"Yeah, all right." He looked around him. "Well I'd better let you out before someone comes." He went over to turn off the light in the copper cage.

At that point my pulse quickened. I could floor him right now and then go berserk in the installation. I turned slightly, my right fist clenched out of sight, and waited.

The light clicked off and he made for the door.

Suddenly it didn't seem such a good idea. I'd need a heavy hammer or an axe to make a real impression on this installation. Even if I had something like that to hand –

which I didn't – there'd be a good chance of electrocuting myself with 20 kilovolts, or raising an alarm, or exposing myself to a lethal radiofrequency field.

He was at the door now.

My fist relaxed. The moment had passed. I opened the door and stood aside.

He led the way back and opened the security door into the main corridor. I went through.

"I'll leave you here," he said. "Got one or two things to do."

"You spend most of your day in there?"

"Nah, that stuff's only part of it. I write software, keep things up to date. Some of the older programs ran too slow, so I've streamlined it. Responds in milliseconds now. Not that you'd notice the difference if you were on the receiving end." He huffed a short laugh. "Just a matter of pride, really. I like to make things state-of-the-art."

"But technology's changing all the time, and you're totally isolated here. How can you stay 'state-of-the-art'?"

He blinked a couple of times, then shrugged. "The hardware's good for years. And I'm not about to rewrite the software in another programming language, even if there is one. This is as good as you're gonna get."

"Okay. Well, thanks again. See you at dinner."

He's too good at his job, this Colin, I thought, as I walked back. If I'd been in his shoes I'd have sabotaged the whole shebang years ago. But then, it's different for him. He enjoys the perks too much. Bedtime, in particular.

Once in my room I sat on the edge of the bed, my chin in my hands, thinking about how I could destroy that transmitter. Four magnetic charges, or maybe a couple of really beefy ones, placed at the base of those columns ought to do it. I grunted.

Great, so how do you get in when there are two security doors on the way? And even if you could get in, where do you get the charges? You don't have explosives, or detonators, or timers.

I thought for a moment. There was a place where they would have explosives of some sort: the LRA camp. But what was the use of that? I couldn't get to it anyway while the transmitter was in operation. I was going round in circles.

I got up and paced the room. There was something at the back of my mind, nagging for attention, but I just couldn't bring it into focus.

After a while I gave up the effort. I lay down on the bed, closed my eyes, and had a nap.

*

I woke with a jolt and sat up, tingling with excitement.

That's the way it goes, sometimes, your brain turning over while you're asleep. It had certainly worked for me, because I knew now why the Toyota was kept outside the fence!

It was Colin's talk of a Faraday cage that had given me the answer. A car was effectively a metal box, a Faraday cage. The radiofrequency field at the fence would be a lot weaker for anyone inside a car. So Müller had placed the garage out beyond the boundary fence in case some bright spark thought they could get into a vehicle and drive away!

I went quickly over the implications. As an escape strategy it was seriously flawed. There was no way of knowing when the Toyota would next be inside the fence. Even if I timed it right and got inside the vehicle the protection wouldn't be complete – nothing like it: the windows were effectively a big hole in the screening and there'd still be enough of a field left to make anyone trying to drive over the cable die in agony.

I went over to the window and looked out, across the patch of tough grass to the windowed corridor of the far wing, the wing that housed Müller, his vicious wife, and that transmitter. And then an idea came to me. The garage might be outside the fence, but the kitchen wasn't, and deliveries had to go up to the back door.

I leapt off the bed and made for the door. I would pay a visit to that kitchen right now.

36

The kitchen staff stopped working when I came in. They stared at me, their expressions curious rather than hostile. I guessed the clientele didn't often show their faces in here, although there'd surely be some girls on kitchen duty to help clear up after meals. Before they could open their mouths I explained I'd just dropped by to congratulate them on their fine cuisine. I started in English, with a heavy American accent.

"I tell you, I've eaten at plenty Mex restaurants back home, and not one served food as great as you guys."

Their smiles flickered uncertainly. They were getting the bonhomie but not the words. I switched to Spanish, also delivered with a heavy American accent, and laid on the praise with a trowel. It worked: their postures relaxed and the smiles were wider now that they knew – or thought they knew – why I was there.

I asked them where they'd worked before. Two of the staff had been chefs in restaurants, one in Mexico City, the other in Guadalajara. They liked working here; it gave them the chance to run an establishment of their own and cook the way they wanted to without an ignorant boss looking over their shoulder. And it was a great package.

Of course it was. They wouldn't mind having the implant when they also had the "privileges".

"But surely," I said ingenuously, "it's much harder to cook for as many people as this."

They laughed. The shorter of the two explained. He was a chubby guy with smooth, Chinese-looking features. "No, no, much easier. Nice full dining room every night, same number of people, same meal for everyone, nothing goes to waste."

"But we're miles from anywhere," I protested. "What happens if you run out of food?"

"We don't run out of food," the taller one replied. He had a more European appearance. "Truck comes every week in time for the weekend." He smiled. "We like to cook something special for the weekend."

It was Tuesday.

"So on Friday you get fresh supplies."

"Sí, Friday morning."

"And I guess you give them the order for the following week when they leave."

"That's right."

I had what I needed – at least, some of it.

I showed great interest in the walk-in frozen store, where I saw whole carcasses hanging. A third member of staff was butchering meat into cuts. He told me he'd worked for a man in Tegucigalpa before, but he was much happier here. I noticed a basket near the door which contained a neat pile of muslin sheets. From the pale brown patches I concluded they'd been used to wrap the meat, but they'd clearly been laundered and pressed and were waiting to go back.

At the end of the kitchen a young sous-chef was busy cutting up vegetables. He didn't say anything. On the floor near him was a stack of crates. Something else that would have to go back.

I was deep in thought as I returned to my room.

I sat down on the chair by the writing desk. I would plan this like any other mission: objective, possible routes to objective, risk assessment, alternative courses of action, questions to be resolved. No need to think about size of force, transport logistics for infil and exfil, and types of weapon. Not this time. It was just me, and I'd be unarmed.

Objective. I have to do more than simply get out of here; that would just leave me in the middle of nowhere, miles from any help. I know a bit about survival, but I see no way I could survive for long in that parched landscape – Baer was right about that – and I couldn't summon help because they took my phone. In any case merely getting outside wouldn't help Delfina and the other girls. So the objective is simple enough. Get out of this bloody place, infiltrate the LRA camp, steal explosives or munitions of some sort, come back, and blow up the transmitter installation.

Yeah, just like that. Well, the details will have to wait until I see what's available in that rebel camp.

Route to the objective? The only way is in the back of the vehicle that makes deliveries to the kitchen. What kind of vehicle is it? The chef said *camión*, but that could mean either a truck or a van. A truck would be overkill; assume it's a van. Will it be refrigerated? This is a hot climate so either the vehicle is refrigerated or the journey's short enough for the meat to stay cold. If it's refrigerated I may not be in great shape when the ride's over. Something else to check.

The two rebel soldiers are rotated once a week, so presumably that happens on a Friday, and they come and go in the van. Does one of the two do the driving? If there's a separate driver there'll be three of them. Can they sit three abreast in the front, or will one ride in the back? Three abreast isn't too big a problem. One in the back is a *big* problem. I could take him out all right but could I do it inside a tin box without making any noise? The slightest thump or cry and the other two would come to investigate, unbuttoning their holsters. So I need to find out how many soldiers, and if there are three, whether one gets in the back.

Do they lock the doors? Van doors work from a lever on the other side of the handle. If the soldiers leave the handle unlocked I can turn the lever, open the doors, wait till the van slows down a bit, and jump. Then what? I may be able to follow the tracks on foot, stop when I'm within sight of the camp, then wait for darkness before going in. Find some explosives, get out of the camp, and wait for sunrise so I can follow the tracks back. I like the idea of going in after dark, but that's all I do like. Why? Because they'll stop the van the moment the doors swing open to see what's going on, and I'll be a sitting duck in terrain like this. No, I have to stay in the van until it reaches the camp, whether the doors are locked or not.

I bit my lip. There were a hell of a lot of open questions. If I could answer most of them this Friday I could be ready to make my move the following week.

With that decided I was impatient for Friday to come around, but it was only Tuesday, so I'd simply have to bide my time.

*

Delfina came to my room at ten o'clock, as before. I closed the door behind her.

"Did you have any problems?"

"No. You were right, the girls didn't ask where I was last night. No one talks about those things – they just understand."

She spoke a nice clear Spanish that was easy for me to follow. Perhaps she was making allowances, having heard mine.

She sat down on the side of the bed. "I did some work today. Maria showed me how to sew part of a uniform. Maria is the supervisor. She is very patient and kind, but you know…" She lifted her chin, and for a moment I got a flash of the old Delfina, the one who initially defied Müller. "At home I was a secretary in a city bank. I typed, I filed documents, I did book-keeping, I made travel arrangements, I took phone calls. And now?" She made a throwaway gesture with one hand. "Now, I'm a seamstress."

I grimaced. "I guess it's better than kitchen or laundry duty."

"I suppose so." She put a palm down on the bed, and her voice lost some of its firmness. "Like before?"

"Exactly the same as before."

She gave me a smile so sweet my heart melted.

When I got into bed next to her she snuggled up against me. It was unexpected, but I put an arm around her shoulders and we lay there for a while in each other's warmth, breathing softly. After a while I said:

"Where are you from, Delfina?"

She raised her head. "Guatemala City."

"What happened – it doesn't upset you if I ask, does it?"

"No, I thought you would ask." She paused a beat, as if collecting her thoughts. "I was at the bank, working late one evening. It was still light when I left and walked to the Transmetro. A small car drew up and the passenger asked me for directions. I didn't see the man on the pavement behind me. The back door opened and he pushed me inside. Something stabbed me in the arm. I struggled but then I must have passed out."

Had they targeted her, I wondered, or was it a random snatch? The outcome would be the same.

"Any time I woke up they drugged me again. They

were horrible men. Sometimes if I was half-awake I knew what they were doing—"

I gave her a little squeeze. "It's okay, I understand." It was a familiar story, just like we'd encountered in Honduras. "Were there other girls with you?"

"Yes. When I woke up again we were in a larger vehicle. We must have been travelling for a long time and making stops. It was like my life was moving in small jerks, and each time I woke up there were more of us. In the end we got out at a sort of camp. Some soldiers arrived and we had to line up. They looked us over carefully, chose me, and then they must have brought me here. I don't know any more – they drugged me again."

"They'll be looking for you back in Guatemala, won't they?"

"Perhaps, perhaps not. You know there are many criminal gangs in the city and kidnapping is not unusual." She became tense and her voice rose. "My family must be frantic – but you know, the police will probably just look at them and shrug their shoulders."

She let out a small moan, and her body went slack against me. I felt her pain and desperation and had an urge to unburden her, take it all onto myself. But there was only one way to do that; I had to break down the invisible wall around this prison.

We said nothing more for several minutes. Then she reached up and gently touched the stubble area on the side of my head. The stitches had fallen out by now. "They did this to you, too."

"Yeah. Told me I had cryptococcal meningitis, whatever that is. What about you?"

She nodded. "He said I should have a vaccination for Q-fever. He is a filthy liar, that man."

I sighed. "Yeah. We've been deceived, both of us."

"What are you doing here, Jim?"

"Oh, I was in Europe, looking into some companies. The trail led here. Now it seems they want me as a permanent guest."

"People will be looking for you, too, won't they?"

"I should think they're moving heaven and earth by now, but what hope do they have of finding me out here?"

"I'm sorry. This should not have happened to you."

I shook my head. It said a lot about her generous nature that, even in her dire situation, she could empathize with someone else.

"I can handle it," I said. "It's a lot worse for you." I took a breath. "You know, Delfina, I'm not sure how long we can keep this up. Sooner or later Müller is going to change his mind and… make you available."

She pulled away from me. "But we could escape, couldn't we? Both of us?"

My mind raced. I knew I couldn't give her even a whiff of what I had in mind. It would take just a careless word, just the tiniest hint, even a lift in her mood, and it would spread through the establishment like wildfire. In any case my plans could still come to nothing; a lot depended on what I could find out this Friday.

I played for time. "How?"

She raised her voice. "I don't know, but you're a soldier, aren't you? You could find a way!"

I said nothing.

She subsided. "I'm sorry, Jim. That wasn't fair."

"It's okay, I understand. We'll just have to make the best of these nights we have together."

Her hair brushed my cheek as she nodded. "Yes, and while it lasts it is worth every moment to me." She ran the flat of her hand over my chest, then snuggled down again. She was ready for sleep.

I smiled and closed my eyes. I could really love this girl. *What a dope you are, Jim! You feel sorry for her and she's grateful to you, and you think that's a basis for a relationship?*

Maybe not, but it would make a great start.

I banished the thought. Right now this was the only place Delfina could feel safe. It had to stay that way. At least I could give her that much. There'd be time enough if my plans did work out.

In the morning I got up early, leaving her to sleep. When I emerged from the bathroom, barefoot and still in my boxer shorts, she was already out of bed. She gave me a tiny smile, reached a hand to my face and kissed me on the cheek. Her skin was like silk.

"I will see you tomorrow night," she said softly. Then she opened the door, looked up and down the corridor, and left the room.

I stepped over to the door and watched her go. It may have been my imagination, but I thought she was walking a little taller. I certainly was.

37

I glanced at my watch. Just after six o'clock. I threw on some clothes and went quickly down to the entrance. I wanted to see whether anyone was on duty yet.

The lobby was empty but as I approached the security door at the other end of the corridor flew open. It was the wing with, among other things, the soldiers' accommodation, and it was a soldier's voice I heard shouting:

"¡sal de aquí!"

A naked girl stumbled out, followed by a nightdress that had been flung at her. She picked it up and set off in my direction. Then she saw me. She lowered her eyes and, gathering the torn nightdress to her, hurried past. But I'd already seen the tear-stained face, the blotchy red defence marks on her arms, and the swelling high on her cheek. I set my jaw. Right now there was nothing I could do about it, but it was yet another score to settle.

The air was cool outside. I turned left and walked along the front of the building in the direction of the factory wing. At this time of the morning everything was quiet. At the far end I turned left and walked right down to the corner of the building. There I stopped and listened. I could hear nothing, so I rounded the corner and put my ear to the kitchen door. Again there was no sound of movement inside. The staff would have to come soon to prepare breakfast. My guess was that it wouldn't be any earlier than this when the delivery arrived on Friday.

I shivered and rubbed my bare arms.

Jesus, it's cold. If they deliver at this time of the morning they may not need a refrigerated van.

I turned to go back in. It had been useful. But next time I'd put on something more than a T-shirt.

*

I spent most of the day working with Baer and his assistant Tilman. To my chagrin it was like Baer had said: the population recruited for the drug trial included enough different nationalities and ethnicities to conduct a valid statistical analysis. I couldn't see any holes in what they'd done up to now so I used the approach I'd outlined in the meeting with Müller. It was many years since the economic geography module in my degree but I had them making pie charts to show the composition of the trial cohort, whisker plots of the results and as many other graphical forms as I could remember. To do this they had to organize the data in different ways.

Baer looked pained. "There is much work to do this. Is it really necessary?"

"Absolutely," I assured him. "There are some red-hot statisticians on that committee and we have to get it right."

It was a curious inversion of the normal consultancy role. The danger wasn't that they'd overrun but that they'd finish too soon. To make sure that didn't happen I'd have to think of something else when they'd finished the present task. I studied the trial design carefully. Some of the evaluations had been conducted at two stages on the same subjects. That meant they should be doing a repeated measures analysis. Of course this would only occur to me after they'd already generated the graphs.

How long could I keep this up before someone realized I was deliberately holding things back? It was Wednesday and I couldn't make a move until Friday week. I could drag my feet over writing the actual application but there were limits even to that. Yet I had to prevent that doctored application going to the US Army.

It was hard, because I was also trying to think through the plan that had been forming in my mind. Right now I had only the barest outline, and I was trying to put up alternative courses of action, based on what could go wrong. After a while I had to abandon the effort; there was too much hanging on what I could discover on Friday morning.

*

When we sat down to dinner Colin entertained me with a new algorithm he'd developed, which saved half a dozen clock cycles. It was a fascinating topic – for Colin.

We'd just started the main course when he said, "What's happened to Delfina?"

My muscles tensed. "What do you mean, what's happened to her?"

"She's not on line yet. Müller usually spits them out quicker than this."

I tried to control my voice. "Perhaps he's got too fond of her to let her go."

He threw his head back and laughed. A morsel of food landed on my cheek and I quickly brushed it away.

"Müller? You're joking. You think he's got feelings?"

"You evidently don't."

"Too right, I don't. Oh, he's a clever bloke, I'll give him that, but feelings? A shark's got more feelings than him."

I thought this was a bit rich from someone with his emotional sensitivity.

"Oh well," he said. "Think I'll have a piece of Maria tonight. Won't be much competition for her. A bit mature for my taste, too, but she's got a nice arse on her. I like 'em big in the beam. Gives you something to grab hold of."

I sighed. "Colin, do you ever think about anything besides sex?"

"I like algorithms," he said cheerfully, and then he caught my expression. "Oh, see what you're saying." He grinned. "All right for you, old son. I didn't get any before I came here. I got a lot of catching up to do."

To switch the topic I glanced round at the other tables and turned back to him. "The surgeon-guy down there, my side…"

"That's Wayne. The one facing him is Chuck, also a surgeon. Want me to introduce you?"

I grimaced. "No thanks."

"They're all right, James. Only doing their job. Mustn't hold it against them."

Oh, but I do hold it against them, Colin. In a very big way.

"Both been here longer than me," he said, adding with a quick laugh, "well, of course they have."

"That's my point. They're the ones who do the implants, so they can't be wired themselves. What's keeping them here?"

"They like it here, same as me. Any case, they can't go back – malpractice suits waiting for both of them if they do."

"So they were neurosurgeons back in the States?"

"Nah. Wayne was a cosmetic surgeon. I think Chuck was what you and I would call a general practitioner. They didn't know each other back then. Both of them answered an advert – clinic in a nice, remote place and a good package to go with it. Not hard – was it? – not in their position."

*

Knowledge is power, and I was acquiring it fast. First the nugget of information in Müller's proud description of his grandfather's technique, which told me that he'd learned to place the electrodes in the brain without image guidance. The indentations I'd seen in the mirror were clearly left behind by a stereotactic frame, which would have been around in grandfather Müller's day, too, but that was the extent of it. The technique was good, but it wasn't that precise. Next Colin's crude account of the way individuals experienced the pain as coming from different parts of the body, toothache and earache in his own case, breasts in one of the girls, abdomen in Delfina, and so on. That was completely consistent; the target was small and the placement wasn't precise, so the results varied. And now confirmation that the procedure was being emulated here by the two medics, Wayne and Chuck, who weren't even qualified neurosurgeons. Conclusion: Wayne and Chuck put the electrodes in without guidance, and because they'd done it so many times they could usually be sure of placing them near enough to the target.

In any *normal* brain.

But my brain wasn't normal. My brain had been transplanted into a different body. I'd read the whole procedure up after my rehabilitation because I wanted to know exactly what had been done to me. People's brains vary somewhat in size, and that means the space inside their skulls, the so-called cranial capacity, varies too. Surgeons don't mind transplanting a brain into a larger skull; what they don't want to do is transplant it into a smaller one. The bigger skull isn't a problem: it gives them a bit more room to work in, and when they've finished they inject a gel to fill the space and make the brain a nice snug fit so it won't shake about. And that's what must have happened to me. I was given the body of a big guy with a bigger head than mine so they would have had to inject the gel. That fact was absolutely crucial. It meant that my brain was sitting lower in the skull than those two clowns in the clinic here were used to. The thalamus wasn't a large target, so there was a fair chance the electrodes they'd put in my head ended up short.

That was the good news. The bad news was that the field under that flimsy fence ran at full whack all the time – Colin had said so when he was showing me the installation. Even if the electrodes in my head were short of the proper target, enough current would probably spread to make me curl up and die in agony if I tried to walk through it.

But I wasn't planning to walk through it. I was planning to ride through it inside a delivery van. If you put together my off-target electrodes with the shielding effect of being in a metal box – even an incomplete one – there was a faint chance I could end up on the other side of that fence and still be alive to tell the tale.

It was dangerous, very dangerous, but what choice did I have? My delaying tactics with the clinical data couldn't last much longer. When the statistical analysis was complete I'd find myself writing an application to get another unsafe drug accepted by the US Army. Meanwhile medics all over the world would still be reaching for the Prescaline in the drugs cabinet, and more soldiers and civilians would die. The kidnapping, the money-laundering, the slavery, and all the rest of it would go on. The Guardians of the Reich would continue to sponsor the drive towards a Europe tyrannized by right-wing fanatics. And Delfina would be put up for grabs by Colin, the two surgeons, the kitchen staff, those brutal soldiers, and anyone else who chose to order her into their beds.

I had no right to consider my own safety. I had to accept the risk.

38

On Thursday Delfina and I woke at about 6 am. We went to the door together and she reached up again and kissed me on the cheek. I fought down a strong urge to take her in my arms and kiss her properly. I knew in my heart that I was right to exercise restraint, but it was getting harder each time I saw her. To get it out of my head I dressed quickly and took another turn around the building. I wanted to make sure nothing had changed. I was also hoping that the visibility towards those mountains would be better at this time of the morning, but a light mist had gathered up there. I was still examining the plan from every angle. It was a tedious process but my military experience had taught me that adequate preparation could make the difference between living and dying.

After breakfast I went to Baer with a brand-new ruse.

"Have we tested Xylozib for cross-reactions with antimalarials? I mean, they're bound to be taken together."

"Yes, of course. Dopranamid and Quinoxocarb."

"What about Quinocitab?"

He blinked. "I have not heard of this drug." He turned to his assistants. "Have you heard of Quinocitab?" They shook their heads.

It was a fair bet that none of them would have heard of it but I hadn't made it up. I knew about these anti-malarials from the operation on counterfeit drugs. I explained it to them.

"Dopranamid and Quinoxocarb are out of date; there are too many places where the organisms have developed resistance. Quinocitab is made by Kappa Pharmaceuticals, the people who made Quinoxocarb. But there's no drug resistance to it. Not yet, anyway."

"And this drug has been adopted by the United States Army?"

"Yes." Here I was being economical with the truth. Last time I heard, Quinocitab was in Phase III trials, but it was doing well. The chances were that it would be adopted sooner or later. "Well it's okay," I said, "we've got a list of drugs being taken concurrently by the trial subjects. We just have to pick out the ones on Quinocitab."

Baer's face fell. "But that will take many hours!"

Great, isn't it?

I shrugged. "All the same, we need to do it."

I left them scratching their heads. They wouldn't find any subjects taking Quinocitab unless they'd been involved in one of Kappa's trials. That was only the most distant of possibilities, but they'd still have to trawl the data to find out.

At dinner I joined Baer and his colleagues again, excusing myself to Colin by saying there was an analysis we needed to discuss. Actually I was seeking refuge from his revolting table manners and his incessant, egotistical, sexist prattle. When we'd finished coffee I left quickly to go back to my room.

At ten o'clock Delfina knocked on my door, a knock I now recognized. There was a certain assurance about her, something of the proud bearing she'd displayed before Müller degraded her. Had I begun to restore her self-respect? I hoped so – and I hoped it wasn't just by keeping her out of the other men's beds.

"I am cutting patterns for the uniforms now." She wiggled her fingers and rubbed them briefly with her other hand; the muscles were no doubt fatigued from using scissors. "Actually it is quite interesting. I never did anything like this before."

It was understandable. She had a receptive mind and this was something new for her.

"I thought clothing companies used lasers these days," I said. "They can cut whole stacks at a time."

"We have nothing like that." Her face darkened. "I don't mind work, Jim, even hard work. But I can't allow myself to be abused by all those men. I must escape from here."

My body tensed. "But how?"

"There is a gap in the fence. I have seen it from the entrance."

"Delfina, the cable runs under the fence and under the gap, too."

"I know, but I will run very fast."

I drew a breath. "It's terribly dangerous. And even if you do manage to get through, where will you go? We are miles from any help, and without help you would not last long out there."

"So I will die. It is better than spending years here as the plaything of men like Colin." My concern must have been obvious because she reached a hand out to my cheek and smiled, and her voice softened. "Don't worry, Jim. I won't do it as long as we can be together. But after that…"

I nodded, my lips tight.

While she was getting into bed I went to the bathroom, preparing for an early night. Tomorrow was Friday and I needed to be outside shortly after six o'clock, waiting near the kitchen. I'd learn everything I could about the delivery and after that I could put together an effective strategy.

When I got in next to her she cuddled up on cue. I sighed and relaxed, my senses flooded with the feeling of that warm, soft body against mine. If only we could keep this arrangement up for another week perhaps she wouldn't have to resort to desperate measures.

*

I'd never needed an alarm clock. It was my army experience: I'd be told "Reveille at 0600" and I'd be awake on the dot.

I got up without disturbing Delfina and washed and dressed. She was sitting on the side of the bed when I came back into the room.

I said, "Okay for tonight?" It was a routine question. It didn't get a routine answer.

She got to her feet. "No, I do not think I can come tonight, Jim. Dr Müller sent one of the soldiers to tell me to go there this evening. Mrs Müller wants to see me."

The alarm clock was going off now, all right, drilling loudly all around inside my head. Clearly Delfina hadn't yet heard about this woman's reputation. It wouldn't help if I told her, either; she'd just live in dread the whole day long.

It was totally unexpected. Colin had said Mrs Müller didn't get the new girls, not until they'd done the rounds for a bit. Maybe she'd seen Delfina and taken a special fancy to her, in her own twisted way. Or maybe her husband had decided to remind me who was in charge. Damn him! Damn the pair of them!

Delfina must have read my expression. "Is something wrong, Jim?"

I took a quick breath. "No, no. You have to do as Dr Müller says. You go back to your room now."

She tilted her head to one side, then put her arms round my neck and I felt her lips on mine, her breasts firm and warm against my chest.

I still had my eyes closed as I heard the door click shut. Then I blinked, and returned abruptly to reality.

I couldn't let her get into that woman's hands, I couldn't. That simply must not happen.

I glanced at my watch, paced around the room, then stood by the window, biting my lip. At any moment now two or three armed rebel soldiers would be driving a vehicle up to the kitchen. The plan I'd based on this routine delivery was near-suicidal – I had no illusions about that – and everything I'd ever learned told me how much the dangers would be multiplied if I wasn't fully prepared. And I was nowhere near it, not yet. What the hell was I to do?

It didn't take long to decide.

Ready or not, I had to make my move right now.

39

I took up a position at the side of the building, just around the corner from the kitchen, waited and listened. It was still and quiet, too cold at this hour for insects to be active. No morning chorus either: I'd only seen one bird since I'd been here, something large that circled over the mountains for a while, then flew off. I was wearing a stout Army shirt over my T-shirt, but despite the extra layer I began to shiver, so I took a break to swing my arms and walk up and down the windowless wall. The minutes dragged by, waiting and listening, walking up and down, then waiting some more. It was during one of these brief spells of exercise that I froze. Something had seeped into my awareness: the sound of a motor, rising and falling, the sound made by a vehicle navigating an uneven landscape. I quickly returned to the kitchen end of the wall and put my head around the corner. The sound got louder, then a vehicle came into view – not a car, not an all-terrain either, taller than that. As it got closer I stayed behind the wall. There was a squeal of brakes and some manoeuvring. The burble of the engine continued for a few moments, then stopped. Peering out I saw a large van, an old model painted crudely in desert camo. At the back were two vertically hinged doors, a wire-reinforced window high up on each one, and a locking handle. As I'd expected, it was a van, not a truck. The front doors opened and I ducked back. I heard the crunch of boots, then the sound of doors being unlocked and opened.

They'll have their backs to you now. Take another peek.

Two soldiers were standing at the opened doors of the van. One turned slightly and I spotted the holstered semi-automatic on his belt.

No full-time driver, then; just two soldiers, and one of them did the driving. Good, that meant there'd be no one in the back – one question answered. It made sense not to have a driver. It probably wasn't too hard to find the way – the van must have worn some sort of path by now and it was probably fitted with a NavAid.

There was no vapour issuing from the inside of the van.

Great, looks like it's not refrigerated. Another question answered.

The door to the kitchen opened and again I ducked back. I heard an exchange of greetings, then the scrape of things being slid across a metal floor. I took a quick look. The soldiers were inside the van, pushing forward crates of vegetables, then handing them down to the second chef and the young sous-chef. There were no other kitchen staff around – the others were probably busy preparing breakfast. I glimpsed carcasses hanging in the depths of the van. Then one of the soldiers looked up.

I pulled back quickly.

Shit! Did he see me?

There was nowhere to hide here and the front corner of the building was too far to get to. I crouched low and manoeuvred my toes for the best purchase on the dusty ground, ready to spring if he came to investigate. Seconds ticked by. My whole body was tense, primed to explode into action, waiting for that soldier's boot to appear around the corner. And the moment it did the whole plan would go to hell.

The sliding noises and the comings and goings continued. It seemed like I'd got away with it. I breathed out. I'd have to be more careful. When I put my head out again, I'd do it at this low level. I reached for a bunch of the tough grass with some sort of weed mixed in with it and tore it out. As an extra precaution I'd hold it in front of my face each time I peered out.

The noises stopped and I decided to risk another look. They were passing down insulated boxes, which presumably contained some kind of perishable foodstuffs. I withdrew carefully and straightened up, my back to the wall, listening to them taking stuff into the kitchen and returning for more. There were probably boxes with other items: cooking oil, wines, spices, and tinned goods. Perhaps there were supplies for the rest of the establishment: articles of clothing, soap, and detergents for the laundry. It seemed like quite a comprehensive delivery.

The sounds took on a different character now and I squatted down for another peek. The soldiers in the van were accepting empty wooden crates and stacking them. The sous-chef came out with the basket of muslins and handed it up. They must be nearly finished.

I waited until it was quiet before I poked my head out again. The kitchen door was still ajar, but the staff had gone inside and there was no sign of the soldiers. Now would be the time for them to change places with the two who were coming off duty. That could take a few minutes: the new arrivals had to be briefed, and they had to go through the routine of registering their handprints on the security panels. The van doors had been left open.

I won't get a better chance than this.

I covered the ground in a couple of quick strides and vaulted lightly into the back of the van. The crates were stacked on the right and there was room to squeeze myself in behind them. I paused, breathing lightly through my mouth, and looked around. The partition behind me was fitted with a rectangular window. No doubt that would be in the driver's rear-view mirror so I'd have to be careful to stay out of his line of vision. Above my head there was a rail with half a dozen S-shaped hooks – meat hooks for hanging the carcasses. I shuffled up with my back to the side of the van, got as comfortable as I could, checked my watch, and settled down to wait. I'd never come in for breakfast at a predictable time – or set a consistent pattern for anything else apart from dinner – so it should be quite a while before anyone noticed my absence.

Twenty minutes later I heard voices. There were two heavy thumps and I saw a couple of backpacks land on the floor of the van. Then I was plunged into gloom as the doors shut with a metallic clang and I heard the squeak of the handle being turned, the lever driving steel bars, one up and one down, into their sockets. There was a further rattle as the key was turned in the lock.

That was it: I was locked in a metal box and unless someone opened the doors again when we got to the other end, I'd be stuffed. My pulse beat a little faster.

Don't panic. Take one thing at a time. Right now your big worry is those windows.

There were three – one in the partition and one in each door – and the wire mesh in the glass wasn't fine enough to keep out a radiofrequency field. It was a gaping hole in the shielding. I thought of Colin's Faraday cage, with its soldered joints and copper spring seals on the door and hinges. This van was nothing like as good. It would attenuate the field, but it wouldn't exclude it. The danger had just escalated.

The heavy tread of the soldiers' boots came around the van, accompanied by laughter. They were happy. They'd had an energetic seven nights. Life was good.

The front doors opened and the laughter was loud now, right behind me on the other side of the partition. The doors slammed. I heard the cough of the engine starting and we began to move off. Then there were shouts and a banging on the side of the van. It braked sharply and the engine died.

I passed my tongue over my lips. Had I been spotted?

The van's front doors opened, boots hit the ground, and there was a rapid conversation. I strained to hear the Spanish but I was getting only snatches. Bottles… cooking brandy… it seemed like something was missing from the list. More footsteps. The rattle of a key, a squeak as the handle to the van doors turned. The doors opened and light flooded in.

They're crazy! There's nothing in here but empty crates and a stack of muslins. But if they come looking…

A shout from somewhere in the distance. *"Está bien, me pareció!"*

Whatever was missing, they'd found it.

The van doors slammed shut, the handle turned, the lock rattled, and footsteps returned to the cabin.

I breathed again.

Once more the engine started and we moved off. I checked my watch by its internal illumination, my wrist wandering back and forth with the sway of the cab.

It would take less than 60 seconds to reach that gap in the fence with the deadly cable running under it. My protection in here was incomplete. Everything now depended on whether I was right about the placement of the electrodes in my brain. If I was wrong then very soon I'd be writhing on the floor in agony. I clamped my jaw tightly, closed my eyes, and counted off the seconds.

Here it comes.

A ghastly wave of sickness swept over me.

The thought flashed through my mind that I was imagining it, simply because I'd been expecting it, but no – I wasn't imagining this.

The nausea was mixed in with an ache – not a physical ache, but overpowering feelings of regret and sorrow and malaise.

I clenched my fists, felt the sweat in my palms. My heart was pounding with fear and anxiety and distress. I couldn't contain it a moment longer, I was going to lift my head and bellow at the top of my lungs—

Abruptly it was gone, leaving just a dark shadow behind.

I opened my eyes, breathing hard. It had probably taken no more than a few seconds but it had felt like an age. With the crisis over, it dawned on me. The radiofrequency field I'd just passed through could have killed me, but I was still alive!

My reasoning had been correct. The field had been attenuated inside the van. And without guidance those amateur neurosurgeons had inserted the electrodes short of the thalamus. Where did they land up? They must have stimulated the limbic system instead – that would account for the sensations. I allowed myself a weak grin of self-congratulation. The anatomical study I'd put in after my transplant had finally paid off, in a way I could never have imagined.

The van jolted and rumbled over the uneven ground, gathering speed. The crates rattled and the meat hooks jangled above my head. My eyes were adjusting now to the little light that entered through the small windows, which rendered the interior of the van dim but visible.

It was time to reassess my situation. I was out, I was

free, I was no longer part of Müller's nasty little empire. All of which was good, except I could be dead inside half an hour. We were about to enter the camp of a rebel militia, and groups like these had earned a well-deserved reputation for mindless violence. I didn't know what their operational strength was but it would surprise me if it was less than a hundred. My immediate future would rest on where exactly the van ended up. What were these guys most likely to do? Thinking about it, they'd want to retrieve their backpacks, so they'd open the doors again. But where?

They could park the van with some other vehicles, take their backpacks, and go away. Then in a week's time it'd be up to the next two on the rotation to take the van round to the stores, unload the crates, empty boxes, and muslin wraps, load the van with fresh produce, and drive it to Müller's establishment. That would be the logical option.

But suppose they didn't take the logical option? Suppose they went to the stores first to unload there? That would drop me right in the middle of a bunch of trigger-happy yo-yos.

I had to work on the assumption that they did the sensible thing and parked the van. What then? I couldn't just let them pick up their backpacks and leave while I waited until the coast was clear. They'd probably relock the door and then I'd be trapped in here for a week without food or water. If I was still alive at the end of a week, which was highly doubtful in this climate, I'd be driven round to face the crazies. No way, I had to act as soon as those doors came open.

I eyed the meat hooks. Would they be any good as weapons? They weren't sufficiently open to stab with, and with a point at both ends they were as likely to injure me as someone else. I could use one as a throwing weapon, but if it landed on a hard surface it would make a ringing noise that would bring the whole camp down on me. I decided against. I preferred to trust my combat skills.

The van shuddered as it encountered an obstacle, and some of the crates slid across the floor. That was handy. I moved forward, keeping low because of that rear cabin window, and inserted myself on the left, two stacks away from the doors.

I could see from the slope of the floor that we were ascending, although not steeply. I braced my back against the side of the van and rocked back and forth with the vehicle as its suspension was tested by the rough terrain. The interior was warming up, and the air was fetid with the smell of fresh meat and stale cabbage.

We'd been going steadily uphill over what felt like rubble, and from the way the engine was revving the van hadn't got out of third gear. Now the ground seemed to be levelling off but the driver wasn't changing up and the engine note was dropping. That meant we were close. I checked my watch: less than ten minutes since we left. At a quick estimate we'd travelled between six and seven ks.

I was pressed a little harder against the side of the van as it took a long curving path to the right. We slowed down, we stopped, we reversed slowly, we stopped again, and the engine died.

Second objective achieved: I was inside the rebel camp. The question now was: would I ever get out again?

40

The moment I heard the driver's and passenger's doors open I was out of my hiding place. I pushed the soldier's backpacks to one side and lay on my back close to the doors, legs raised, knees bent. The lock rattled, the handle turned, sliding the bars out of their sockets, and just as the doors were about to open I jerked out my legs so that the soles of my boots landed on them with maximum force. Two cries went up as the doors flew back and bounced off the soldiers standing there. I vaulted out.

The one on the left was sitting on the ground, his hand clamped over his nose. The other had staggered backwards against another vehicle. He was the first to recover. He hunched, reaching for his holster. He didn't get there. I took one step with my right foot and my left heel strike caught him on the forehead. Again he flew back, then bounced off the vehicle and I caught him on the rebound with a straight punch to the throat. In the gym you'd pull a lethal strike like that, but I wasn't in a gym – this was for real. The blow was all the more devastating because he was coming onto it. I felt the crunch as the delicate bones of the larynx collapsed, and he went down choking.

I whirled quickly to engage the other one. He'd

257

struggled to his feet, his face spattered with blood from his nose, and he was fumbling for his pistol. I kicked that hand away, and chopped for the bridge of his nose, but he jerked his head back and countered with a left hook. I stepped inside it, threw him over my hip, and applied a choke hold. He jerked, he struggled, the struggles got weaker, then he went limp. When I finally let him go he dropped like a bundle of rags. I checked the other one, but it was all over for him as well.

I straightened up and quickly looked around me. It seemed that of the two options they'd taken the sensible one and backed into a parking area. I was astonished at the number of jeeps, large all-terrains, and trucks, all camo'd, standing in line abreast and three deep. Above me was camo netting, stretched over a frame. This was a sizeable unit. They probably kept all the rolling stock in here to avoid detection from the air. I scanned the area but there was no one else about.

I took a breath and listened to the sounds outside. The doors had made a bit of a clang as they'd hit the soldiers, but it was mixed in with the noise of slinging them open, so shouldn't have attracted undue attention. I could hear no shouts, no running footsteps.

My attention returned to the two soldiers. I'd never enjoyed killing people, but this was a question of survival. Nor could I feel a lot of sympathy for them. They'd committed fourteen rapes between them in the last week, and one of these bastards was responsible for beating up the girl I saw a couple of days ago. But now I had to move quickly. The van would have been seen coming in and it wouldn't be long before someone asked why these two hadn't emerged.

I bent down to the soldier lying at my feet and relieved him of his belt with the semi-automatic. I noticed there was also a pouch with an extra magazine. Then I stripped off his shirt and put it on over my own, just in case someone saw me. I fastened his belt over the top of it. There were two pens in the shirt pocket but also something heavy. Dipping inside I found a phone. I checked that it was on and put it back. Then I patted his trouser pockets, felt something inside the left-hand one and withdrew a vehicle remote. I hefted it approvingly and dropped it into in my own pocket. Earlier the van had been a potential prison; now it was my passport to freedom.

I rolled the two bodies under a truck where they'd be less visible. Then I went over to the rear corner of the parking area, parted the netting, and peered cautiously out. We seemed to be on a natural plateau, backed up against a steep limestone cliff. I could see camo tents, some quite large, and there were people moving about. The slopes above the cliff were heavily forested with pines and junipers. I dropped the netting, then threaded my way back between the vehicles to the opposite side. There was less to see out here, some open ground and the triple strands of a wire boundary fence. Somewhere further up there'd be the gap we drove through when we came in, but I couldn't see it from here.

It was time to find what I came here for. In my experience guys looked after their own rifles and pistols, but anything heavier had to come from a secure and well guarded ordnance depot. It would be different for an outfit like this, which depended on instant mobility. I began to explore the contents of the trucks.

The first three I came across were equipped as troop carriers, with benches down both sides. The fourth contained a lot of long wooden boxes; I recognized the characters stencilled on the outside as Korean. My lips formed in a soundless whistle. Whatever was inside these boxes, it was political dynamite. I took out the phone, selected the camera app, and took a couple of photos. The lids were loose and I lifted one. Inside it was packed with automatic rifles. I took another photo. Then I lifted out one of the weapons, checked it had a full magazine, and put it on the floor. In a smaller box I found spare magazines. I took out three and put them with the rifle. Deeper inside the truck there were some even larger boxes. The stencilling on these was Cyrillic. I took more photos. Then I opened one up and saw a lot of RPGs, bigger than any I'd seen before. In another box I found the launchers. These guys were not just equipped for sporadic raids; they were lining up for full-scale war.

It took several journeys to transfer the rifle and magazines, a couple of launchers and two of the big grenades to the back of the van. I packed the crates around the stuff as best I could to stop it sliding around. Then I closed the doors, turned the handle as quietly as I could, and leaned against them, thinking.

Normally I'd want to carry out an operation like this after dark. There were a number of reasons why that wasn't an option. For one thing, the soldiers I'd killed would soon be missed. For another, it'd be impossible to see the path back to Müller's compound at night. And by the time I got there it would be too late to save Delfina from the attentions of Mrs Müller. I could scarcely believe what I was about to do but there was no alternative. I was going to make my move right now, in full daylight.

I pushed myself upright and returned to the other vehicles. I had a plan in my head and it didn't include being pursued by a horde of heavily armed rebel soldiers. It took a search of several more trucks before I found what I was looking for: explosives. After sifting through what was in there I took out ten magnetic bombs, each fitted with a timer. I took a careful note of the time, then attached six to the undersides of the half-dozen vehicles in the front rank, each set to explode in twelve minutes. Even if nothing else went up they'd obstruct the vehicles behind them. I put another bomb on the truck among the rest of the explosives, set for thirteen minutes. Another went on the truck with the RPGs, set for fourteen minutes, and then two more, the last set for fifteen minutes.

As I returned to the van I checked my watch again. It had taken me seven minutes to place those charges. That wasn't bad going but it meant I had just five minutes to haul ass.

I opened the driver's door of the van, only it wasn't the driver's door. Idiot – I'd got used to driving on the left in England. I hurried round to the other side, got in, and carefully pulled the door to until it clicked shut. A glance down confirmed this was a stick-shift, not an automatic transmission, which wasn't unusual for this type of vehicle. No problem. I depressed the footbrake and pushed the start button. Nothing. Absolute silence, not even the slightest grunt or whirr. Something went down inside me like a lift. I took the remote out of my pocket and looked at it, blinking in disbelief. My gaze shifted to the instrument panel, then back and forth between the two.

Finally it registered. It was the wrong bloody remote! It came from the guy on the right side of the van. I'd assumed he was the driver, but he was the passenger!

I got out quickly, went to the back, and reached under the truck where I'd pushed the other soldier. I drew him out by his feet, then hastily felt in his pockets. No remote.

I was breathing fast now, my scalp prickling with sweat. On either side of me precious seconds were ticking away on those bombs. I might just have time to stop the countdown on one of them, but on ten? – no way. If I made a run for it across the open ground I wouldn't have a snowball's chance in hell. In any case I wasn't going to leave without the weapons – they were the whole point of coming here. I took a deep breath and made a desperate effort to think more clearly. There was only one way I could get out of this place, and it was in that van. Where was the bloody remote? We drove in so it had to be around somewhere. It was probably with the key that unlocked the rear doors, but that hadn't been in the lock. I dropped to my knees and looked under the van, then under the truck he'd fallen against – and saw it. The remote was lying there, with a key on the same ring. He must have lost it when I kicked one of those van doors into him.

I edged under the truck, scrabbling with my fingertips until I could feel the key ring, clawed it, lost it, clawed it again, and this time I hooked the ring and drew it out. Then I rushed back and jumped into the driver's seat. Did I lock the van doors? Ah, the hell with it – with just two minutes left I wasn't hanging around. I slammed my door, pressed the start button, and this time the engine, still warm, coughed instantly into life. There was a pair of sunglasses on the console. I put them on, threw the stick-shift into gear, and lumbered forward. Remembering the way the van had turned in at the approach I followed a long, curving path to the left, all the time scanning for the entrance, and—*Oh shit!*

The entrance was a hundred metres ahead of me. But it wasn't an open gap: there was a barrier and a sentry box, and standing by it was a soldier toting an assault rifle.

41

Of course the entry point would be manned – why the hell hadn't I anticipated that? The van hadn't paused on the way in – that must have been because the sentry raised the barrier when he recognized it. But right now the barrier was down. And in less than two minutes the first bombs would detonate.

My mind raced with possibilities. The fence was just three strands of barbed wire. If I hit it fast enough I could break through, but I wasn't going to do that because it could be mined as well. The barrier wouldn't be mined, but if I crashed it the sentry would rake the van and take out the tyres. I could cruise up and just pretend I was driving back to the factory, but if I had to speak my accent would give me away. If I got out of the van he'd see my US Army blue trousers right away. I could sit still and take him quietly if he came close enough, but if he was well trained he'd stand off with his weapon levelled. It was an awful lot of "if"s.

Steering with one hand I drew the pistol out of its holster, took the safety off, and placed it on the bench seat, close to my thigh. It was a last resort; a shot would bring a bunch of soldiers running and shooting before I could put a reasonable distance between us. I coasted forward.

Was it the van he'd recognized on the way in or the guy driving it? He was standing just outside the sentry box, so I was about to find out. I lowered the window, my left hand placed casually at the top of the steering wheel, trying to look relaxed.

To my relief he went towards the switch at the side of the gate. I breathed out and prepared to give him a cheery wave as I drove through. Then he hesitated, turned, and came back. He was wearing mirrored sunglasses and it was hard to read his expression, but he barked something at me. I didn't understand the words, only that it was some sort of challenge.

Here we go.

In a conspiratorial gesture I put my finger to my lips and jabbed a thumb towards the passenger side. He approached and craned to see inside. Thank God for human curiosity. I snaked my left hand out, grabbed him by the back of the neck, and slammed his head hard against the frame of the window. I did it again, then jerked the handle down and kicked the door open. It hit him squarely just as he was straightening up and sent him backpedalling into the sentry box. I jumped down and I was on him almost before he'd hit the ground. First I grabbed his rifle by the barrel and yanked it off his shoulder. He half-rose, fumbling for his pistol, so I swung the rifle butt. It hit him hard behind the ear and he toppled sideways. He was out of it – no need to kill him. I took his pistol in one hand and with the rifle in the other I went up to the barrier and tossed both weapons over the wire fence. Then I threw the switch at the side of the barrier. The barrier didn't move. Maybe there was a remote interlock or something but it made no difference, this wasn't the moment to piss about. I climbed back in the van, slammed it into gear, brought the engine revs right up and let out the clutch. The van lurched forward and the barrier splintered with a noise like a rifle shot.

My window was still open, so I could hear shouts behind me over the roar of the engine. Ahead, the path weaved like a white snake through the coarse grass and scrub. I was going as fast as I dared and the vehicle was staggering and plunging over the rough ground. The weapons I'd stolen had already broken loose – I could hear them sliding around behind the partition. I was at the limit of the plateau when the first bullet thunked into the back of the van. And another.

In my head the seconds were ticking away. It must be less than a minute to detonation. I badly needed that distraction to put off my pursuers.

A moment later I was over the edge of the plateau and on the descent. I'd covered about fifty yards when there was an enormous clang, and the rear-view mirror lit up with brilliant daylight. The van's doors had swung open.

Fuck it! I should have locked them.

I braked to a halt. I'd worked hard to get that stuff and no way was I going to have it scattered all over the hillside. With the remote and the key in my hand I opened the door and jumped down. More bullets went singing overhead. I hesitated. Right now they'd be running to the top of the rise and from there they'd have a clear line of sight. They'd rake the van and at this range I'd be a sitting duck. They could even toss in grenades. Did I have time to lock the doors before they could get there? Where were those bloody bombs? The answer came almost immediately. The timers had hit zero.

There were four explosions in quick succession and the shockwaves sent a wall of pale dust out over the plateau and down the slope. I just had time to get an arm over my face and eyes before it hit me with stinging force. To steady myself I put a hand out to the van and felt it rocking on its springs. Another explosion, then another, and the air was foggy with dust. This was much better than a distraction. Even if they were standing up there now, this lot would screen me.

I ran back, closed the rear doors and locked them, then jumped into the driver's seat again. The steering wheel was gritty and the windscreen almost opaque, but I was already on the move as I raised the side window and set the windscreen washers going. They made a grating sound and muddy water trickled from the ends of the sweep. It didn't help; outside, the visibility was still zero, and I had to drive blindly towards where I'd last seen the path. Eventually the dust thinned and I found myself careering over hummocks of coarse grass. I steered quickly back to the path and ploughed on, listening for the succession of explosions as the remaining charges detonated – seven, eight, nine, ten. More explosions. That would be the munitions going up.

Through the cleared sectors in the windscreen I could see the path stretching in front of me and I pressed on as fast as I dared over the rough ground, slackening speed only to put the safety back on the semi-automatic and replace it in the holster. At the moment those soldiers would be running around in circles wondering where the hell the attack was coming from. Sooner or later they'd realize what had happened. Even if they had a few vehicles left somewhere most of them would have to grab whatever weapons they had to hand and chase after me on foot. But I knew I'd stirred up a hornets' nest and it wouldn't be long before the hornets came swarming after me.

I switched on the NavAid, just to get the compass bearing. It seemed I was travelling pretty much due north all the way. By the time I was half-way down I could see my destination clearly – the big double-E-shaped building and the smaller garage outside it. I followed the path round to the rear of the main building and when I saw the gap in the fence I braked to a halt before I reached it.

This was different to the journey out. Then I was in a metal box with a couple of small windows in the doors and one in the partition. Up here in the cab I had windows on the driver's and passenger's side and a great big windscreen in front of me, and I was massively vulnerable to that radiofrequency field. The floorpan would absorb some of it but I couldn't rely on that; I wouldn't drive through a minefield, and I wasn't going to drive through this. While the engine was still running I used the NavAid to get the coordinates for my current position, grabbed one of the pens from the shirt pocket, and wrote them on the back of my hand. Then I switched off the ignition, opened the door, and hopped down. I stepped away from the van and looked back along the way I'd come. The mountain top was obscured by heat haze – or it could have been dust – but above it a column of black smoke was rising high into the sky.

I took the phone from the pocket of the soldier's shirt and checked there was satellite reception before punching in the number for my own office at Fort Piper. It was answered by my ADC, Sergeant Bagley. That pained, put-upon voice was almost music to my ears.

"Sergeant, Colonel Slater here. Give me Major Geiger – on the double."

"Yes, sir."

Pause. Click. "Geiger."

"Tommy, this is Jim Slater."

I heard a gasp. "Jim? Where've you been? Everyone's looking all over for you—"

"No time for explanations, Tommy, I'm in a tight spot. I need air cover. Can you put me through on a secure line to United States Air Force West Texas? Tell 'em it's coming from the highest level."

"Sure thing. And you're where, Jim?"

"Mexico."

"Jeezus! We're still in deep doodoo over the Honduras thing and now you want the USAF to fly through Mexican airspace—?"

"Can't help it, Tommy. We'll pick up the pieces later. Hurry, man."

I waited, biting my lip. Finally I was through.

"United States Air Force West Texas. Sergeant Bellamy speaking. How kin I help yew?"

"Sergeant, this is Colonel James Slater. I want air support here, fast. Are you operating Rotofans?"

"Yes, sir, we sure are."

"Well what sort, dammit?"

"Transport configuration, sir." Triumphantly.

That's a fat lot of use.

"Sergeant, I've got a rebel militia on my heels. I need ground attack. Haven't you got any GA versions there?"

"No, sir."

"Don't you have any GAs at all?"

"Yes, sir. We have Buzzards."

I sucked in my breath. One of these literal types, straight out of the quartermaster's stores.

"Listen to me, Sergeant. Scramble those Buzzards right now. And then follow up with three of your transport Rotofans."

"Where to, sir?" He sounded shaken.

I turned the back of my left hand and gave him my coordinates.

"Your people are to attack camo'd men and any vehicles in the vicinity of a building at those coordinates – it's shaped like two capital letter E's, back to back. They are not, repeat not, to attack the building itself or civilians in that area. Then they need to hit the rebel camp. It's just six ks to the south of this position. It won't be hard to find; there's a damned great column of smoke coming from it. Got all that?"

"Yes, sir."

"Repeat it."

He read back the coordinates and the targets.

"Good, now do it. And I mean now, Sergeant. Shift your butt, or I'll kick it all the way to Washington. Understood?"

I heard him swallow. "Yes-sir, right away, sir."

I clicked off and checked my watch. I knew he wouldn't take orders from me – I wasn't in his chain of command. But if he ran straight to the Commander's office there was a good chance his boss would see it was an emergency and overlook the impropriety. How long would it take them? If they got off the ground quickly they could be here in maybe forty minutes. Those militiamen will be running downhill; they could be here before that.

I sucked in a breath and was about to return the phone to my pocket when I noticed I was still wearing a camo shirt myself. I tore it off, dropped it on the ground, and put the phone and pens in the top pocket of my own shirt.

Right. Now to do what I came here for.

42

I unlocked the van doors. Everything had slid up behind the cabin so I climbed in, picked up the two launchers and loaded them both. The RPGs were big and heavy with hardened tips. I shoved both the launchers as far as the doors, got out, and with one in each hand walked to a point level with the middle wing. Then I went down on one knee, placed one launcher on the ground and hoisted the other to my shoulder. I pointed it at the far wing, targeting the windowless end section. In my head the wall wasn't there, just a mental picture of the transmitter installation: the copper cage, the tall metal columns, the high tension cables… I lined up the sights to hit the centre of the copper cage, squeezed the trigger, and the grenade roared off and struck the wall.

The blast made me flinch and duck my head. Pieces of masonry arced through the air – even at this distance I could hear some landing behind me. Smoking bricks bounced end over end across the grass and one came to rest just feet away. I lowered the launcher and blinked. I wasn't expecting it to ping off a brick wall; these things were designed to pierce heavy armour. What I hadn't expected was the sheer size of the charge it carried. Where there'd been a solid wall there was now a black hole several metres across, belching smoke and dust. I cast an incredulous look at the grenade loaded in the other launcher at my feet, and returned my gaze to the hole. How much of the blast had gone outwards? I wasn't interested in the wall, it was what was inside that I needed to destroy, and the pressure wave could have been dissipated. I couldn't take the chance. I picked up the second launcher, sighted the centre of the hole and fired. The grenade went through, the hole lit up with a brilliant flash, and the windows blew out all down the adjacent corridor. I ducked my head again as splinters of glass and debris flew out and hailed against the middle wing. Seconds later they were still pattering to the ground all around me.

Now fresh clouds of smoke were pouring from the enlarged breach in the wall. Had I done enough? Colin said the transmitter equipment was built to last. Had it withstood the explosion? Was that deadly signal still radiating unseen from the underground antenna? I'd know soon enough. I dumped the launcher, got to my feet, and ran back to the van. There I paused, took a deep breath, clenched my teeth, and ran right through the gap in the fence. I felt nothing, not even the nausea and sorrow and anxiety I'd experienced earlier on when I rode through it in the van. I punched the air. I'd done it! The transmitter may have been secure, and it may have been over-engineered, but it wasn't bomb-proof.

I turned the handle of the kitchen door. It was locked. I didn't hesitate, just drew the pistol and shot the lock out.

The kitchen staff were rooted to the spot, watching me wide-eyed as I ran through.

I was out of the kitchen, into the dining room, then out of the dining room and along the corridor to the factory. The moment I burst through the door a siren close at hand set up a deafening wail. I winced, looking all around me. Above my head was a metal detector arch, and the siren was in the corner of the ceiling. The semi-automatic the detector had picked up was still in my hand so I raised it, fired twice, and the siren flew to pieces. The combined noise of the siren and the pistol shots was tremendous in this relatively confined space, and the silence that followed it was so thick you could almost reach out and touch it. I turned around. All the machines had stopped. I saw a sea of pale faces, all looking in my direction. I returned the pistol to its holster.

I spoke in Spanish, loudly and clearly. "I am Colonel James Slater of the United States Army. I have destroyed Dr Müller's transmitter. He cannot hurt you any more. There is nothing to keep you here."

The silence continued for several seconds, then a cautious, questioning sound, a murmur of disbelief. Most of them had been here too long to harbour a hope that this might happen. The murmur grew louder. I held up a hand.

"I have arranged transport to fly you all to Texas. It should be here in less than one hour. We will see about getting you home from there."

Someone shouted *"Somos libres!"*, and a huge gabble started up. A girl sitting at a nearby machine dropped on her knees, grabbed my hand and kissed it again and again. Then I noticed Maria. She'd picked up a large pair of scissors, and she was brandishing it open like a dagger.

"Queremos venganza!"

Now they were all grabbing scissors and shouting *"Venganza!"* Maria led the way through the door and out into the corridor, the others pouring after her. The arch would only let through one at a time so the crowd was soon backed up.

I couldn't see Delfina anywhere but I recognised a girl

waiting impatiently for her turn and stepped forward. "Beatriz, where is Delfina?"

She shrugged. "I don't know." She tugged at the sleeve of another girl. "Camila, do you know where Delfina is?"

Camila met my eyes and her face fell. "Mrs Müller asked for her."

I blinked at her. "When?"

"This morning. I'm sorry."

This morning? Oh my God.

I pushed past the girls and raced down the main corridor towards the far wing, passing more yelling girls on the way. I was barely aware of the entrance lobby coming up on my left as I ran through to the end of the main corridor and turned, ready to shoot my way through the security door. There was no need – it was hanging open, suspended precariously by the top hinge. The corridor beyond was filled with smoke, drifting out slowly through windows in which only a few shards of glass remained. The once-blue composite on the floor was white with dust and pieces of plaster which crunched under my boots as I rushed on. On my left, the door to Müller's office had been blown flat, the doorway a gaping hole. The next door was skewed half in and half out of the opening, held in place by a stubborn bottom hinge. Behind it would be the room that connected internally with Müller's office. I figured the room after that would be the one I wanted.

I paused in the threshold. The room was a shambles. The doorframe was empty, the door lying among the wreckage inside. Items of furniture were tipped over, a large part of the ceiling had fallen in, and the air was fogged with dust. I picked my way through the debris, coughing, my eyes smarting.

Looks like no one in here. Perhaps it's the next one.

I turned and noticed some sort of padded table almost upside-down. It was hung with a variety of leather straps. I was about to pass it by when I pulled up short; one of the straps was fastened around a slim ankle. I gently detached the strap, gripped the edge of the heavy table, and tipped it back.

Delfina.

I put an arm round her shoulders and as I lifted her gently to me her head flopped loosely onto my chest. My blood turned to ice. I looked more carefully, put my cheek next to her open mouth, felt for the pulse in her poor twisted neck. Then I clasped her to me and buried my face in her hair.

Delfina…

I heaved a deep, despairing breath and with the movement her dress shifted and I caught sight of a smudged trickle of blood down one thigh. There were no rips or bloodstains on her dress.

This wasn't caused by the explosion.

A heap of plaster and ceiling tiles on the floor moved and I heard a groan. As I looked up, grey hair emerged, then the face of an elderly woman, white with dust. She was trying to lever herself up with her right hand alone. Her left arm was dangling oddly.

There were shouts from the corridor and four of the girls burst in. They hesitated for a moment as they saw me cradling Delfina. Then they spotted Mrs Müller and converged on her with whoops of triumph. Two of them grabbed the woman's left hand and yanked her out of the debris by her broken arm. She screamed. The girls shouted with elation, and she screamed louder still.

"Hilfe! Hilfe!"

Should I intervene?

I looked down at Delfina, at the blood on her thigh. Did she cry for help when that woman was doing things to her? Did the other girls? And did anyone help them? No. So do I help her? Do I hell.

I lay Delfina down. There was nothing I could do for her now. I had other business to attend to, including the one person responsible for all this.

I went back down the corridor, Mrs Müller's screams echoing behind me. Almost as loud were the exultant cries of the girls as they extracted their revenge. But my resolve had hardened.

I wanted Müller.

43

Müller's office, being furthest from the blast, was in slightly better shape than the one I'd just left. All the same everything was in disarray. There was no sign of him in here. I pushed through the connecting door at the back, the one through which he'd taken Delfina.

Müller was facing me on the far side of the room, legs apart, palms flat against the wall. He looked dazed. His already pallid features were white with dust, and fragments of plaster were stuck in his hair.

I strolled over and stopped in front of him. He must have perceived my manner, because his eyes narrowed to puffy slits. His voice was hoarse. "What have you done?"

I folded my arms. "I just blew your radiofrequency transmitter to bits."

His eyes widened, then he blinked. "Impossible!"

"Not really. I paid a visit to the LRA camp. Your friends have some nice little toys over there. In the right hands they make one hell of a mess."

"I don't believe you. You could never get out of here!"

"No?" I snorted. "I couldn't, but I did. You'd love to know how – wouldn't you? – but I'm not going to tell you. All I'll say is this. In ways you could never imagine in your wildest dreams, Dr Müller, you came up against the wrong person, and you lost. Your reign of terror is over. I've opened the prison doors and set the girls free. You're fucked, Müller, finished."

His eyes blazed. "Traitor!"

"No, not a traitor. To be a traitor you have to start by being loyal, and I was never loyal to you. On the contrary, I despise you and everything you stand for."

"It was a different story when I let you take Delfina to your bed!" He spat the words.

The mention of Delfina, whose lifeless body was lying in the next room, sent a shaft of pain and anger through me. I clenched my right fist, about to smash it into that chalky face. But standing there now Müller appeared aged, shrunken, and I knew it would provide no satisfaction; on the contrary, it would be degrading..

The urge subsided. "You really fell for that, didn't you?" I thrust my head forward. "I have news for you, Müller. I never touched that girl. I took her to my room so she wouldn't have to endure any more than she'd suffered already." I poked him in the middle of his bony chest with two fingers, hard enough to make him gasp. "At your hands."

He was breathing hard. "What are you going to do?"

I stepped back and folded my arms again, contemplating him. My loathing of this man was so intense that just taking him to face justice wasn't enough; I wanted him to stare into the abyss. "You're going back to Germany – I'll let them charge you there. What will they throw at you? Rape, torture, kidnap, unlawful imprisonment, forced labour, prostitution, money-laundering, providing assistance to proscribed organisations… They'll have a bloody field day."

He scowled. "Never, my lawyers will oppose extradition."

"They won't get the chance – you're coming with me. You know all about the SS, don't you? Remember what happened to Adolf Eichmann? He was kidnapped by Mossad and he stood trial in Israel. Well, he was a war criminal, and so was your grandfather, and so – in your own way – are you. And your prosecution will be just the start of it. I'm going to dismantle the rest of it: Lipzan, the Guardians of the Reich, the whole nasty network."

He moved, then winced, clutching at his thigh. He'd probably fallen or been knocked over. He hissed, "That you will never manage."

"Oh, but I will."

I went back into his office and glanced around. The display screen on the desk was smashed, but it told me where to look. I peered under the desk. It was a familiar, if slightly antiquated, set-up: a small – no doubt well specified – computer, connected to an external data storage unit for continuous backup, and a secure modem/router. The presence of that local data storage unit was significant. It meant that everything I needed was right there, on something no bigger than my phone. I detached it from the connecting cables, took it back into the other room, and waggled it in front of his face.

"You see? It's all here, all the evidence I need."

"Encoded!" His thin lips curled in a smug smile.

"So well that my friends at the NSA won't be able to decrypt it? I don't think so."

The smile faded. I unbuttoned the flap of the other shirt pocket, the empty one, and made a show of dropping the unit in and refastening the flap. He followed it all with his eyes, his mouth making small movements as if he were chewing words that refused to emerge.

Then more screams came down the corridor and he grimaced. "What is that dreadful noise?"

"That dreadful noise is your wife, Müller. It seems the

girls hate her even more than they hate you. But perhaps only slightly more."

I glanced around the room, saw a padded table with straps, similar to the one in the other room. I returned my gaze to him and jerked my head at the table. "Is that where you 'entertained' Delfina? And all the others?"

Another scream sounded, longer and even more agonized than the others, then it cut off abruptly. There was an ominous silence.

He passed his tongue over his lips. "Get me out of here."

"All in good time. First—"

A loud explosion made both of us jerk round. It seemed to come from the other wing. Thoughts flashed through my mind. The rebel soldiers are out there. Some have jumped into the remaining vehicles and this is the advance guard. Or the Buzzards have arrived already and, ignoring my orders, they're shooting up the building.

I pointed at him as I turned to hurry out. "I'll be back. You'd best stay just where you are if you don't want to run into those girls."

I crossed the room and ducked through the gap under the dangling door. Outside acrid smoke was still billowing along the corridor and I could hear crackling from the transmitter installation. The generators were probably still pouring out their high tension electricity into ruptured cables.

In the main corridor I encountered a group of girls running towards me, scuffs of dirt and soot on their clothes and faces. Behind them, more smoke.

Maria was with the ones in the lead. I caught her by the arm.

"Maria, what happened back there?"

She was breathless, but her face was flushed with triumph. "We set fire to the kitchen. That was one of the gas canisters."

"What about the staff?"

She smiled.

I had a fleeting mental image of the four: the chubby, Asiatic chef, his tall European-looking partner, the man from Tegucigalpa who'd been butchering the meat, the young sous-chef.

She must have registered my expression, because her smile faded. "Mr Müller gave them one plastic disc only. Every night all four would take turns with one girl." Her eyes flashed. "I expect it was his idea of a joke."

Half a dozen girls came hurrying out of the middle corridor, Camila in the lead, her plaits bouncing, her dress spotted with blood. Two of the others were carrying bottles. I pointed and looked at Maria. "What's in the bottles?"

"Cooking brandy. It burns very well."

Camila dragged at Maria's sleeve. "What are you waiting for? Come on."

"Maria," I said. "We need to get all of you outside to wait for the transport. The rebel militia could be here any moment. For your own safety you must go out at the front."

I was hoping the factory supervisor would have some authority over these girls, but she had other ideas.

"Not yet." She brandished her scissors above her head. With a cheer the others did the same, and they ran on down the corridor. Their shouts receded.

I looked along the middle corridor. My room was down there but I couldn't concern myself with that. At the far end a fire had taken hold and in the flickering light I saw the dark shapes of two bodies. It wasn't hard to put together. Those two must have retreated to their bedrooms and barricaded the doors. The girls had piled up combustible materials, sprinkled them with brandy, set them alight, and then waited. Smoke would have trickled underneath the doors and built up in those small rooms with the windows that didn't open. And smoke meant fire, and fire made a person panic. The men opened the doors and ran out and the girls were waiting for them with their scissors. Who were they? Baer? Tilmann? The two surgeons, Wayne and Chuck? I'd have few regrets about those two…

A thick cloud of smoke billowed up from the kitchen end of the main corridor and I had to back away. I'd made a serious miscalculation. In my anxiety to tell the girls they were free I'd left the automatic rifle in the van. That was when I found out Delfina was already with Mrs Müller and all I could think of was to run to her. But now the corridor was ablaze and it would be impossible to get out through the rear door. The rifle was all I had now to fend off that militia, so I'd have to get there via the front entrance and hope they hadn't arrived yet.

I ran back to the lobby. The girls were reappearing from Müller's corridor, pursued by yet more smoke. Either the high tension cables had finally ignited a fire, or the girls had set one with those bottles of brandy. But I wanted Müller; I needed him to give evidence. I was about to go back for him when the security door opposite slammed open and Wayne and Chuck appeared.

There were two soldiers with them, and each was fanning a semi-automatic pistol. My own pistol was in its holster, and I was directly in the line of fire.

44

Before I could react the girls surged forward, shouting and screaming, and heedless of the danger they hurled themselves at the men. At that range the soldiers couldn't miss. Above all the noise I heard the shots ringing out and watched in horror as they went down, one after another: Camila and Victoria, and others whose names I'd never known. I'd drawn my own semi-automatic by then but the girls continued to press their attack and I couldn't get a clear shot. The four men backed steadily towards the entrance. They made it as far as the lobby when the magazine on one of those pistols ran out. I saw the panic on the rebel soldier's face as he reached for another magazine; then there was a blur of movement, a flash of steel, and he was clasping his neck, blood pumping between his fingers. All around him open scissors rose and fell, rose and fell, and he disappeared from view. The two surgeons and the remaining soldier continued to back away, and the soldier levelled his weapon. At last I had a clear shot. It took him in the chest and he dropped. Through the glass doors behind him I could see the two surgeons running around to the right. They were heading for the garage.

Smoke was now pouring into the lobby from every side. With the pistol in my right hand and the sleeve of my left arm over my mouth and nose, I herded the over-excited girls out through the glass doors and into the open. The ones supporting wounded friends were last; all that was left was a pathetic tangle of dead bodies. Was Müller still alive? I bent low and headed in that direction, ready to make a dash for it to bring him out, but the corridor was already burning fiercely and I was forced back by a wave of heat. It was hopeless.

I hurried outside and shouted to the girls, "Wait here." Then I turned to the right and ran around the end wing. Too late: the garage doors were open and the camo'd all-terrain was already racing off, bumping and lurching over the uneven ground. I dropped to one knee to fire at them, but they made it to the worn path that led to the front of the building. I watched helplessly as they accelerated away.

I got up, returned the pistol to the holster, and stood there, gritting my teeth in frustration. After the Müllers those two were the ones I'd most wanted to nail, and now I never would. I heaved a sigh and turned to look up at the mountain – and my back went cold. A dark river of rebel soldiers was flowing along the mountain track. I could already hear faint shouts, and the nearest ones were close enough for me to make out the undulating movement as they jogged down the path, assault rifles glinting in the sun. My pulse quickened.

There's well over a hundred of them, and what do I have? A handgun!

I had to slow them down somehow. If I could get to the van I had an automatic rifle in there with three spare magazines. But would I get to it? The rank and file were at the limits of the useful range of those assault weapons but they could spray bullets in my direction and one of them was sure to get lucky. I bit my lip, weighing up the distance to the van. I had to try. I took a deep breath and steeled myself for the sprint.

There was a swishing sound and I whirled just as the all-terrain with the two surgeons exploded in a ball of fire. I blinked in disbelief. A ragged cheer went up from the girls. Rooted to the spot, I registered the rapidly dissipating streak of white smoke that ended in the burning crater. In my head I saw Scottie running through the grass, the drone banking in, the rocket ripping through the air, and the fiery blast that blew him to pieces. The image vanished from my mind as the Buzzard flashed low overhead and I ducked instinctively. It banked sharply right, then left, following the line of the mountain path, the thunder of its engines accompanied by the eerie sound that always sent shivers down my spine: the buzzing wail of fast-firing cannon. A long plume of dust rose into the air, stretching all the way up the hillside. The rebel militia had got close, but they wouldn't be getting any closer. Two more Buzzards were flying towards the mountains, their wings underslung with bombs and rockets. The air was ripped apart by the noise as they streaked over the scrub landscape and soared up into the foothills. Then multiple explosions, and white smoke erupting from the hill to the south.

I heaved a sigh of relief and went back to where the girls had gathered.

Behind the entrance doors the lobby was in flames and, even as I looked, the glass shattered with an enormous bang. Fanned by the draught the fire roared, erupted from the entrance, and began to lick over the outside of the building. The girls moved further out to escape the heat. They were still breathing hard, faces flushed and sooty, hair dishevelled, dresses spattered darkly with blood. I noticed the scissors some were still carrying and went round collecting them and tossing them into the inferno.

Someone else could work that one out.

Twenty minutes later the slower Rotofans came in to land. The crews jumped down and I went to meet them. The senior pilot spoke to me.

"Colonel Slater?"

"That's me."

"This lot will fit into two Rotofans. You asked for three." There was a slight note of accusation in his voice.

"Yeah, that was before a couple of rebel soldiers opened fire on them. They killed quite a few. We had to leave them behind." I pointed to the blazing building, and for a moment I couldn't speak as I thought of the tangle of dead girls in the foyer, and Delfina lying in the debris of that dreadful room, all of them being consumed, even now, by the flames.

He grimaced and nodded.

I took a deep breath. "We should make a move. Some of these girls are badly hurt."

"Sure. I'll radio ahead." He glanced again at the girls. "We can't handle that many at the base. There's a major incident unit at the local hospital. We'll call them in. The cops, too. It'll all be there by the time we get back."

We decided to use one of the Rotofans to transport the wounded girls on their own. A couple of crewmen were waiting inside with medical kits to do the best they could for them and they would attend them during the flight. That Rotofan took off immediately; the rest of the girls got on the other two.

I boarded last, with Maria. A glance down the cabin showed me this craft wasn't a modified civilian one like the SAS had used in the Yemen. Those had aircraft style seating; these were in full military transport configuration: no windows and a long bench down either side of the fuselage. I could guess that they were also armoured in the vulnerable spots. A jihadi with an automatic rifle wouldn't bring one of these beauties down with a fluke shot.

Maria and I took the last two places. "Did you see Colin?" I asked her.

"The engineer? No, we couldn't find him anywhere. Pity. He was near the top of our list."

Colin must have been inside the secure wing when I fired the grenades into it. The blast would have distributed him all over his beloved transmitter installation.

Sorry, Colin, but you had your fun. And a quick death was probably a lot more pleasant than what these girls had in store for you.

"What about Müller? Did you kill him?"

"No, we did not kill Mr Müller. We put him on that table of his, fastened the straps the way he did on us. He could not move. Just to make sure, we soaked his trousers in brandy." Her smooth, round face shone with the satisfaction of a job well done. "You do see, don't you? You are the only man to come out of that building alive." She raised her voice. "But then, you are not just a man, my dear Colonel; you are a saint." And she leant over, cupped her hand around my neck, and kissed me long and hard on the lips. I became aware of a roaring in my ears and as she drew away I realized it was the girls cheering, clapping their hands, and stamping on the floor. I don't embarrass easily but I could feel the heat in my face. I lifted a hand in acknowledgement and gave them a uneasy smile. Then, to my relief, the cabin doors closed. I pointed vigorously at my seat belt, the girls looked round and fumbled for theirs, and the awkward moment had passed. The engines whined up and the Rotofan took to the air.

We flew at low level for maybe ten minutes, then we ascended to an operational cruising height. I guess by then we'd crossed the border into Texas.

I thought about what Maria had just told me. I couldn't feel any sympathy for Müller, even as I couldn't feel any for his wife. Nor did it lessen my admiration for these women. After being tortured and cowed into submission, after suffering abuse night after night for months – in some cases years – they'd hung onto a fierce hatred, nurtured it like glowing coals until it was fanned into life by their sudden freedom. It was a triumph of the human spirit, even if the resultant orgy of violence was more like an animal frenzy. But there could be consequences. I turned to her.

"Maria, as soon as we land, get the girls together. You didn't kill anyone, you understand? The soldiers were shooting at you and I shot them, both of them. The fire was started by my grenades, and the other men were trapped inside."

She met my eyes. "Why?"

"What you did could be called justifiable homicide, but a court might take a different view. It's better this way. You're just the victims of a people-trafficking operation. Okay?"

Her lips tightened and she nodded slowly. "Okay."

I settled back. Behind us the Müllers, and their ugly neo-Nazi outpost, would soon be no more than a charred patch on a remote stretch of landscape.

But the job wasn't finished. It was time to go after the rest of Hitler's legacy.

45

As the pilot had promised, emergency services were already at the West Texas Air Force base, waiting to deal with twenty-eight displaced South American women. An ambulance team took charge of the ones who were wounded, but all of them would be receiving hospital attention in due course. The Texas police were well-organized and cooperative. It helped that they were used to dealing with illegal immigrants, and not one of these young women was seeking asylum; they simply wanted to be repatriated. A skilled group of Spanish-speaking policewomen went with the girls. They would interview them and make all the arrangements for their return. Thinking ahead, I told the policewomen it was vital to keep a record of the contact details, because there could be prosecutions arising from this and the girls would be needed as witnesses. They looked at me as if I'd just landed from another planet and one of them, a lady of ample proportions, said "We know our job, sir" in a tone that lacked deference. So I left it to them, just glad it had been taken off my hands. The vehicles drove away and the apron was suddenly empty.

The control tower winked in the sun. At the far end of

the airfield the last of the Buzzards was taxiing into line, the image rippling in the heat coming off the runways. The sound of its engines swelled and died.

I turned to the base Commander, who'd joined me to watch the proceedings, and we walked back to the base buildings together. Colonel "Red" Nicholson equalled me for height, and although he must have been knocking fifty still had a brush of carrot-red hair. I'd already thanked him for his prompt and effective response but I felt the need to say something more.

"You saved those girl's lives, Commander. Not to mention mine."

His freckled face creased in a grin. "Colonel, it was real good for my boys to carry out a genu-iyne mission instead of th' usual exercises. So long as you can explain to those Mexican folk why we went in there—"

"I'm sure Washington can handle it," I said, with a confidence I in no way felt.

The air-conditioning hit me with an icy blast as we entered his office.

"You need a coffee? Something stronger? I got some real powerful liquor in that filing cabinet." He jerked his head towards it.

"Thanks, I'd love to, but some other time. Right now I need to move quickly. Do you have a holoconference suite on site?"

"We sure do."

He picked up a phone, held a brief conversation, and put it down again. "Master Sergeant Chuck McKenzie going t'help you with that." We waited in silence for a few minutes, then there was a knock at the door. "That'll be him now. Cm'in!"

McKenzie was in his early forties, rosy-cheeked and overweight. He led me back into the baking sun, rocking from side to side as he walked, arms out wide, a dark patch spreading under each armpit. We entered another block and he pointed along the corridor.

"The suite's down there, last door on the left. You want some help running it?"

"I just need the conference settings for this guy. Is there a phone round here I could use?"

"C'n use mine. This is my office in here."

He opened the door and we went inside. It was crammed with communications equipment.

He gathered some spare cables off his desk chair and gestured with an open hand to the seat and the phone. Then he made for the door, saying, "I'll jes' make sure it's all switched on fer you."

Business cards have their uses. Müller had stolen my phone, but Viktor Schröder's card was still in my billfold. I checked my watch. It would be late in Berlin but I was counting on him still being at the *Bundeskriminalamt*.

"Schröder."

I heaved a sigh of relief. "Herr Schröder, this is Jim Slater. I'd like to pay you another visit. It's about that European network we were discussing."

"Yes, Colonel, you would like some more information?"

"No, I have information for you, a lot of information. I know it's late for you but could we set up a holoconference?"

A brief pause. "Yes, that is possible."

"Good. Could you let me have the conference settings?"

I found a scrap of paper on the crowded bench and wrote them down. We agreed to make the connection in ten minutes.

McKenzie was holding the door of the holoconference suite open for me. "All ready for you, Colonel. I'll be in my office if you need me."

"Thanks."

I went inside and closed the door behind me. There was a warm, musty smell in the windowless room, so perhaps it wasn't used that frequently. I sat down in the single chair and let my eyes adjust to the dim red lighting.

Originally I'd intended to take the data storage unit to Washington for decrypting. I could give it to Peter Richardson; he worked at the NSA and I knew him well. But there was a downside to that plan. For one thing it would put me in Washington, where there were probably a bunch of people baying for my blood because I'd asked USAF combat aircraft to make an unauthorised incursion into Mexican airspace. More importantly, though, Peter was a busy guy, and it could take a day or two to decrypt this lot. Time was of the essence now. Lipzan no doubt made a good profit on their pharmaceuticals, but the flow of illegal money from Mexico was even more important. Holle and Müller would be in touch on an almost daily basis. If Holle once suspected that his colleague's operation had been compromised the element of surprise would be lost, and with it any hope of cracking the network. So I wouldn't be going to Washington. I'd be flying to Berlin.

The red digits on a wall clock showed me that ten minutes had passed. Time to get this going. I entered the settings and Schröder's holoimage stuttered in blue and white, then consolidated in colour.

After a brief exchange of greetings I said, "Herr Schröder—"

"Please, you should call me Viktor."

"Yes, okay, and I'm Jim. Look, Viktor, you were right about the Guardians of the Reich but there's a lot more to it than that. Lipzan doesn't just support it. Lipzan *is* the Guardians of the Reich."

His eyes widened as I explained the set-up. I told him

about the partnership of Holle and Müller, the nature of the small empire Müller had built for himself in Mexico, the trafficking of drugs and girls, the money-laundering, the manipulated trial data that resulted in a profitable product line for Lipzan and provided a legitimate façade for the whole enterprise.

"The bottom line, Viktor, is this: you have to move on Lipzan right now. If we wait any longer Holle will know something's happened. He's smart, very smart. By the time you get to him there'll be nothing left for you to find."

Schröder swallowed. "Jim… I cannot just descend on that company. I need warrants for entry and for arrests to be made, and I cannot get them without solid evidence."

"I'm bringing you the evidence. Do you have a decryption section at the BKA?"

He blinked. "Yes, we do."

"I thought you would. I have all the data from Müller's computer. It will have the emails, the money transfers, everything."

His voice was breathless with excitement. "That is wonderful. When you get here we will start to work on it immediately."

I sighed and shook my head. "No good. I'm in Texas. Even if I get the supersonic it won't be a direct flight. I'll have to change planes somewhere and I probably won't be with you before tomorrow afternoon. It could be too late by that time…" I held up a finger. "Wait a moment. Don't go away."

I opened the door and hurried back to McKenzie's office.

"Y'all done?" he asked mildly.

"No, I'm still on the line. I need to transmit some important data to this party. What's the best way to do it securely?"

"You c'n do that in the suite. Use the data channel

instead of the imaging channel. That's the best way – it's secure and it's real fast."

I unfastened the shirt pocket and handed him the data storage unit. "It's on this."

He turned it over in his large hands and sucked in a breath. "While since I seen one of these. No way you can plug that into the console. It only takes memory tiles."

"Damn."

"Want me to port it over to a tile for you? Shouldn't be a problem."

"Will it take long?"

"Nah, not long, if I can find the right stuff. I'll bring it down when it's ready."

"Thanks."

I left him rummaging in drawers, no doubt looking for the right cables, a d.c. power supply, and memory tiles.

I got back to Schröder. "I can send you that data now, over this line. Can you record it?"

"Excellent. Yes, I can record it here."

"Okay, we're just putting it on a memory tile. It'll be here shortly."

"Very good. Jim, I do not understand how you obtained the data from Mr Müller's computer."

I gave him a brief account of my escape, the trip to the rebel camp, and the destruction of the transmitter.

"I wanted to bring Müller with me to face justice but in the end it was impossible. He died in the fire." There was a knock at the door and a triumphant McKenzie was standing there, holding up a memory tile. I gave him a smile and a nod. "Okay, Viktor, I have the data ready to send. We'll have to close down the imaging channel now and I'll send the data right away. I'm still coming out there, though – I'll send you my arrival time once I'm en route."

"Okay, Jim. I'll see you tomorrow. Goodbye for now."

I turned to McKenzie. "Go ahead. We're still

connected."

He came forward, closed the imaging channel down, plugged in the memory tile, and went through a sequence of button presses. Then he stepped back.

"It's going."

We waited in silence, watching the steady creep of a progress bar on the panel. It completed its traverse and a message appeared, confirming that it had been received. I pulled the memory tile from the slot in the panel and put it in my billfold.

I clapped McKenzie on the shoulder. "Great job, Sergeant. Thanks."

He handed me the data storage unit and I put it back in my shirt pocket.

Once everything was shut down McKenzie closed the door of the holoconference suite behind us. "Want me to take you back to the Commander's office?"

"No thanks. I can find my way."

Nicholson looked up as I came in. "Okay?"

"Yeah. Sergeant McKenzie was a real help."

"So where y'all off to now?"

"I have to fly to Europe."

"I'll get a corporal t'drive you to Dallas/Fort Worth."

"Are you sure?"

"No problem at all." As he picked up the phone he pointed at my belt. "Mebbe you should leave that piece with me, though. They don't take too kindly to those things at th' airport."

"My God, I'd forgotten it was there. Thanks." I handed over the semi-automatic. "It's Russian. Someone might ask questions about it."

"Okay, I'll put it in the safe."

I took the data storage unit from my shirt pocket. "Would you mind putting this in with it?"

He took it from me and raised his eyebrows. "What is

it?"

"The girls I liberated were kidnapped and held as sex slaves. The guy behind it all had links with organized crime as well as the rebel militia. What you have there is the data from his computer. I've transmitted it to a security service, but the original may be needed in a court of law. It'd be more secure if I left it with you for the moment."

"Sure, we c'n do that."

There was a knock at the door. The driver was here. I shook hands with the Commander and left.

As I settled into the back seat I felt a flutter of anticipation. I was looking forward very much to my second – and no doubt final – meeting with Mr Holle of Lipzan Pharmaceutica.

46

At Dallas/Fort Worth International I bought a ticket for the next flight to Berlin Tegel via London Heathrow. I had some time before departure so I purchased a disposable cell phone, which I'd use from now on; the rebel soldier's phone would have to be handed over at some stage and I didn't want any of my private calls to be on it. Next I found a men's outfitters. I purchased a complete change of clothes and put them on in the changing room. The casual jacket, T-shirt, and lightweight trousers felt comfortable, and it wouldn't hurt to look like a civilian for a while. I rolled the old stuff into a tight bundle and dumped it in the first trash can I came across.

With that done I went through security and into the departures lounge. It was fairly busy but most of the people were near the coffee counter or by the big windows looking out across the runways. At the back I found a quiet corner, took the new phone out, and switched it on. It was just a cheap burner but it would do the job. I took a good look around, making sure there was no one near enough to overhear me.

First I phoned my own office in North Carolina and spoke to Tommy Geiger.

"Tommy, I should have been in touch earlier. You did great and so did the Air Force boys in West Texas."

Was that a sigh of relief? "You're okay, then, Jim?"

"Yeah, I'm okay."

"So when are you coming in? I can't wait to hand this job back to you."

I smiled. "Not too long now, I hope, Tommy. Right now I need a couple of numbers. Could you look them up for me?"

"Go ahead."

"One's the Federal Drugs Administration in Washington. The other's the CO at SAS 'A' Division in Hereford, England. His name's Colonel Owen Gracey."

"Sure. Just take a moment."

I'd kept the scrap of paper I'd picked up in McKenzie's office. When Tommy came back to me I added the two numbers to it.

A bell-like signal came over the public address system, followed by the announcement of my flight to London. It was only the first call and I ignored it. Instead I phoned the FDA. I no longer had the direct line I wanted, of course, so I had to settle for the switchboard. A woman answered, and I asked for Dr Norman Harries. She tried to stonewall me, as I knew she would. I cursed Müller for taking my phone. They say you shouldn't speak ill of the dead, but in his case I was prepared to make an exception.

I became more assertive and pulled rank all over the place, and finally she put me through.

He answered in his usual stiff fashion. "Hello, Colonel. Did you have any luck?"

Luck was not how I'd describe it, but I passed over that.

"Your suspicions were right, Dr Harries. The data on

Prescaline was manipulated to exclude the side effects. And they were aiming to do the same with Xylozib."

"My God, how did you find that out?"

"It's a long story. The bottom line is, I'm expecting to have the original trials data in my hands shortly. You should be able to compare it with the highly modified version they sent to your people."

He emitted a low whistle, which was unexpected coming from someone as rigidly correct as Harries. "Revelations like that would put a bomb under the company! The US Army will sue for fraudulent misrepresentation of the product. There'll be class action law suits on behalf of every family with someone who responded adversely to the drug. The company won't be able to withstand the onslaught: they'll go under."

I was aiming to put an even bigger bomb under the company myself, but I said nothing.

"When can you get the data to me?"

I thought for a moment. "Look, I can't say precisely when, but I have to return to Washington soon and I can bring you a copy then. It'll probably be in German."

"German? Well, all right. I'm not fluent but I think I have a sufficient grasp. It's the data I'm interested in."

"Dr Harries, I don't want the Army to use Prescaline any more."

"I can put out a notice. It's not uncommon for side-effects to emerge when a drug's been in circulation for a while. The fraudulent aspect can be pursued later."

"What about the Brits? They've been using it, too."

"I'll make sure they get the notice as well."

"Thanks."

"No, it's for me to thank you. As soon as you can with that data, Colonel."

"You bet."

My next call was to Owen Gracey. I was feeling bad

about the way I'd treated him. He gave me a safe billet, and I went walkabout in a big way without telling him. I punched the number in.

"Owen? This is Jim Slater."

There was a miniscule pause. "Jim? Where are you?"

"Er, right now I'm at Dallas/Fort Worth Airport."

"Good God, what are you doing there? Never mind. Are you all right?"

Now that was generous. He had every reason to chew me out.

"I'm fine now, Owen, but I've been in tight spot. I'm really sorry, but there was no way I could get in touch with you."

"All right. Look, General Harken's been asking for you. I had to tell him I had no idea where you were. Trifle awkward, of course, but he didn't seem all that surprised. Anyway he wants to see you urgently. So does the Deputy Secretary of Defense."

The Deputy Secretary of State, too, no doubt. The shit must have hit the fan already. It'll be a bloody miracle if I'm still in a job after this.

He went on, talking rapidly. "So you're in Texas. Are you on your way to Washington now?"

"Er, not just yet. But I'll be there in a couple of days."

"Good. If they call again I'll tell them. And are you coming back here after that?"

"I will, one way or another." I wasn't speaking loudly but I lowered my voice still further. "Owen, I found out what sent Scot Hayward round the twist."

I heard the intake of breath. "You did?"

"Yes. I can't say too much now, but the blame lies elsewhere. Scot reacted badly to a drug that was supposed to protect him."

Seconds passed. Then he said, "Jim, I want to know more. So will Alan."

"I'll give you both the full story when I come."

"Good. Make it soon, won't you? Take care, now."

"You too."

I clicked off and looked around again as I replaced the phone in my pocket.

International Airways announces the departure of…

Time to go to the departure gate.

*

The BMW saloon swept down the autobahn, heading for Taufkirchen. Next to me in the back seat Viktor Schröder gazed impassively ahead. Two hours ago he was waiting in the Arrivals Hall when I landed at Berlin Tegel. A quick handshake and he was whisking me off to another departure gate.

"Come, Jim, we are not staying in Berlin. We will fly immediately to München. Everything there is arranged."

And it certainly was. Ours was just one vehicle in a convoy that consisted of several big four-wheel-drives and three police vans, all travelling at speed, blue lights flashing.

It may have taken three flights to get me here from Dallas but I didn't feel tired. Soldiers acquire the knack of grabbing sleep whenever the opportunity presents itself. On the transatlantic leg I settled down as soon as the evening meal had been cleared away and didn't wake up until the engine note changed for the descent into London's Heathrow. Any residual travel fatigue I might have felt had been banished by the prospect of imminent action.

I looked out of the side window, watching apartment blocks and factories rush by, windows flaring in the afternoon sun. The last time I made this journey it was pouring with rain. Back then Lipzan was just a name on a slip of paper that Major Alan Wicklow had taken from a carton of Prescaline. Was it really less than two weeks ago?

It seemed like a hell of a lot longer.

I glanced at Viktor. He was outwardly calm but no doubt he was still turning things over in his mind, making sure he'd covered every angle. He'd told me he had staff working on Müller's data all night, and even while the computer was still decrypting it they were already poring over the material that was emerging in clear. It was a revelation. With the thoroughness that Colin had grudgingly admired, Müller had recorded everything in minute detail, and even the small fraction they'd seen so far was deeply incriminating. There was more than enough evidence, Viktor said, to justify waking up a man rather early this morning to get the necessary warrants signed.

The convoy exited the autobahn and negotiated an interchange to join another, all without slackening speed.

"Viktor," I said, "It's Saturday. Can we be sure there'll be someone there?"

He turned his head, the faint trace of a smile on his lips. "There is only one road in and out. I have had a man watching it since before dawn. He reported that between 8.00 and 8.30 am six cars arrived. Four of them were expensive, top-of-the-range models, not the cars you would expect laboratory or secretarial staff to drive. He would have phoned me immediately if any of them had left. So yes, I believe we will find the top management there, and they are the ones we want. Of course, we will get a list of personnel and all of them will be under arrest by tomorrow night."

I thought about the young Californian-trained computer scientist I'd met briefly on my tour of the facility, the one Frau Schenk had called Franz.

I said, "Most of the lab workers wouldn't have known what the company was up to. They were just doing a job."

"I know this. After questioning we will probably let most of them go."

I returned my gaze to the window. That was probably why the senior staff were at the company now. They did the sensitive work at the weekend, while the rest of the staff weren't around.

I took a deep breath. Holle could be trying to put in a call to Mexico at this very moment.

Pray God we're not too late.

47

The convoy stopped well short of the main building and we approached it on foot from one side. I was still looking around, trying to spot Viktor's observer, but I couldn't see him. There wasn't a lot of cover out front, so this guy must be good.

I pointed to the older building in the grounds. "That's the original 1947 building, Viktor. Holle said it was used for conferences and guest accommodation. My guess is that's where you'll find the central administration of the 'Guardians of the Reich'. He'd want to have it close by, but separate from the research establishment."

Viktor nodded, then went to have a word with the *polizei*, who were waiting patiently to go into action. They were armed and in full riot gear, and looked menacing enough to scare the shit out of any opposition. Viktor divided them into two groups. One group went over to the old building. We went with the other group to the new building, keeping wide of the entrance.

Viktor nodded to the officer in charge and he gave the signal.

The entry was quick and efficient. By the time Viktor and I were through the doors the security man on reception was lying on the floor with a policeman fastening the cuffs on him. He wouldn't have had a chance to warn the people on the next floor, which was the general idea.

I took the stairs two at a time, strode down the corridor to the end, and burst into Holle's office. Holle leapt to his feet in alarm, but recovered quickly.

"Colonel! This is an unexpected pleasure—"

"Unexpected, yes. A pleasure? I doubt it." I faced him across the desk. "Right now you're wondering how I escaped from your Mexican prison."

"Prison?" He laughed. "Surely not. There must be some mistake—"

"It won't work, Holle. The Mexican operation is over. Erich Müller is dead. There won't be any more money from the trafficking of people and drugs and the forced labour and sexual slavery that went with it."

He smiled uneasily. "This is pure fantasy!"

"Is it? Like your charitable object, the 'Guardians of the Reich', which supports right-wing organisations all over Europe?" I pointed at him. "Lipzan is nothing but a conduit for money-laundering with a convincing cover: a pharmaceutical company, your company. Which you made profitable by manipulating trial data. It was all on Müller's computer records, you see."

The smile had frozen solid now. "Why are you here?"

"Your drug Prescaline had serious side effects which you concealed from the FDA and the US Army. A lot of people died because of you." I leaned in. "One of them happened to be a close friend of mine. That's why I'm here. You and your pals are going to face justice at last, and I wanted to be the first to tell you."

The silence lasted several seconds. His eyes flicked to the top left-hand drawer of his desk an instant before his hand darted to it. I vaulted up, one hand on his desk, and drop-kicked him in the chest. He staggered backwards, hit the wall hard, and sank to the floor, gasping for breath. I eased myself off on the other side of the desk, opened the drawer, and removed the pistol lying there. I held it up between finger and thumb by the knurled grips so as not to disturb any fingerprints.

"Well, well, a Luger P.08. Standard Nazi issue. Did this belong to your great-grandfather, then, Holle? How many innocent civilians did he shoot in the back of the neck with it?"

Viktor appeared in the doorway with two policemen. He looked at the pistol, still dangling from my fingers, then at Holle, crouched against the wall.

"Are you all right, Jim?"

"Yeah. He's all yours." I tossed the pistol onto the desk. "You may want to bag this."

Downstairs the police were bundling six men and a woman into a police van. The woman was Frau Schenk, Holle's PA, and she was protesting loudly right up to the moment they banged and locked the doors. Then Holle emerged, his hands cuffed, walking between Viktor and another officer. The lenses of his gold-rimmed spectacles flashed angrily at me, then he was pushed into one of the four-wheel-drives. The officer got in next to him.

Another police van was coming back across the grass from the old building, where I presumed more arrests had been made.

The riot police had taken off their helmets and visors now, and some were standing around chatting. Among them was one in NATO combat uniform, his face smeared with brown and green camo paint. Viktor's observer.

Viktor walked over to me. "These buildings are empty now. We've secured them and after this we'll move our investigators in. Between the two there will enough evidence to give us entry to the whole network."

He led the way towards the BMW. "Do you want to return to Berlin with me or are you flying straight back?"

"I'd better fly straight back. There are people in

Washington who want to see me."

"Very well. We have much to thank you for, Jim. Is there anything we can do on our side?"

"There is, actually, Viktor. This company's drugs aren't safe to use. Some are downright dangerous. We need to have them withdrawn – for good. Lipzan got them adopted by tampering with the drug trials. The details are in that data I sent you. I'd like a copy for my contact in the Federal Drugs Administration."

"This is not a problem. Let me know when you are back and we will send the data to you or your contact."

As we reached the car he said, "So, now a return to normal duties?"

"A return to normal duties."

I wonder what the hell they are.

48

The heat hit me as I got out of the cab and walked over to the Concourse entrance of the Pentagon. After my recent trips to Washington it was nice to encounter the city under blue skies.

Bob Cressington's PA met me at the E-ring checkpoint and took me to his office. Bob stood, gave me a quick handshake, and gestured to the chair on the other side of his desk. Then he sat down and leaned back, as if to get a good look at me.

He took a deep breath. "Well, Jim, you've been at it again."

"You could say that."

"We've had the Mexican Ambassador here—"

Just as I expected, cries of outrage, major diplomatic rows all over again.

"Bob, I'm sorry but it was the only way—"

He held up a hand. "The Buzzards you called in took aerial footage of the rebel installation and army throughout the operation. The Commander at that Air Force base had the good sense to send a copy to the Mexican Ministry of Defence."

Colonel "Red" Nicholson! The second time the man's

come up trumps! I must pay him a visit and have that drink with him. In fact I'll take a damned good bottle with me.

Bob continued, "The Ambassador wasn't all that pleased about the violation of their airspace, but he was over the moon about the result. They've been expecting an incursion of major proportions but they didn't know where it was coming from. The size of that rebel force left no room for doubt: not only had we located the base but we'd destroyed it, too. Well, what was left of it – I gather you did a pretty good job even before the Buzzards arrived. How the hell did you find it? And how did you manage to get in there – and out again?"

I gave Bob the short version, leaving out the stuff about the thalamus implants. He listened without interruption and when I'd finished he nodded.

"The Mexicans want to know where the weapons came from and how they were paid for. Can you help them with that?"

"Some of it."

I dipped into a pocket and came out with the phone I'd taken from the soldier I'd killed. I put it on his desk. "You'll find photos of some of the crates on this. From the writing it looked to me like they came from North Korea and Russia."

Bob gave a low whistle.

"By the way," I went on, "this phone came from the pocket of one of the rebel soldiers. It could have some useful contacts on it. And this," I opened my billfold and removed the memory tile, "is a copy of the data on Müller's computer. It's possible there are records of his dealings with the militia and the drug cartels on it."

Bob drew them over to his side of the desk and smiled. "I think we won't be handing these to the Mexicans just yet. I'd like to give the CIA first shot."

Which was exactly as I'd expected. "They'll need to pass it by the NSA. It's encrypted and it's in German."

"Okay, no problem." He got to his feet. "Well done, Jim. State Department's pretty pleased about this. Seems to have eclipsed the fallout from that Honduras episode."

I realized I hadn't told him anything about the falsified drug trials that were responsible for that episode. Well, it would all come out in good time.

As we shook hands he said, "Have you seen Wendell yet?"

"No, I thought I'd see you first."

"He wants to have a word with you. I should go down there now."

*

"Jim!" Harken waved me in. "Where the hell have you been? I've been trying to get you for days. Did you switch your phone off or something?"

"No, actually it was taken from me."

He gave me a long, appraising look. "I'm a tiny bit surprised anyone could do that."

"So was I. It won't happen again."

"I got through to Hereford, but the CO there didn't know where you were either."

"It wasn't his fault, Wendell. I got involved."

He sighed. "I thought it would be a nice safe posting. I should have guessed you couldn't stay out of trouble."

"Yeah, well it started when one of their officers went on a killing spree, same as Sergeant Bill Archer. I thought there might be a connection. There was."

"Really? I want to hear about that, but hang on a moment. Have a seat while I make a call."

He spoke to someone. "He's with me now, debriefing…" He glanced at his watch. "Fine, yes, my room."

He clicked off the phone. I looked at him, but there

was no explanation. He just said, "Right, Jim, go ahead."

I gave him a brief account of the drug business.

When I'd finished he said, "Poor Archer, it wasn't his fault after all."

"I think there are going to be class action law suits. His family should be able to get some heavy compensation from Lipzan. But it may be from their executors by then. Right now the BKA are taking the company apart."

"And the other soldier who took the same drug? Who was it?"

I felt again the ache of loss. "Major Scot Hayward. We served together when I was in the SAS. He was a good buddy. Someone on our side of the water decided the way to put a stop to his activities was to take him out with a drone. He was blown to bits."

"I'm sorry."

"Yeah, me too."

There was a knock at the door and Harken said, "This will be the man I wanted you to see." And louder, "Come in."

The man he wanted me to see was Mr Mark Godstall, Special Agent with the US Army Criminal Investigation Command. We stood as he entered.

Harken said, "Jim, you remember Mr Godstall."

It was a statement. We shook hands, then we all sat down.

Harken said, "Go ahead, Godstall."

Godstall inclined his head and turned to me. "The law suit brought against the Army by a woman who demanded the return of her one-time partner's body—"

"My body."

"Yes."

"It's been to court?"

"Yes." He leaned forward. "Colonel, are you familiar at all with the work of the English playright William

Shakespeare?"

I stared at him. I wanted to know the outcome. What the hell did this have to do with it?

"We studied some of the plays when I was at school. Why?"

"Did those plays include *The Merchant of Venice*?"

"I think so. I can't remember. Do get to the point."

He leaned back again. "I'm sorry. It's just that the play was used to good effect by the Attorney for the Army. It's not legal precedent, of course, but it carried a lot of weight. You see, in the play Shylock has exacted a bargain from Antonio, the guarantor of a loan: if he fails to repay it, he will forfeit a pound of his own flesh. He defaults and the matter is brought to trial. The court finds in favour of Shylock; he is, indeed, entitled to his pound of flesh. It is Portia, posing as a doctor of the law, who makes the telling point: in essence, that he may take only the flesh, not the blood. Of course the one is impossible without the other and Shylock is defeated."

"And the attorney produced this in court?"

"He did. It tried the patience of the judge but the defence was rock solid. The parties who were suing were not prohibited by law from reclaiming your body. They were, however, not allowed to endanger your life. The suit was dismissed. Congratulations, Colonel."

I looked from him to Harken and back again. "So... so that's it? I can return to work?"

"Yes. Whenever you like."

I felt a flood of relief. The case had been absurd from the start, but it had still settled an unnecessary burden on me. Now that burden had been lifted.

Godstall rose to his feet. "Curious, isn't it, Colonel? William Shakespeare could scarcely have imagined that a play of his would be cited in an American court four-and-a-half centuries later."

"Good old Shakespeare," I said, as we shook hands again. "I should have paid more attention to him at school. Thanks."

He nodded. "I'll leave you to your debriefing."

The door closed behind him. I smiled at Harken and shook my head. "Strange, how a piece of history can catch up with you. That's the second time in three weeks."

"Oh? What was the other piece of history?"

"A fortune bequeathed over a century ago by a German dictator called Adolf Hitler."

His eyes opened wide. "I think you'd better explain…"

Acknowledgements

The vast wealth accumulated by Adolf Hitler is a matter of historical record, and the documentary evidence is to be found in two books: *Hitler's Will* (The History Press, 2009) by Herman Rothman, edited by Helen Fry, and *Hitler's Fortune* (Leo Cooper, 2003) by Cris Whetton. Although I am indebted to the authors for these accounts, which formed part of the inspiration for this story, I have not quoted from their texts in the present work. The quotation from Hitler's Private Will is, however, an authentic translation. The fate of much of the dictator's fortune remains a mystery, and the solution provided in this book is a product of my imagination.

I'm grateful to my wife Paula, sons Graham and Daniel, and daughter Debby for their encouragement and feedback. Special thanks go to my friends in the Liverpool-based writers' group Wordsmiths – Neville Krasner, John Clarke, Mary Gillie, Emma Mackley, and Rachel Sayle – who listened to successive chapters and provided invaluable critical comments.

Printed in Poland
by Amazon Fulfillment
Poland Sp. z o.o., Wrocław